PE

SO

RICHARD ALDINGTON

SOFT
ANSWERS

Richard Aldington

PENGUIN BOOKS
IN ASSOCIATION WITH
CHATTO AND WINDUS

FIRST PUBLISHED 1932
PUBLISHED IN PENGUIN BOOKS 1949

MADE AND PRINTED IN GREAT BRITAIN
FOR PENGUIN BOOKS LTD, HARMONDSWORTH, MIDDLESEX
BY C. NICHOLLS AND COMPANY LTD

CONTENTS

'YES, AUNT': *A Warning*   7

NOW LIES SHE THERE: *An Elegy*   55

NOBODY'S BABY: *A Mystery Story*   107

A GENTLEMAN OF ENGLAND:
    A Speculation   156

STEPPING HEAVENWARD:
    A Record   198

*

'Yes, Aunt'

A WARNING

Who doth ambition shun,
And loves to lie i' the sun.

I

IF Mr Oswald Carstairs had not inherited the almost competence of three hundred and fifty pounds a year, most probably he would never have been a great man. Not that Mr Carstairs pushed himself forward and upward to greatness. Indeed, if that worthy dissenting divine, holy Mr Baxter, had been gifted with prophecy as well as holiness, he might have had Carstairs in view when he penned his celebrated tract entitled 'A Shove Up Behind For A Heavy-Arsed Christian'. Only, in this case it was Mrs Carstairs who did the shoving. Her efforts to thrust greatness upon her husband were energetic and pertinacious, only equalled by the speed with which he invariably collapsed under the load.

Just after the War, Oswald Carstairs lived in a small but comfortable service flat near Regent's Park – the compleat bachelor. During the War he had been the perfect Cuthbert of the gutter press. Perceiving with a flash of intuition that scenes of indiscriminate slaughter were no place for a man of parts, Oswald wrote to his well-connected Aunts (in trouble, he always wrote to his Aunts), and the Aunts pulled wires. It may seem incredible that anybody's War-time Aunts should say anything to a young man but 'Your King and Country Need YOU', or do anything but lead him kindly but implacably to the recruiting sergeant. But Oswald's Aunts were placid, humane creatures, much concerned with the fates of

7

stray cats and masterless dogs, and while they continued to say to each other and to the world that 'EVERY young man's place is in the Trenches', they made an inward reservation that Oswald was too delicate for a rough army life. Besides, he was a Carstairs – which made a difference. Oswald's Aunts were used to playing the part of Providence to him. When he over-spent his income – as he almost invariably did – one or other of them as invariably handed over a hundred or so or a very aged one would die and leave him five hundred and her miniature and several aged animals, which Oswald with prompt humanity always conducted to the lethal chamber.

'Oswald,' they said to each other, 'is delicate, but *unselfish*. He loves animals. And he is really *gifted*.'

So Oswald was found to be unfit for active service, and received the Order of Indispensability as a clerk in the Ministry of Munitions; later, an ironical administration transferred him to the Ministry of Health. Apart from air raids, rations and the necessity of appearing at the office every day, Oswald spent a rational and not unpleasant War. His salary, added to his little patrimony, enabled him to purchase those little comforts which are so essential to the delicate. Hence the comfortable service flat which he continued to inhabit, after he had been dismissed from the ardours and endurances of his War service with politeness and an O.B.E. The Aunts were delighted about the O.B.E. It was an official recognition of Oswald's 'gifts' and of their own acumen in placing him in a Sphere where 'gifts' were rightly appreciated. While careful not to *spoil* him with too much praise, they frequently discussed his 'brilliant career', past and future.

The Aunts eagerly awaited the next step in Oswald's career, 'now that he had left the Government'. But Oswald did nothing, and even laughed at a hint that he might 'stand for Parliament'. This finicky little man was a living symbol of a race exhausted by the immense and comparatively futile effort of the Industrial Revolution. Just as the hierarchy of iron Crusaders eventually petered out in coquettish *abbés* and diminutive *petits maitres*, so the industrial hierarchy of England much more rapidly collapsed into a generation of supine Oswalds. His business ancestors (men who, like Dogberry, had had losses) apparently overstrained the family vitality. Oswald didn't want to do anything in particular, and was comfortable living in a gay but trivial series of elegant nothings. In appearance he was rather like a desiccated and diminutive Colonial, a sort of Chelsea cowboy. A brownish skin and very dark birdy eyes gave him 'that foreign look', as his Aunts called it, but though he was naturally lean his extremely sedentary habits already betrayed themselves in a small but noticeable pot-belly. His thin brown fingers were stained yellow from innumerable cigarettes, which he smoked with a finicky stiff elegance of gesture. His legs, however, were rather thick and stumpy, and there was a tiny, thin patch of hair which showed the skin on the top of his head. As he hopped about a drawing-room, smoking and talking in a high civil-servant voice, cocking up his bright birdy eyes, he looked like a member of a Colonial concert party disguised as one of the chorus in the Birds of Aristophanes.

Oswald's Aunts never paused to ask themselves what sort of career Oswald's nature fitted. In their view a man was almost inseparable from the 'career' which brought him both profit and honour. They yearned to see Oswald honourably and profitably careering, but the means to this desirable end they left entirely to him – it was up to him (they felt) to know what he wanted to do, and to do it. But Oswald didn't want to do anything, especially anything long and difficult. If his Aunts had examined him with the impartial eye of cool criticism, they would have observed that the only thing for which Oswald was naturally fitted was to be what the Americans call a dilly-tant and the English a dilly-tanty. Oswald 'went out' a good deal, as any presentable young bachelor of apparently independent means can go out, if he possesses a dress suit and can chatter. And Oswald could chatter all right. He was enthusiastically punctual in his attendance at the Russian Ballet. He went to first nights at the theatre and the right concerts. In a small way he collected – Piranesi engravings and small Japanese figures of seated women which when turned upside down afford the beholder an agreeable surprise. And he read a lot – everybody does nowadays. Apart from that ever-renewed stream of immortal nothings which everybody reads, Oswald had made peculiarly his own the study of Elizabethan drama and the more scandalous memoirs of the Bourbon Court. Among the moderns he affected, and perhaps felt, a peculiar kinship with the works of Mr Lytton Strachey and Marcel Proust – writers gracefully at ease among the great, and seldom concerned with that vast dull mass of humanity which earns its living, with or without a career. Oswald was as comfortable in his silken nest of habits as any winter dormouse in its ball of lined grass. If he had condescended to prayer it could only have been to supplicate that our unexampled prosperity might last.

Alas, it did not last. Economics, what crimes are committed in thy name! In 1919-21 things were really *too* dear. Of course, we know there must be profits – otherwise where would our dividends come from? – but, hang it all, there ought to be a decent moderation in everything. So Oswald had thought more than once, when forced to painful payment for some indispensable nothing. And he thought so with even more pain one morning when his Bank Manager called him into his private office.

'Will you look over this statement of your account, Mr Carstairs?'

Mr Carstairs looked, and saw with a thrill of horror that he was overdrawn to the extent of £382 16s. 3d. How the

devil had he spent all that? Under the shock his mind vacil-
lated, and dwelt vaguely but bitterly on the longevity of
well-off Aunts.

'I'm very sorry to trouble you,' said the Manager with
almost excessive politeness, for, after all, Oswald had several
thousand pounds of securities in the Bank's vaults, 'but
Headquarters don't like these big overdrafts. We must all
draw in our horns. Trade isn't what it was, and the War's
got to be paid for, hasn't it?'

'Ye-es,' said Oswald doubtfully. 'Yes. I – I suppose it has.'

He was wondering why on earth a peaceful person like
Oswald Carstairs should have to pay for the War. Oughtn't
that to be the job of the fire-eaters who dashed into it?

'Well,' the Manager went on with brisk and, as Oswald
felt, misplaced cheerfulness, 'what are we to do about it? Can
you pay in something to reduce it? Say, a hundred and fifty
this week, and the remainder next month?'

Put like that, it sounded extremely easy, but Oswald was
tragically aware of its impossibility. The very word was like
a knell.

'Impossible,' he murmured, shaking his head, 'impossible,
I'm afraid.'

'Then we'll have to think of something else,' said the Manager more crisply, but still politely. 'Now what about those
Tono-Mala Oils of yours?'

The Manager knew that Tono-Malas were due for a rise
in the near future, since bears were over-sold. Oswald did not
know this. The Manager rustled over the pages of *The
Times*.

'Here we are,' he said cheerily, putting his finger on the
previous days' quotation, 'Tono-Malas – 17s., 16s. 9d.,
16s. 6d., 16s. 9d.' 16s. 3d., 16s. Still falling a bit, I'm afraid.
It might be as well to get out of 'em before they go down further. I daresay we could get you 16s. 6d. for your five hun-

dred. That'd wipe out the overdraft and put you on the credit side. What about it?'

Irresolution has its advantages. Oswald hated to act, even by signing a share transfer. Besides, he was honourable; and he had promised Aunt Ursula he would not sell those shares until she gave the word. But the thought of Aunt Ursula depressed him still further – one of those painful interviews. Oswald suddenly remembered that a taxi was ticking up useless threepences against him outside the Bank. Must economise.

'I'm awfully sorry,' he said, adding vaguely, 'and all that. I must see my ... Come back to-morrow morning ... Settle up ... Decent of you to wait ...'

And Oswald incoherently fled, intending to pay off his taxi-man, and to reflect soberly as he walked home. Alas for economy. Outside, it was raining; Oswald was wearing a new suit; evidently, it was very false economy to save a taxi-fare and spoil a fifteen-guinea suit. Oswald entered the taxi, bowed under the bludgeonings of Fate.

I must economise, Oswald informed himself repeatedly, strict economy; and I must see Aunt Ursula at once. (Aunt Ursula was the richest and most indulgent of his Aunts.) Oswald was not a man of steel. He liked the idea of saving money but he could not bear deprivation, and he felt terror at the thought of facing Aunt Ursula with the confession of so monstrous an overdraft – more than a year's income. Then, for some reason everything went wrong and was very expensive. The taxi was constantly held up in traffic blocks, ticking up shillings and pence with revolting rapidity; and Oswald tried to calculate how much money is lost to the nation by incompetent traffic regulation. Outside his flat he met a District Messenger Boy who firmly desired payment for a stall at the Russian Ballet, which Oswald had cheerfully commanded before seeing the Bank Manager. Twenty-five shillings! As he picked up the telephone receiver to speak to his Aunt, he remembered that he owed more than a quarter's telephone and telegraph fees. At lunch he was horrified to discover that in a fit of gluttonous anticipation he had ordered the day before that the meal should be enlivened with plovers' eggs, asparagus and forced strawberries. Economy! He spent a gloomy afternoon, which was not improved by a steady patter of rain. Oswald had intended to take a bus to Piccadilly Circus, change there and take another to Knightsbridge, where Aunt Ursula lived. Against this sacrifice and hardship every nerve in his delicate body protested. What! Walk along damp pavements under a dripping umbrella, watch overcrowded buses arrive and depart without shedding a single place, struggle in among steamy raincoats and wet umbrellas and damp humanity, and confront his Aunt for this important interview with mud-splashed shoes, wet trousers and an exhausted frame? Oswald telephoned for a taxi ...

Aunt Ursula lived in a flat which was several sizes too large for a solitary female, but she felt she owed it to the memory of her deceased partner to keep up appearances. He had 'done well', by selling agricultural machinery to South Africa, and then, smitten by paralysis, had tormented her for five years by his helplessness and pathos, finally atoning by a swift death and a generous will. In early Edwardian days, Aunt Ursula must have been a beauty of the blonde, fluffy, exacting kind.

Recoiling from the austere tubular forms affected by the younger generation – so unfeminine – she concealed flaccid rotundities with abundance of silk and lace. A gold watch with a diamond monogram was invariably pinned to the left of her lacy bosom; she wore a number of ruby and emerald rings of antique design, and a gold-handled lorgnette was suspended from her neck on a richly chased gold chain. Impossible to say what distinguished dowager of her youth she was now imitating. But for the fact that she had never moved in Exalted Circles, you would have sworn she was one of the now ageing female intimates of his late lamented Majesty. The well-doing of her husband had left Aunt Ursula well-off, but she had hobbies. The most expensive was the collection of poor but exceedingly elegant young men of musical genius, who appeared to be much devoted to each other, avoided the company of young women and were very much at ease with elderly ladies. Oswald disliked these young men, and they discreetly disparaged him to his Aunt. Yet – so thick is blood – Aunt Ursula would willingly have wasted on Oswald at least one half of her annual investment in the least promising of her 'young men', if *only* Oswald had invented a career.

Aunt Ursula did not receive Oswald in her large and over-furnished drawing-room, but over a small fire in the 'snuggery.' The 'snuggery' had been fitted up by her late husband for meditation and incessant mental labour. It contained a cigar cabinet, two deep and comfortable armchairs conducive to intellectual activity, a bookcase of handsomely bound uncut English classics, and a fireplace decorated with horrific African gods in polished wood. Aunt Ursula, all for European culture, would gladly have abolished these 'dreadful indecencies', but she felt that among the duties of keeping up appearances was an obligation to maintain her husband's house exactly as he had left it. Oswald, more enlightened, would have liked those African carvings – he knew their value was rising, while Aunt Ursula thought them valueless lumber.

It would be straining the truth to say that Oswald faced his Aunt with pleased anticipation. Indeed, he was in a hell of a dither. He kissed her forehead vaguely, and put into her hand a volume of French memoirs which he had snatched from one of his shelves as he left.

'What pestilential weather!' he exclaimed languidly, trying to hide his uneasiness with the airs of an *évaporé*. 'My dear,

14

I'm quite worn out. You'd never believe the trouble I had to find that copy of *Tilly*. Positively scoured the bookshops.'

Aunt Ursula knew Oswald well enough to be a little suspicious of his Greek gifts, but could not help being flattered by his attention.

'Poor Lamb!' she said compassionately, meaning Oswald hunting a book for her in pestilential weather. 'How thoughtful of you! What a career dear Count Tilly had – a man of genius ruined by that dreadul Revolution. But, Oswald, it worries me when you spend valuable time and money in trying to humour my little whims. I should be so much happier if I felt you were devoting yourself to a *career*.'

'That,' said Oswald recklessly, 'is exactly what I've come to consult you about.'

'Indeed! And what are you going to do?'

Now, since Oswald had made this remark entirely on the spur of the moment, he was more than a little embarrassed. He felt he needed to gain time. He said:

'May I have a cigarette, Aunt?'

'Yes, my dear, but don't scatter the ashes. And now tell me *all* about your plans.'

Oswald lit a cigarette very slowly, surprised to find that his hands were shaking.

'When I left the Government service after the War,' he said deliberately, 'I felt I needed a rest.'

'Poor Lamb,' said Aunt Ursula.

'But,' Oswald invented lavishly, 'I find idleness does not suit my temperament.'

'Of course not!' she agreed enthusiastically.

'Nor,' he added cautiously, 'will my means permit it. In fact, I'm very much worried by the state of my finances.'

'Ah!'

Aunt Ursula sat very upright and looked at him fixedly.

'In fact,' Oswald blundered on, 'I'm overdrawn.'

'How much?' Quite a pistol-shot of a question.

'About three hundred and eighty pounds,' he confessed miserably.

Aunt Ursula clapped her hands together in outraged horror. Three hundred and eighty pounds! Then she let Oswald have it, with all the heat and strength she had never dared to display in matrimonial debates. What had he been doing? How had he spent it? Was he entangled with a woman? Or women? She had never heard of such a thing. Did he think that a poor old woman like herself, beggared by income-tax to pay for that dreadful War, could be expected to sell the clothes from her back to liquidate the debts of a licentious wastrel? Three hundred and eighty pounds were an immense fortune, almost sufficient to redeem the National Debt. What had Oswald been thinking of? Was he trying to ruin and disgrace them all?

'Then,' said Oswald pathetically, 'I must sell my Tono-Malas.'

But this only made matters worse.

Any one who has observed the remarkable and siphon-like protest of an outraged and terrified cat will have a clear idea of Aunt Ursula's reaction to this impious sugges-tion. Oswald, who had not yet learned the profundities of the religion of money, was amazed by her vehemence. Selling shares, except to make a good profit, was apparently an ignoble turpitude, wherein folly and wickedness were almost equally mixed. It was the Rake's Progress. She sketched his future in tragical colours. Selling shares to pay debts reduced your income; a reduced income meant more debts, more impiety of selling out, and another reduction – result: beggary, disgrace, ruin and suicide! Oswald, gazing helplessly at the little fire which was going out, wished he could go out too. This it was to have served one's Country in bare and hostile Ministries! What was she saying now?

'Who is this woman, Oswald? I insist on knowing!'

'What woman?' he asked in feeble bewilderment.

'Why, the woman for whom you have squandered your capital in this outrageous way.'

'But I haven't! There isn't any woman.'

'Oswald!'

Poor Oswald appealingly held out his hands, rather like little Davy Copperfield to his Aunt Betsey.

'Please, Aunt, *please!* There isn't any woman. I swear there isn't.'

'Do you mean to tell me you've spent all that money on yourself?'

'Things are frightfully dear,' he murmured.

'However you could have contrived to spend so much I for one cannot conceive,' she said severely, overlooking the fact that in the same period of time she had contrived to waste about five times as much. 'What are you going to do about it?'

It is said that in moments of acute danger the thyroid gland pours into the system a beneficent stimulant. Oswald had a bright idea.

'I intend,' he said, 'to take up writing as a career.'

'But,' said Aunt Ursula, forgetting her patronage of elegantly-dressed young male genius and reverting to type, 'that is a life of intolerable idleness!'

'On the contrary,' said Oswald firmly, as if speaking with the authority of a veteran, 'it is the most exacting of professions. An author is *always* at work. Ceaseless mental activity. It is *the* career for men of energy and intelligence.'

It is a remarkable fact that whenever a young man announces that he is going to write – and almost all young men at some time or other feel the call of genius – the most sceptical at first are his nearest relatives. Oswald found his Aunt extremely sceptical. Stimulated by dire necessity and the thyroid gland, he became eloquent. Inventing boldly, he said that he had long been considering the matter and had thought everything out. He would give up his flat and retire to a small cottage in the country – all authors did. He would join the London Library and write a book on Elizabethan drama. He had planned a series of witty and satirical portrait-biographies in the manner of Mr Strachey. He also intended a long novel, somewhat in the manner of Monsieur Proust, depicting the social and intellectual life of London. And he would 'criticise for the newspapers.'

'I'm quite sure,' he cried, 'that I could turn out something better than *most* of the stuff that gets published.'

That remark would have cooked Oswald's literary goose with anybody who had experienced young literary genius, but Aunt Ursula was struck by it.

'I don't like the idea of your going off alone to the country, Oswald. You'll get bored and fritter. Besides, a literary man' – she was already quite proud to think there was a literary man in the family – 'a literary man needs distraction and to keep up useful relations. Before you publish your book you must give dinners to all the important critics and praise their wives' novels.'

It was now Oswald's turn to be struck by her literary acumen.

'Why don't you write too, Aunt?' he exclaimed. 'We could work together.'

Exquisitely flattered, Aunt Ursula resiled from the compliment in such a way that Oswald found himself committed to a joint work on the Court of Louis XV. How delightfully easy it all seemed! You have an idea, you write a book, publishers compete for the profit and honour of issuing it, you square the critics – *et voilà!* Fame and fortune!

Apparently Aunt Ursula's thyroid gland was also in full blast.

'I have it!' she cried. 'Oswald, you must marry!'

'What, a woman?' he exclaimed in horror.

'Of course. What ridiculous things you say, Oswald.'

'But I should have to keep her on my overdraft,' he said apprehensively.

'Don't be silly. You are a presentable young man of *very* good family, with some means, and a distinguished career before you. There is a real shortage of eligible young men, Oswald. Those who didn't *throw* away their lives in that dreadful War seem to prefer to amuse each other. Within reason you can pick and choose. We must find you a nice sensible girl with a little money, who'll look after you and further your career. Now, let me see, who is there?'

And Aunt Ursula began running over possibilities and families and bank accounts, rather like an expert punter running over the form of racehorses. Oswald sat in silent dismay, cowed by misfortune. He had enough sense not to interrupt, realising that Aunt Ursula had him squashed like a tender flower between the leaves of her cheque-book. Rendered enthusiastic by the thought of so much interest and activity – life is really very dull at times – Aunt Ursula behaved with exemplary generosity. She gave him a cheque for a hundred and fifty, to fill the Manager's maw for the time being; and undertook a whip-round among the other Aunts to raise the balance. Oswald murmured incoherent and mournful thanks. So much time had been expended in these exhausting scenes that he would have to rush to the Criterion for a bite of dinner and then gallop round to the Alhambra. He muttered something about an important engagement.

'I was going to suggest that you dine with *me* and discuss your future,' said his Aunt with some asperity, still entertaining suspicions of an expensive woman somewhere in the background of Oswald's existence, a suspicion which had been rather strengthened than destroyed by his obvious horror of matrimony. 'But *if* you have an important engagement, you must of course keep it. To-morrow you must start work in earnest in your new career. Meanwhile, I shall begin to put down my little ideas' – she bristled with modest conceit – 'for the book on dear Louis Quinze, and you shall make *any* use you like of them. Come and dine with me to-morrow. No, to-morrow evening Rupert has a piano recital. Come the next evening, and we'll talk it all over. And I shall do my best to find you a *charming* fiancée.'

'Thank you, Aunt,' said Oswald meekly.

It was a sad and sober Oswald who that evening beheld the fairy world of the Russian Ballet. True, he had the cheque in his pocket. True, he had saved his bacon for the time being, but at what a cost! Somehow the glory had faded from the Ballet; and even from Massine the halo had fallen. Oswald went to bed, utterly exhausted and extremely depressed.

II

The life of virtual idleness as a literary genius was poisoned for Oswald by his servitude and the fiendish activity of his Aunt Ursula. Historians have observed that in declining dynasties the primitive virtues of the early males tend to survive only in the females. At any rate, this was true of the Carstairs dynasty. Examining his conscience with minute care, Oswald was unable to find any trace of the slightest ambition for a career and public consideration. He wanted to live an easy, peaceful, padded life of unhurried trifles, as in the golden days before the appalling shock of the overdraft. He felt languid, and wished he were an old maid who would not be expected to do anything violent, especially in the shape of a career. During the forty-eight hours which elapsed before he saw his Aunt for dinner, Oswald by grim and exhausting determination succeeded in accomplishing three pieces of business. He paid in his cheque, and was allowed to draw ten pounds for current expenses. He wrote 'Elizabethan Drama By Oswald Carstairs' at the head of a sheet of foolscap. He strolled into the London Library and recoiled with horror at the number of books on a subject he had considered peculiarly his own. Like La Bruyère (whom he had not read) Oswald made the discovery, so fatal to literary productiveness, that everything has been said. He was disgusted by the plodding industry which had scraped together so much useless comment. Writing, he felt, was not the occupation for a gentleman.

Aunt Ursula, on the other hand, seemed to Oswald's diseased imagination to have multiplied herself by abominable witchcraft into several active and pernicious meddlers. They were scarcely seated at dinner, with the discreet butler standing white-gloved in the background, when she poisoned Oswald's first mouthful of soup by saying:

'Well, my dear, and *how* have you progressed with your new work?'

Concealing the facts that he had written nothing but the title of a work he now felt sure he could never begin, still less complete, and that he now felt as much distaste for authorship as for any other kind of activity, Oswald plunged into an elaborate but embarrassed version of his researches at the library.

'There is far more material than I had imagined,' he said, 'and though I've made a start, I can see there'll be a lot of preliminary work.'

Aunt Ursula was so eager to boast of her own doings that she scarcely noticed Oswald's sullen reluctance, and failed to interpret it correctly. She said:

'Now, my dear, you mustn't overdo matters in your first enthusiasm. Steadiness and persistence, steadiness and persistence.'

'Yes, Aunt.'

'I'm eager to tell you the little I've been able to do to further your plans.'

'Yes, Aunt.'

'I've filled nearly half a notebook already with jottings for our joint volume. Do you know, my dear, I'm *surprised* to find how much I remember of those far-off days? I think I must have an affinity with the splendours of Versailles.'

Oswald mutely cursed the felicity of his Aunt's memory and totally failed to visualise her as a Bourbon Duchess. He murmured something which might have sounded like a compliment.

'I've discussed your career with Rupert,' she went on, 'and I am bound to say he has been most sympathetic and helpful. I've arranged for you to call to-morrow on a friend of his, an editor, who will allow you to review books for him every week. The salary, I understand, is slight; about five shillings a week, I believe, but it will be admirable practice for you and bring your name prominently before the public. Isn't that splendid?'

'Splendid,' said Oswald in a kind of frozen melancholy. More work! He felt he would like to grind Rupert's head in the dust.

'Thirteen pounds a year,' his Aunt calculated, 'is equal to the interest on two hundred and sixty pounds of War Loan. You must look at it in that light. Moreover, I understand that the books will be presented to you, and will in time form a handsome library.'

Oswald gulped half a glass of his Aunt's sweet Graves, and tried to look ravished with happiness. Nevertheless, he made a feeble attempt at defence.

'You don't think,' he ventured, 'that this will occupy valuable time which might be – er – otherwise employed?'

'Of course not! It's merely a matter of reading books, a most pleasurable occupation, and noting your impressions and judgment.'

Oswald sighed inaudibly, and wondered feebly why his Aunt would serve gooseberry tart with a white wine. It put his teeth on edge.

When they drank coffee alone in the 'snuggery', Aunt Ursula continued her agitating revelations.

'About that overdraft of yours, Oswald ...'

'Yes, Aunt?'

'I haven't had the response I hoped for from your other Aunts, who all have had the singular experience of simultaneous money losses in the past few months. I feel this is very strange, Oswald, since my brokers tell me the markets have been booming recently. I have promises of only a hundred pounds, which still leaves you with a serious deficit. You will have to be very careful, very careful indeed.'

'Yes, Aunt.'

'Yes, Aunt' might have been taken as the keynote or motto of a life which Oswald felt was absolute hell. He suffered with extreme indignation the officious tyrannies of Aunt Ursula, most ably supported by the inventions of her sisters and sisters-in-law. Once he was out of this mess, he vowed he would never again put his head into such a nest of preying termites. They were eating him raw. And the devil of it was that they dribbled out their subsidies so mingily, and Oswald's economy was so imperfect, that he found himself with a permanent floating debt to the Bank. If he had dared, he would have sold out some shares and made himself solvent and self-respecting again. But he didn't dare, partly because he didn't know where the process would cease, and partly because Aunt Ursula had taken to inspecting his pass-book in the cause of reformation. He felt his Aunts had con-spired together, in their own economic interests, to see that henceforth he lived within his means. And what was so in-furiating was that they wouldn't leave him alone. They were always ringing him up and inviting him to tedious lunches or dinners to meet some egregious imbecile who had written a book, or some flat-chested girl who was on the market. It was infuriating, infuriating. He hardly ever went out now among the people he really liked. He had a sus-picion that 'everybody' knew of his plight and was laughing at him. He spent dreary, dreary hours in his dressing-gown, struggling over reviews which appeared very much cut down and altered, or trying to make some sense out of Aunt Ursula's helter-skelter observations about Versailles. Such utter nonsense! Oswald could see that she had got everything mixed up in a jumble of ill-assorted memories. Sometimes he would groan aloud and mutter to himself: 'If only I could get out of this, if *only* I could get out of it!' He poured out some of his resentment in a most vindictive 'portrait' of that other managing woman, Elizabeth Tudor. The liveliness of its denunciations secured its publication in one of the heavy magazines, and it was proudly read by Aunt Ursula, who never perceived that it was a biased description of herself.

Oswald did 'get out of it', but only by exchanging the frying-pan of his Aunts for the fires of matrimony. To say that Oswald fell in love with Julia Heathcote would be a manifest exaggeration. Oswald had never been much attracted by women, and in his pitiable state of mind high passion was an impossibility. But Julia seemed an escape, and as girls sometimes marry to get away from disagreeable parents, so Oswald married to get away from the nightmare of his Aunts. It was a queer marriage in many ways, particularly from the fact that the usual *rôles* seemed to be reversed.

Oswald was rather a feminine man; Julia rather a masculine sort of woman. She had a deep throaty voice and black hair cut very short, and she was far more 'managing' than Oswald had ever dreaded in his most pessimistic reflections on the opposite sex. Julia was older than he and had rather more money, but, if Oswald and his Aunts didn't know, *she* knew that three or four 'affairs' had rather knocked the gilt off her matrimonial gingerbread. This female *rouée* was extremely taken with the idea of marrying a dear little virgin man. Weary of the subterfuges and dissatisfactions of adultery, she felt it would be charming to have a comfortable little man of her very own, one who was not always having to hurry away or to elaborate fantastic lies to deceive the vigilance of a suspicious wife. Julia was much more sophisticated than Oswald, having lived in Bloomsbury for years. Moreover, she was ambitious.

The ambition of Julia cannot be considered as unique. She belonged to a comparatively large class of females who have inherited a certain amount of money, but not enough to become famous for negro lovers or to buy a title. She wanted to be 'someone', a figure in society, in the public eye. At first she had tried to do something on her own, but several years of failure to paint her way into notoriety had convinced her that success did not lie in that direction. She felt that the alternative was to attach herself legally to a coming man. Luckily or unluckily for Oswald, she had only the sketchiest notions of the ingredients of a literary celebrity. She listened credulously to Aunt Ursula's optimistic forecasts of the brilliant career before Oswald, and was duly impressed by the contribution to the heavy magazine. And as soon as she saw Oswald's ingenuous face and bird-like dark eyes, she determined to make him peculiarly her own. Their united incomes (she calculated) would be something over eight hundred a year, apart from Oswald's growing gains as a literary celebrity.

With care they could manage a studio, a small country cottage, and a two-seater, while awaiting the Bugatti, the house in Eaton Square, and the Riviera villa which would be the reward of Oswald's genius. Until that happy day arrived, they would entertain in an economical but distinguished manner, concentrating on persons in the public eye. When Oswald had done his bit by making them both famous, *she* would take her place in the polite world – somewhere between Lady Lavery and Mrs Baldwin.

The Aunts were agreeably fluttered by this marriage, taking a keen vicarious interest in an event which in their own lives was either remote in time or missed for ever. Indeed their vicarious enjoyment was probably greater than that of Julia and Oswald, who had to endure realities, while the Aunts were free of an imaginary paradise of per-petual honeymoons. From the first they insisted on a con-vention that this was *the* ideal match, combining in perfect proportions romantic passion with affinity of character and material advantage. If their premises had been exact, no doubt the Aunts would have been right; but unfortunately their premises came from what they hoped and not from what was. The Aunts based high hopes on the convention they had established that Oswald was 'so devoted' and Julia 'so sensible', the assumption being apparently that in matri-mony the man must always be a little deluded and the more clear-sighted woman let him down lightly. And certainly too much romance is as dangerous as too little – no couple has ever yet succeeded in playing Romeo and Juliet for forty years. It can't be done. *If* Julia and Oswald had been very much in love; *if* their characters had been harmonious; *if* Oswald had been the sort of man who can't be happy without a wife; *if* Julia had been the sort of woman who delights in devoted monogamy; *if* Oswald had possessed talents and had really wanted to work; and *if* Julia's ambitions had been less vague and mountainous – why then, the Aunts *might* not have been wrong. But since none of these 'ifs' was true ...

About a week before his marriage, Oswald received an unexpected visit from his Aunt Ursula, who entered his room with a kind of portentous benevolence which frightened Oswald very much. He had a desperate suspicion that she meant to give him good and possibly intimate advice about the duties and responsibilities of a husband. In this he was only partly right; Aunt Ursula was too much of a lady to peer directly into alcoves.

She began with a fatuous solemnity which filled Oswald with mingled apprehension and glee, saying:

'Oswald, you are about to take a most important step in life.'

'Yes, Aunt.'

'Marriage is a serious thing. You young people ...'

She paused, having forgotten that part of her prepared speech.

'Yes, Aunt?' Oswald asked innocently.

'I was going to give you a warning from my own experience, but I think that is better left to your own delicacy.'

'Yes, Aunt.'

'Where is your passbook?' she asked with unexpected abruptness. Oswald rummaged through a drawer and presented her with a calf-bound small book, beautifully inscribed 'Mr Oswald Carstairs.' She studied the pages carefully through her lorgnette.

'Um. I see you are still overdrawn to the extent of ninety pounds, in spite of the money that has been given to you and your own income. How do you account for *that*?'

'My dear Aunt,' cried Oswald desperately, 'hang it all, a fellow must *live*.'

'Not beyond his means, Oswald. Above all, not when he is responsible for Another and Precious Life.'

Now it is characteristic of an English gentleman that the more he feels and the more he has to say, the less capable he is of expression. Oswald vaguely felt and wanted to say a number of things – that his Aunts had been responsible for his education and therefore to some extent for his character; that it wouldn't have hurt them to give him some of the money they hinted they were going to leave him, so that he could live the life of bachelor comfort he wanted to live; that they had taken advantage of his helplessness to boss him confoundedly; that they had forced him into the hypocrisy of pretending that he wanted a career; that Aunt Ursula had suggested almost commandingly that he assume responsibility for 'another and precious life', and had introduced him to the same. All this and more he wanted to say, but to his own extreme annoyance and confusion, could only utter the fatal and feeble words:

'Yes, Aunt.'

'Now listen to me, Oswald,' said his Aunt, pointing her lorgnette almost threateningly at him. 'We, your other Aunts and I, have talked this matter over carefully and thoroughly. With all our affection for you, we are bound to admit that you have disappointed us. When we consented to your own earnest entreaties that you should take up authorship as a Career, we did *not* expect that you would use our consent as an excuse for frittering. But let that pass. We hope and believe that a fuller sense of the responsibilities of Manhood will make you work conscientiously for success in the Career of your own choosing. But let that pass.'

'I ... ' Oswald burst out desperately, and then stopped He had an insane desire to tell his Aunt to go to blazes, to yell at her that he didn't want a beastly career, that he didn't want to get married, that what he wanted from her was three hundred a year and his liberty. But, alas, he realised he was now so deep in blood that he might as well go on as attempt to run back. And telling his Aunt to go to blazes certainly wouldn't induce her to give him three hundred a year, though it might give him the dangerous privilege of liberty – to live on overdrafts and a dwindling capital.

Aunt Ursula waited for what Oswald was going to say, but as he only looked sweaty and uncomfortable and said nothing, she waved her lorgnette at him again, and proceeded:

'We, your other Aunts and I, have decided that you are not to be trusted to look after money, and we feel we should be entirely failing in our duty if we allowed you by your careless extravagance and frittering to bring Julia and yourself to beggary and ruin. Read that.'

'That' was a document which his Aunt took from her handbag and presented to Oswald at arm's length, almost as if she were holding a Webley to his head. With acute horror Oswald gradually discovered that the document was an order to his Banker authorising him, after deduction of income-tax, to pay into Oswald's account the sum of fifty pounds annually, the remainder to be paid to the private account of 'my wife, Julia Carstairs' so long as the marriage continued. Oswald had that feeling of complete gasping helplessness which comes from a violent blow in the stomach. He became dimly aware that his Aunt was talking.

'Julia is a sensible girl,' he heard, 'and devoted to your interests and Career, Oswald. She will arrange all your expenses for you, and see that you live in decency and comfort. Meanwhile, you will have a pound a week for your pocket-money and everything you earn – which I hope will be considerable – in your Career. If by any chance – which God forbid – you two should separate, the arrangement automatically becomes void.'

'But, Aunt,' Oswald pleaded feebly, 'why *should* I give Julia all my income?'

'I've already told you, Oswald. It's the only means to ensure your safety and comfort, and Julia's. Now, sign the document like a good boy. You may trust us to do all for the best. As soon as it is signed, I shall arrange for the settling of your overdraft, and I shall place three hundred pounds to your credit. Out of this I want you to buy a nice two-seater as a wedding present for Julia. Now, hurry up, my dear, there isn't much time before you.'

'But, Aunt ...' Oswald began again.

Aunt Ursula pointed the lorgnette at him so ferociously that Oswald quailed.

'Let us have no nonsense, Oswald. You don't want to be disowned by your family on the eve of marriage and left to beggary, do you?'

'No, Aunt,' said Oswald, now thoroughly cowed. Julia, he felt, could never be the tyrant that these harpies of Aunts were.

'Then take your pen and sign.'

'Yes, Aunt.'

And a fevered, agitated, yet hopeful Oswald signed away his last vestige of freedom.

III

After all this drama, very over-heating to the blood of a peaceful young gentleman, Oswald looked forward to matrimony as a sheltered nook of honourable tranquillity. No more Aunts, no more detestable careering. By a process of specious reasoning he tried to convince himself that it was better to be kept and have fifty pounds pocket-money than to enjoy the dangerous freedom of contracting overdrafts, with all the subsequent horrors real and imaginary. Like the hero of Corneille, Oswald aspired to descend. And for a while, at least, Julia was very good to him. Eight hundred a year and a little man of one's own seemed to her solid blessings in an uncertain world. And she enjoyed perverting his ignorance. The feminine instinct for dominion (inherited no doubt from the happy matriarchy of the Stone Age) is slow to develop, and only waxes with the inevitable waning of the prestige of the captured male. In the warmth of gratified senses she smiled indulgently on his caprices, and Oswald had almost the privileges of a favourite concubine. Quite as often as not, she allowed him to do what he wanted, and for some months the Court of Louis XV, Elizabethan drama and the Proustian novel were allowed to rest in peace, a relief for which Oswald was truly grateful.

In one matter, however, Julia was firm; and if Oswald had not been so trusting he would immediately have suspected, what was the fact, that the chain of a Career had only been temporarily loosened. She insisted that Oswald should continue his important functions as critic.

'But, my darling,' said Oswald, mildly uxorious and reasonable, 'it's perfectly ridiculous for me to spend all that time and trouble for the utterly paltry sum they pay.'

'I want you to do it for *my* sake,' Julia replied sweetly. 'It keeps us in touch with people, and I'm proud to see *our* name before the public. As to the pay, leave that to me.'

Involuntarily Oswald almost said 'Yes, Aunt,' Julia's tone was so like that of Aunt Ursula when she was gently bullying him for his own good. But, like Aunt Ursula, Julia had practical sense, and justified her 'leave that to me.' She invited the editor to a week-end in their country cottage, an idea which would never have occurred to Oswald, who disliked the man as one of the instruments of career-torture. She flattered the editor, she fed him with a lavish extravagance which made Oswald's eyes pop wide open with innocent amazement as he contrasted this luxury with Julia's ordinary frugality, and she had two long private conferences with her guest. Oswald was staggered to learn that his weekly contributions were now valued at two guineas – a rise of more than eight hundred per cent. Nor was this undeserved, for if Oswald's productions were scarcely worth reading, they were not so very different from lots of others which were paid just as much. But while the distinction was flattering and the extra money more than welcome to one almost in the position of a ward in Chancery, Oswald still felt that he would exchange willingly this fame and fortune for a little peace and quietness. *He* was not ambitious. The preparation of one short article occupied most of a week, and worried his waking and sleeping thoughts. But for Julia's bright ideas and gentle but insistent bullying, the article often would never have been written at all.

Bullied Oswald undoubtedly was, not in the slightly truculent *in loco parentis* manner of Aunt Ursula, but with a firmer sweetness, a more determined pretence of weakness and injury, a more precise ambition. Oswald instinctively knew himself. He knew that he would never be guilty of his country's blood, and that the ecstasy of the living lyre would never be awakened by him if it cost more than half an hour's effort. Dante would have put him in Limbo, a poor colourless creature. Like many self-indulgent persons, he was peculiarly sensitive to the moods of those near him. He was not observant; he hadn't the swift intuition which enables us to detect real motives and feelings under the altruistic disguises which are quite as often self-deceptive as meant to deceive. Julia soon found out how to 'manage' him. If she wanted to make him happy, either as a reward or to hoodwink him or as a preliminary to an attack, she had only to see to his little comforts of bed and board, and for the rest merely leave him alone to 'fritter', as Aunt Ursula so energetically put it. When she wanted to coerce him, she had a splendid arsenal of weapons. She would meet his ardours with a gentle indifference which distressed Oswald and left him *triste*. She would give him cold mutton for dinner on the plea of economy; and Oswald loathed economy and cold mutton. She would harry him about that wretched weekly article until he had indigestion and a sleepless night. But her most potent method was to brood over Oswald's real or imaginary sins of omission until she oozed disapprobation and a sullen, injured self-righteousness. She wouldn't say anything, but gradually filled the atmosphere with a kind of ectoplasm of reproach and gentle misery. Oswald would try to combat this by an affectation of tremendous cheeriness, which invariably broke down and reduced him to the ignominy of asking with palpitating timidity and meekness, 'What is it, dear?' And very soon he would learn to his cost what it was.

Julia was not long in losing that 'pride of possession' which American advertisements tell us invariably comes if you purchase the right car, and which young women of strong temperament are supposed to feel when they acquire a beautiful new husband. Oswald lived as far as possible like an idle but harmless bachelor with a woman about the house. And Julia began to feel this would never do – it was far too dull and undistinguished. What about that house in Eaton Square and the crowds of guests paying homage to fame and beauty? Upon the whole, that dream was rather more distant than when they had married. Julia was bored and disappointed and boredom and disappointment made her resentful. She chose the week-end cottage as her terrain, started brooding on Saturday evening, and by Sunday night had worked up such an atmosphere that Oswald felt almost as nervous as a Venetian when politely informed by two masks that their Excellencies desired to speak with him. Over dinner, a nasty cold dinner, he laboured frantically to stave off the inevitable 'What is it, dear?' Never much of a hand at making conversation to a hostile audience, he cocked up his birdy eye with comical distress, waved his cigarette-yellow fingers unhappily, and made inane remarks.

'The blue lupins are coming on marvellously.'

'Are they?' A very listless Julia, picking at her food with an air of injured melancholy.

'Yes. Don't you think those big red poppies look lovely with them?'

'Do they? I hadn't noticed.'

Oswald nearly said, 'What is it, dear?' but instead gulped at some bread and cheese. A pause. Julia sighed, and imparted a pathetic droop to her swarthy and masterful head.

'By the way,' Oswald broke the uneasy silence with abject flattery, 'how would it be if we put one of your pictures in the spare room? Brighten the place up, and look awfully well ...'

'Don't pretend, Oswald. You know my pictures are no good, and you know you know it.'

'Oh, I say! You know I'm always urging you to go on with your painting.'

'Yes,' Julia put in swiftly, 'I know you'd much rather do that than do the slightest stroke of work yourself.'

Oswald gasped and took a swig of cider which he rather disliked, but he wasn't allowed anything more expensive. He sighed. She sighed. His sigh meant 'Why is this woman so confoundedly disagreeable and unreasonable?' Her sigh meant 'Why does this man make me so unhappy with his selfishness, instead of cherishing his dear little wife?' Oswald remained obstinately silent; he would *not* say 'What is it, dear?' He tried to think about pleasant things – baskets of fruit, the Russian Ballet, the elegance of Swann, the Ritz Bar ... He was violently interrupted:

'Oswald!'

'What? I beg your pardon!'

'Oh, never mind. I can see you don't care about me any longer.'

'Oh, Julia! How unkind of you! You know ...'

Julia interrupted him again with stern but gentle determination.

'I want to talk to your seriously, Oswald, and you sit there without uttering a word. It's very cruel of you, and I sometimes feel I was wrong to let you marry me. You're not the sort of man who takes the trouble to look after his wife.'

If Oswald had been as clear-headed and swift-tongued as his wife, he would immediately have attacked and destroyed the false assumptions and insinuations in her remarks. Was it he who had not uttered a word? Had he married or been married? Was it for him to 'look after' a wife who so obviously looked after him and so promptly suppressed any signs of independence? But he was as tongue-tied as when his Aunt had wrested his signature from him. All he was able to say was:

'Oh, Julia! How can you?'

'I'm not going to argue with you, Oswald,' said Julia with gentle dignity (I'm only telling you, Oscar), 'but I do think you might have a little consideration for me.'

Oswald collapsed:

'What is it, dear?'

'There ought to be no need for me to tell you,' she retorted more severely, 'since it concerns you more than me, and if I weren't so foolishly devoted to you, I shouldn't care.'

'*Now* what have I done?' asked Oswald, with a feeble effort at petulance.

'You haven't done anything, that's the trouble. It's what you ought to have done. I want to talk to you about your career.'

('O God! thought Oswald, 'Aunt Ursula all over again!')

'Before we were married,' Julia went on sadly but firmly, 'you drew alluring pictures of what our life was going to be, how you were going to work hard and write books and make an interesting life for us both.'

35

'Oh!' Oswald exclaimed. He was going to add 'you liar!' but prudence restrained him. She ignored this anguished protest.

'I know you've got great talent, Oswald, but you're lazy and indifferent. Yes, you are! I blame myself – and your Aunt Ursula blames me – for encouraging you to idle when you ought to be at work.'

'My God!' said Oswald, gazing at her in helpless amazement.

'I have made up my mind – I will *not* ruin your career. I will not allow you to do yourself that wrong.'

Oswald was so bewildered by what seemed to him a devilish perversion of the facts that he hadn't the wits or courage to say that if only she *would* ruin his career and make it impossible for the subject ever to come up again, he would be her obedient, idle slave for life. In any case, Julia didn't give him time to speak.

'To-morrow, Oswald,' she said solemnly, 'we begin a new life. I've talked it over with your Aunt, and she agrees with me that it's my duty to work with you and keep you up to the mark. I won't have you make use of me as an excuse for wasting your life. I've decided to work with you, and we'll start as soon as we get back to town to-morrow. There! I've had my say, and it's all determined. Come and kiss me, darling, and say you agree.'

A new epoch of 'absolute hell' now afflicted the lamentable Oswald. All energy seemed to him mysterious and frightening, but the energy which tried to bully him into action was always painful and hellish. The only philosopher Oswald approved of was Epicurus who, far from recommending tumultuous pleasures, exhorts us to shun publicity and the pursuit of wealth and power, and to live in peaceful, sober retirement. Timidly he tried to make Julia read Epicurus, but she belonged to the modern philosophic school of go-getters, and scorned Epicurus heartily. Nor had Oswald himself reached that stage of *ataraxia* where the mind controls the body and enjoys ideal freedom even in material chains. When you consider that the oppressors and robbers of mankind are frequently highly rewarded, when you observe the enormous number of insignificant people who try to thrust themselves into prominence from mere vanity, it does seem hard that Oswald couldn't have been left alone to enjoy his harmless indolence. To be thwarted of peace of mind by a pack of restless females – what a sinister but what a common fate!

Julia installed herself as Oswald's muse and collaborator. Hers was that lowest-common-factor 'modernity' which despises everything not immediately topical. Anything (and that was most things) outside the circle of her immediate interest she called either 'sticky' or 'mouldy'. Her use of these critical terms was perhaps not very exact, but the distinction existed for her, since she said Epicurus was 'mouldy' and Proust 'sticky'. In her view anything more than ten years old was 'mouldy', with the notable exception of those eternal banalities which have existed ever since there have been banal people in the world, which is a very long time indeed.

'Now,' said Julia, taking up the rather dusty papers on Oswald's 'work' table, 'what are these?'

'Oh, those! They're notes for a book on Elizabethan drama.'

Julia sniffed with the enlightened scorn of a gallery first nighter.

'And these?'

'Aunt Ursula's notes for a joint book on the Court of Louis Quinze.'

'And do you suppose any one's interested in that mouldy stuff?'

'Yes,' said Oswald with unexpected boldness, 'I am, and so is Aunt Ursula.'

'The public isn't,' said Julia, well aware that she was the public. 'I don't wonder you can't do anything with this stuff. It isn't up to date. Why, if Shakespeare or What's-his-name wrote a play to-day they wouldn't be able to get it on!'

'Whose fault is that?' asked Oswald, with an attempt at sarcasm which Julia ignored.

'Why don't you write something like Noel Coward?' she asked.

'For the same reason that about fifty thousand other people don't,' said Oswald simply, 'because I can't. If I could write new plays, do you suppose I should bother about discussing old ones?'

'Well,' retorted Julia, a little surprised at the justness of his reasoning, 'why not write something about the Russian Ballet? It's still popular in some of the sets.'

'My dear,' said Oswald, almost firmly, 'if you will go down the Charing Cross Road, you'll see a shop full of books on the Ballet. The meanest of those writers knows more about it than I ever hope to.'

'You're finding excuses for being lazy,' she denounced him.

Oswald shrugged his shoulders.

'You don't care about a single thing but yourself,' she stormed. 'You're selfish and lazy and mean-spirited. All you want to do is to sit about and smoke cigarettes, and go to the theatre, and drink at bars with *beastly* young men a decent man wouldn't know. Why can't you be like other men, Oswald, and *do* something?'

Poor Oswald! He wished very much that he *could* do some things – control his wife, for instance, and get his money back. He also wished that he could do another very simple thing, express himself in domestic debate. For instance, could he not point out that trying to write books you didn't want to write wasn't worth doing? He could not ...

Julia abandoned the hopeless task of making Oswald either a 'man' or a 'modern', but she prodded him with such effect that within six months he had compiled a hodge-podge about the Court of Louis XV, and was fairly launched on a verbose novel about the seventeenth century. This historical effort was to combine the manners of Jacobean comedy with the method of Proust. Oswald groaned under his fardels, cheered only by the hope that the failure of both books would convince his tormentor that he was inapt for literature, and thus secure him the peace for which he pined.

But he had reckoned without his Julia. As publisher after publisher rejected these works with alacrity, Oswald's hopes rose, but Julia's brow grew dark. What! Reject the works of *her* husband in which *she* had collaborated, thwart *her* progress to hostess-ship and the social column? What were these publishers? Were they men? She planted Oswald in the country with two thousand cigarettes and a gramophone, and investigated. Some refused to see her, some granted an interview but refused, with firm politeness, the honour of publishing Oswald, and rang a concealed bell for a typist-secretary when Julia's eyes turned kind. At last she found a small publisher who was, in fact, rather a big man with a cheery red face and horn-rimmed spectacles. But his office, his business, and his staff were undoubtedly small.

At first he was nearly as politely emphatic against Oswald's works as the others had been. But Julia looked at him, and he looked at Julia. He faltered in his eloquent description of business depression and the lack of public interest in French memoirs and the historical novel. He looked at Julia again, and she looked back charmingly. He offered a cigarette, which Julia accepted. They ceased talking about manuscripts,

39

and discussed actors and types of cars. He displayed wit, and Julia's laugh was exquisite and flattering. Julia hinted at the lonely life of self-sacrifice imposed on the wife of a studious recluse (at that moment smoking cigarettes and chaffing the barmaid in a pub over a gin and vermouth), and the publisher pitied and praised her. Time passed. The secretary came in with papers, but was waved away.

'Half-past twelve,' he said. 'How'd it be if we had lunch together, and talked this matter over?'

Julia demurred coquettishly, but yielded to his big-man argument that business is best conducted over a cheerful meal. The lunch was certainly cheerful, but Oswald and his poor old works were not once mentioned, although they discussed a great variety of topics and discovered an amazing number of mutual interests and sympathies. They parted at half-past three, with an appointment to dine together the next evening to 'see what can be done about these books.' Julia wrote Oswald that she might be delayed a day or two longer than she had expected, and Oswald's spirits rose, not only at the extension of his holiday, but with glee at the thought of the difficulties she was encountering in her obstinate efforts. If he had known precisely what she was encountering, he might not have been so pleased. The discussion of business is often protracted, and yet not unpleasant to those who have an aptitude that way.

About ten days later Oswald was reclining on a couch, smoking and wondering if it hurt the gramophone to let it run right down when it was too much of a fag to get up and stop it. Suddenly from the lane he heard the loud, familiar hooting of a klaxon, and knew his temporary peace was shattered. It was Julia, of course it was Julia. He was surprised by the warmth and almost humility of her greeting, as if she were trying to placate him. Oswald had spent so much of his life in a pleasing vacancy of thought, that he had never formulated the great law that infidelity is frequently the parent of domestic charity. He was only grateful that she wasn't in one of her energetic fits.

Now, Julia was still so far duped by the mistaken propaganda of Oswald's Aunts that she firmly believed he 'wanted to write', and was convinced that he would be delighted by receiving a contract for two books at once. Oswald's scarcely disguised hatred of writing was interpreted by her as a sign of 'artistic temperament.' She therefore immediately produced from her handbag a long envelope folded in two, and said to Oswald:

'Guess what I've got here?'

'Not *another* income-tax form?'

'No, of course not! It's something that will please you.'

A wild hope shot into Oswald's mind like a bright meteor through dark skies – had she brought him back that fatal transfer of his income?

'Is it a legal document?' he asked cautiously.

'Yes.'

Oswald could feel his heart beating.

'About money?' he pursued eagerly.

'Partly. But it's more important still – it concerns your Career.'

Oswald's disappointment can only be expressed in metaphor. He felt the utter flop of spirits which came to a wartime subaltern who thought the Orderly Room had sent for him to go on leave, and found it was only that he had been chosen for the honour of leading a trench raid.

That fatal word 'career' – why had God suffered such an abomination to be?

'Let me see it,' he said weakly.

'I must explain it to you,' said Julia, half drawing the document from its envelope and then putting it back again.

'You see, it's very difficult to get anything published now. I saw lots of publishers, and they all said that the book market is in a hopeless state. So when I did get an offer, I accepted it. You'll like Merriton – he's the publisher, and he's coming down to stay with us next week. I think he's awfully jolly. Anyway, he gave me the best contract he could. It's what's called a "deferred royalty" agreement. The first edition's a thousand and you get ten per cent, but you don't get anything until fifteen hundred copies are sold.'

And she handed Oswald a neatly-typed, rather important-looking document, which he received with as much bewilderment as chagrin. Nevertheless, he could not restrain a thrill of honest pride when he read the words 'Oswald Carstairs of The Cottage, Primpton, in the County of Bucks, hereinafter called The Author.' Never before had Oswald realised that he was a genius. A publisher had accepted his books, and believed they would sell at least fifteen hundred, since he did not propose to pay anything to The Author until that number had been reached. He forgot the miseries of a Career in the glory of its rewards.

'Are you pleased?' asked Julia.

'Naturally,' said Oswald, trying not to appear too delighted, 'I think you've done very well, very well indeed.'

She came over and kissed him with a perfidiously complex female kiss, the hardy kiss of one who feels that indeed she has done her duty.

To those who glory in the complete identification of interests in a married pair, it would have been a delicious privilege to observe how completely Julia made Oswald's career her own. Her devotion was more than exemplary, it was heroic. Merriton arrived for his week-end on Friday night, and paid Oswald a great many compliments on his literary accomplishments. On Saturday afternoon, Julia suddenly remembered that she had no lobsters for lunch on

Sunday and that she 'must' have some. Oswald was therefore despatched in the car to the nearest market town with strict injunctions not to return without a supply of fresh crustaceans. During the two hours he was absent, Julia made full use of the opportunity for a really heart-to-heart talk about the whole situation. And, satisfactory as this was, she found that another conference was necessary on Sunday afternoon, and therefore took a long walk in the woods with her guest. He departed on Monday, assuring them that he had had a splendid time and that things were coming along nicely. Julia felt a glow of pride and hope. Far from spending in anticipation the large sums which Oswald was about to earn, she practised an extreme economy, so that they might the sooner begin to entertain on the grand scale demanded of a fashionable author.

Unfortunately, difficulties and many unforeseen delays arose. Six months elapsed before Oswald received proofs, although Julia, with indomitable self-sacrifice, made no less than four lengthy visits to London to smooth the way. Finally, Julia returned triumphantly with the proofs, and, since Oswald was rather languid about them, Julia corrected them, and then took them back to London herself in case they should get lost in the post. Two more months elapsed, during which period Julia spent a great deal of time in London, 'seeing the books through the press', and (what was even more important) getting to know influential critics who might be induced to take an interest in Oswald's genius through heart-to-heart talks with his wife. Merriton wrote Oswald that he was 'having trouble with the binders', but hoped to get one of the books out within a week. Judge therefore of the surprise, grief and rage at The Cottage when Oswald opened and read a letter from some low creature who described himself as a 'Receiver', stating that Merriton and Co. were in bankruptcy and that no doubt Oswald would wish to buy the sheets of his two books for the trifling sum of three hundred pounds.

Julia read the letter and turned pale. She went upstairs, locked herself in her room, and cried for an hour. So much ardent self-sacrifice, all in vain! What a tragedy it is to play Alcestis to an ineffective Admetus! Julia sincerely pitied herself. And, with her, pity took the form of contempt for Oswald. What a poor creature he was, how ineffective, how spineless, how almost insultingly unsuspicious! Any other man with a wife of such self-sacrificing dispositions would have done something about it – either have made a row or a fortune. But the maddening thing about Oswald was that he simply smoked cigarettes and did nothing. Too late Julia realised that the best and most self-sacrificing of wives cannot make a silk purse out of a sow's ear, an Arnold Bennett out of an Oswald. And the most maddening thing was that Oswald didn't seem to care, obviously didn't care, so long as she was there to look after him and *keep* him. To fail her like this after all she had done for him! No wonder Julia wept.

Yet who dare say that English womanhood has lost its ancient virtues of courage and hope, not to mention self-sacrifice? From the depths of defeat and despair Julia wrested courage and strength to try again. If a poor creature like Oswald, she argued, could write books and very nearly get them published – with a little assistance from her – why shouldn't *she* write something really up to date and popular and, if sacrifice was necessary, sacrifice herself for herself? It was obvious to Julia now that Oswald would never have succeeded, whatever she had done for him. People simply were *not* interested in that sort of highbrow stuff. You have to give them life, life as they know it, life as it is lived by those summits of human evolution, the Julias of London. As Julia was never tired of pointing out, there is more real life in a kitten playing than in all the stuffy old famous poets from Shelley to Lawrence Hope. She was always telling Oswald this, and he *never* would see it.

So, without saying a word to any one, Julia began to write a book. Of course, it was a novel. How on earth can you write about 'life' except in a novel? The theme of the novel was Julia's life, and the heroine of the novel was Julia. It was not the Julia that the world knew, it was not even Oswald's Julia, it was a Julia known only to God, as they say in the soldiers' cemeteries. It was unmistakably Julia, but a Julia whose existence nobody had hitherto suspected, one who possessed fascinating charm and a wit which invariably triumphed over opposition. In the end this dream-Julia married a dream-husband who was very unlike Oswald in every respect. Oswald passed a comparatively peaceful time during the months when this work was gestating. He was compelled to write his weekly review, but otherwise was left almost entirely alone. At times he wondered why on earth Julia spent so many hours moping in her room, and dreaded the revelation of some awful plan which would entail action on his part. But nothing of the kind happened, and Oswald began to feel that there might be something in life after all. He was even allowed to go and spend a week alone in London, and renewed his acquaintance with one or two smart but sympathetic young men with bright ties and winning manners.

After dinner one evening in the country Julia said:
'I want to talk to you seriously, Oswald.'
'Yes?' he replied apprehensively.
'Have you written anything this year?'
'No.'
'Do you intend to?'

'I – I haven't planned anything. I –'

'In other words, you admit that you've failed as a writer?'

'I never really thought I should succeed,' he broke out, with almost desperate determination. 'You see, I didn't really want ... I mean ... if it hadn't been for Aunt Ursula and the Bank and you ... It's very difficult to explain,' he ended up feebly.

'So difficult that I don't know what you're talking about,' Julia retorted with dignity. 'What I do know is that you have utterly failed to do what you pretended to me you were going to do. You do admit that?'

'I didn't pretend I was going to do anything,' Oswald protested. 'It was pretended for me.'

'What utter nonsense! But we won't discuss that. The point is that *I* have done what you have failed to do – I have written a novel, and it is accepted for publication.'

'Good God!'

Julia was not quite sure what he meant by this pious or impious exclamation, but she chose to regard it as a compliment.

'I have a copy here,' she said. 'Would you like me to read it to you?'

What could Oswald say but 'Yes'? After all, on such occasions, you can always smoke and think of something else. Moreover, he was still amazed at Julia's declaration, and oddly enough felt a little jealous. He had always understood that *he* was the genius of the family, and it seemed rather cheek of Julia to usurp his functions. But he listened meekly enough to the reading of the novel and, passing to a different set of feelings, began to be rather proud of having a wife who could actually write a novel. Whilst modestly making no claims in that direction, he couldn't help reflecting that his own example and conversation had at least moulded her genius. And he pleased Julia very much by remarking that she had genius.

For a short time Julia was happy. She believed in her book, and especially believed in the fame and social prestige it would bring her. She had the proud feeling that she had done what her lawful protector in life could not do. There were constant journeys to London, and quite a dizzy and orgiastic series of heart-to-heart talks with all sorts of men who were supposed to 'have influence' in making a literary success. On the day of publication Julia triumphed. She gave a small dinner to the four most influential critics obtainable, and during the evening scores of people dropped in for drinks, and were given signed copies of the great work. These were bread upon the waters, which would be returned a hundred-fold – sprats to catch whales of circulation. Everybody was very flattering and foretold an immense success. Perhaps the very peak of the evening came when a young man, who had taken the heart-to-heart talks rather seriously, and had been impressed by the number and fervour of the visitors, said to her shyly:

'What does it feel like to be *famous*?'

And Julia replied honestly:

'It's wonderful, quite wonderful.'

With masculine caprice Oswald was more than a little jealous of all this success and adulation. He need not have been. It would be unkind to say that Julia enjoyed her happiness on false pretences, but at least she built her dream of greatness on crumbling foundations. True, the heart-to-hearters played the game, and her book had a good press, the kind of too good press which damns a book by arousing too much expectation. It made a sharp false start, rapidly dwindled to nothing, and was soon obliterated under the endless floods of new novels which pour from the presses to the circulating libraries to the pulping machine. Julia struggled hard against Fate, and multiplied heart-to-heart talks. The power and the glory, the wealth and the splendour remained obstinately aloof – she was just one of the legion of young women who have written a first novel.

Every one, including her publisher, said: 'You must write another novel.'

Here a distressing difficulty arose; she found she had nothing to write about. The first book, devoted to that fascinating subject, herself, had written itself with surprising facility. The next obstinately refused even to start. Julia worried terribly, and her worrying was not diminished by the discovery that the financing of her glory and of all these heart-to-heart discussions had been exceedingly expensive. She retired to the country to think it all out.

Among the admirers Julia had won – perhaps as much by her talents for intimate conversation as by her literary genius – was a pale blonde young man, who was 'serious'. He was rather dirty, read a great deal of foreign literature, had platonic leanings towards communism, cultivated Style, and contributed to a very 'serious' review which was eagerly read by its contributors.

On his advice, Julia decided to become a Stylist. From the young man's earnest but exceedingly elliptic conversation, and from the models he put before her, Julia grasped the essentials of Style. These were almost wholly negative. To have Style, she gathered, you must not write about anything which would even faintly interest ordinary human beings, and you must put it all in such a way that no ordinary person will have the slightest idea what you mean. Your stream of consciousness must flow, no matter to what purpose, so long as it flows. Above all, you must have a superior air of 'suggesting' – oh, infinite things. The young man even gave her a theme, 'the conflict of the dual ego.' Julia was not quite sure what it meant, but this was rather a help than a hindrance to the attainment of Style. She pegged away, and quite often reached that supreme consolation of the artist, a sense of being greater than she knew.

Unluckily, when this remarkable work was finished, polished and re-polished in consultation with the young man, typed out with beautifully wide spacing and a red headline, nobody would publish it. Julia went frequently to London, the young man recommended lavishly, she became almost reckless in the matter of heart-to-heart talks – but she had to pay for the publication. And the book was an utter flop, in spite of a really lavish Publication Party where myriads of critics were almost miraculously fed on caviare and cocktails. Julia was almost broken-hearted, and again retired with Oswald to the country to think things out.

The position was almost tragically unpleasant. Julia was forced, against her will, to say farewell to all her dreams of greatness. Oswald had failed, if he can ever have been said to have attempted; and she had failed. And the clouds which gather round the setting sun of greatness were menacing. They found themselves strangely neglected by their friends, for the plain ones had been intimidated by Julia in her days of grandeur, and the distinguished ones were not anxious to associate with two unsuccessful amateurs. This might not have been so bad – though it was bad enough – if there had not been quite a formidable hill of debts incurred by Julia in her gamble for the Great Life of the social columns. She hinted to Oswald that he might beg a subsidy from his Aunts, but he refused with brutal terror. Oswald was getting fat, 'gross and sensual' Julia called it, and grumbled continually because she cut down his little luxuries.

In this crisis Julia showed that there was the stuff of a sensible woman in her. She sold the car; she let the studio in London; she abandoned literature, and decided to have a baby. Breaking off all visits to London and heart-to-heart talks, she betrayed the innocent Oswald into paternity. This action on the surface may not seem as economically sound as her other measures, but Julia knew Oswald's Aunts better than Oswald did. As soon as there was no possible doubt that Julia was about to increase the human species by at least one, Oswald was despatched to the Aunts after being carefully drilled as ambassador, and returned with almost opulent subsidies. Even Aunt Ursula said nothing about his Career, and all the Aunts behaved as if paternity was the one career of which Oswald was capable – which, in a limited sense, was no doubt true. As for Julia, she let them think what they liked so long as they paid up; but an unprejudiced observer would have gathered from her manner that parthenogenesis was not confined to insects. She felt she had saved something from the wreck of a noble life, and spent much time working out a scheme of training and education to enable her son – she was certain it would be a son – to do all that she had failed to do.

Oswald, still in the thirties, was already middle-aged – timid, comfort-loving, indolent and upon the whole fatuous. Julia left him very much to himself; she preferred to do her breeding unassisted, and spent week after week day-dreaming the future of the child which was to be not only hers, but Herself projected into the future.

How it happened Oswald never quite knew, but one day he went to Julia's abandoned writing-desk to find something, opened a locked drawer and found a large number of letters tied in different-sized bundles. Julia was upstairs, resting. Oswald knew perfectly well that it is ungentlemanly to read other people's letters; he even knew that it is one of a husband's primary duties never to look at his wife's correspondence – and yet he read those letters, and by reading shattered his comfortable little pot-bellied world. For these letters were undoubtedly compromising, and left no possibility of doubt even to the most obtuse and supine of husbands Beginning with Merriton's, Oswald read letter after letter with feverish haste and frantic indignation. The whole course of Julia's perfidious double life during the past three or four years became painfully obvious to him. What a disgustful mess of intrigue! Oswald clutched his head in despair and rancour.

'The trollop!' he muttered. 'The beastly little trollop!'

Aunt Ursula was napping cosily over tea by the 'snuggery' fire, and didn't hear the new maid's rather timid knock. When one reaches a certain age it is rather startling to find a servant standing beside one all of a sudden, as if the creature were a spook or a pagan divinity. Aunt Ursula spoke a little sharply in reprimand, and then asked why she had been disturbed.

'If you please, Ma'am, it's Mr Oswald to see you.'

'Mr *Oswald*?'

'Yes, Ma'am.'

Aunt Ursula wagged her head, as if shaking the last drops of sleep from her hair.

'Are you sure it's Mr Oswald?'

'Yes, Ma'am, and he particularly wants to see you.'

'Show him in.'

A pale, lugubrious, rather distracted Oswald silently entered the door, carrying a small leather portmanteau. He kissed his Aunt's forehead tragically, made no answer to her voluble enquiries, but placed the bag beside a chair, sat down heavily and hid his face in his hands. Aunt Ursula felt faint with apprehension.

'Oswald!' she exclaimed sternly, 'take your face out of your hands! Why are you here?'

Oswald looked up piteously, opened his lips as if he were going to moan, and made no sound.

'Is anything wrong with Julia?'

Oswald nodded.

'Don't tell me that you've come away and left her ill?'

Oswald shook his head.

'Then what *is* the matter? Don't sit there like a dumb idiot, Oswald. You frighten me.'

'I've run away,' said Oswald gloomily, beginning already to feel a little frightened at what he had done.

'You've *run away*? What on earth for? Are you mad, Oswald, or trying to bring on one of my attacks?'

'No, Aunt,' said Oswald pathetically, 'I've nothing but you left in the world.'

'Don't talk nonsense,' Aunt Ursula cut short this unseasonable sentimentalism, 'and try to explain yourself.'

'Julia ...' Oswald began, and then, unable to express himself, handed his Aunt the small bag.

'Look in that,' he almost wailed, and once more hid his face.

Aunt Ursula opened the bag very cautiously, as if she thought that Oswald had brought the new baby in it or even a small crocodile. Finding only letters, she adjusted her lorgnette and began to read.

'God bless my soul,' she exclaimed, 'what is all this indecent twaddle?'

'Love letters to Julia,' he explained weakly, 'from other men.'

Aunt Ursula read two or three of the letters, put them back in the bag, snapped it shut, and then gazed at Oswald, tapping her knee with the closed lorgnette.

'When did you find those letters?'

'This morning.'

'And then you quarrelled with Julia about them?'

'No, Aunt. I came straight away.'

'What! Without saying a word to her?'

'Yes, Aunt.'

'God bless my soul,' she said indignantly, 'is that how you treat the mother of your child in these critical days?'

Oswald was used to shocks from his Aunt, but he was utterly unprepared for this reception of his news. All the way up to London he had been rehearsing a most pathetic little scene in which his Aunt wept and embraced him, promised to free him from Julia, and to set him up once more in a nice comfortable bachelor flat near at hand. He protested:

'But, Aunt, she's been unfaithful in the most horrid way. Read those letters.'

'I don't want to read them. I never read other people's letters, and I'm surprised at your indelicacy in doing so. And *what* a state of mind poor Julia must be in now, You're risking my godchild's life. Ring the bell.'

As one in a hag-ridden nightmare, Oswald feebly rang the bell, and the maid appeared.

'Baylis,' said Aunt Ursula energetically, 'ring up Mrs Oswald at once in the country, and ask for a six minutes' trunk call. As soon as you are through, come and tell me. I want to speak to Mrs Oswald.'

'Yes, Ma'am.'

'What do you mean ...' Oswald was beginning in a sort of hesitating bluster, when his Aunt interrupted:

'Listen to me, Oswald. You did a foolish thing when you read those letters, and a still more foolish thing when you "ran away", as you rightly put it, like a silly schoolboy. Have you ever read Balzac?'

This last question was snapped at him, and the unfortunate Oswald hadn't the least idea what his Aunt was driving at. Meekly he replied:

'Yes, Aunt.'

'Then you will have learned that there are some husbands who are predestined to ... well, to make certain discoveries. I suppose you think you want to divorce Julia?'

'Yes, Aunt.'

'Well, you don't. You're so accustomed to being looked

after by Julia that you're incapable of looking after yourself. And I'm not going to do it for you. In any case, you can't desert your child. It will be the only heir of the Carstairs name – and estate.'

'But how do I know it's mine?' Oswald protested.

'I'm ringing up Julia to find out. If she assures me it is yours, then I shall absolutely forbid you to leave her. No doubt she has been foolish, many women are' – a veil of reminiscence clouded Aunt Ursula's brow – 'and I've no doubt she's heartily sick of it, and regrets it. Do you hear me?'

'Yes, Aunt.'

'Julia is very fond of you, and I've no doubt whatever that this dear little child coming to you was partly meant by her to express her sincere repentance and her real love for you.'

'Yes, Aunt?' Oswald enquired hesitatingly.

'I've no doubt about it whatever,' she said energetically, frowning at him, 'and I'm ashamed of you for running off to me like this. Take those letters, tear them up, and throw them in the fire. Don't throw them all on at once or you'll put the fire out.'

Very slowly and reluctantly, as if under the influence of hypnosis, Oswald began to tear up the letters and to put them primly on the hot coals. His Aunt went on talking:

'As soon as I have this assurance from Julia, I shall take you straight back to the country. After an upset like this, Julia's health must be tended. As for your relations in the future, I shall take care to see that this sort of indecency doesn't occur again. I'm very angry with you both, and if it weren't for the child, I should send you both packing. Do you hear me, Oswald?'

The sharp ring of the telephone bell rattled on the drums of Oswald's ears as he languidly tore another letter, and answered submissively:

'Yes, Aunt.'

Now Lies She There

AN ELEGY

Any one remarkable, from the clown to the philosopher, can inspire love in these creatures, who will always astound their males. REMY DE GOURMONT

I

THE first winter gale began last night, a rough but very competent dismissal of the sun. These sou'-westers sweep over England like an invading army, pivoted on some imaginary point out in the northern seas. Like an invasion, they seem lugubrious and destructive, particularly at the fall of the leaf. The pelting barrage of rain, the flying terror of the leaves, the groans of the half-stripped trees, the heavy roar of the main body of wind passing, and the sudden shrieking assaults of violent gusts – it all gets on one's nerves. Last night I lay awake listening to the long rumble in the chimney and the creaking, dry-bones rattle of the big chestnut outside the window. For some reason I kept thinking of Constance, the beauty and destructive power of her, as if she were a gale in men's lives to set them whirling to destruction like leaves, only to subside herself in an even more squalid self-destruction. This grey lugubrious morning, with its hurry of clouds and soaked, leaf-scattered lawn and wrecked flower-beds, again makes me think of Constance and her ruined life. You wouldn't imagine that God would want to wreck flower-beds and the lives of beautiful women. I suppose God thinks He knows all about it. I wonder. Anyhow, I'm not God. I'm not responsible, and I don't know everything. I can only surmise and imagine from the little I do know, which isn't much.

I wish I did know more about Constance, but I really think

she was as mysterious and inexplicable to herself as to other people. Sometimes I've thought the mystery was only a void that where we imagined in her a *mêlée* of motives and desires and instincts and thwarted ambitions, there was simply nothing at all. She had to invent caprices from the top of her head, so to speak, in a vain effort to fly the inexorable boredom of that void. I wish I could quite believe that – it would simplify everything. But I don't. Constance is a wreck, but she is the wreck of a noble woman. Yet destructive, right enough; for in destroying herself she destroyed plenty of others. It does seem odd that a woman should have talents and beauty and charm and freedom and wealth and every sort of privilege, and make such a mess of it all as a basket of eggs dropped on a station platform. Nothing to do but sweep up the mess – and such nice eggs! Again I ask myself if it were not a noble discontent, the pursuit of an *O altitudo*, which made her despise all these things the world calls good? She was lovely enough to seduce a saint. What if a saint had seduced her? She lived at the wrong end of the Christian era – Anthony would have sterilised that destructive despair into a fanatical hermitess. Yet I can't imagine a scraggy, sun-blackened Constance, with tangled white hair and filthy rags, wandering about the sands of Egypt, quavering cracked psalms to the glory of God. She might just as well be where she is – one excess is as good, or bad, as another.

It must be less than three years ago that she suddenly appeared in my London flat, and kissed me with that promiscuous indifference she always showed to her male friends, whether they had slept with her or not. I had imagined her at Taormina with the Russian ex-general ('a divahn creature'), and had even envied her a little with the envy of the worker, chained in a sunless London winter, for the happy rich who can live in the sun. She was in evening dress, made of some sort of gold stuff which looked exactly like a golden suit of armour – rather appropriate, I thought nastily, for where would she be without the old man's money? She sat down, unasked, in an arm-chair, and crossed her legs, quite indifferent to how much silk stocking I might or might not see – they went so far I thought they must be trunk hose.

'Surprising to see you,' I said, 'in London, in November. I thought you were still at Taormina.'

She took no notice of that. What business was it of mine or any other insignificant creature to watch her goings and comings? Whether she went to heaven or hell was her business. I rather liked her for that. She said:

'Have you got anything to drink? Give me a cocktail.'

'I haven't got any ice,' I said, taking bottles from the cupboard.

'All right. Straight gin will do.'

That was another nice thing in Constance; she never fussed over trifles or tried to make herself important about nothing, as so many silly females do. Her vanity was more like a man's. Perhaps that was one reason why people thought her such a good friend. She only wanted genuine flattery.

She sat up very straight in the chair, sipping her gin. She looked pale, but there was nothing extraordinary in that. If you rush about all day with feverish activity, doing nothing, and drink a good deal, and go to bed about five in the morning you're not quite sure with whom – well, you're apt to look pale. Suddenly she said:

'Bob! I think I'm going to pieces.'

I'd thought so for some long time, but had felt the remark would not be well received. I said:

'What do you mean?'

'I said I'm going to pieces. You can understand that, can't you?'

'It always sounds rather meaningless to me. At best it

means one's dropped by the dullards, at worst that one's lost money ...'

She cut me short:

'I mean in myself. I'm bored, bored, *bored*.'

'So's everybody who doesn't have to work. Anyway, you were interested enough in Boris three months ago.'

She turned her head away and shrugged contemptuously. I could see she thought I was a fool, the sort of dullard who can't understand a *real* sorrow. She drank more gin, thereby increasing her depression.

'Have you ever taken drugs?' she asked.

'No.'

'Well,' she said, with violent gloom, 'I feel I'll have to take to drugs or suicide.'

This was something new from Constance. Her friends occasionally committed suicide and more took drugs, but I couldn't connect either practice with her. If you can imagine an expensive, quite useless, extremely active machine, made of platinum and jewels, and functioning like mad just because some demented engineer had started the thing going – that was Constance. I could only suppose that drugs and suicide were the two imbecilities in life she had never tried. I said:

'They come to much the same thing. Drugs are a bit slower, that's all.'

'Boris is a brute,' she said, 'a sot and a fool.'

I felt instinctively that Boris had nothing to do with her mood. By now she must have been quite used to seeing her beauties turn into beasts – such a poor taste in men she had! As gently as I could, I said:

'You've got over that sort of thing easily enough before now, Constance.'

She turned on me, palely vehement.

'I never cared a damn for one of them. I used them – all except one.'

'Which one?'

'You don't know him – he was killed in the War.'

Again I felt instinctively that this was false. Perhaps I was unjust, but I simply could not imagine Constance caring enough about anyone to carry a grave in her heart. I said as lightly as I could:

'My dear, we were all killed in the War. At the Armistice we rose again from the dead and ascended into heaven. Forget it.'

'He was rather like you,' she said unexpectedly. 'You have the same sort of ugliness.'

I was staggered by this – it sounded sincere. But I believed Constance and I were too good friends for her to try to seduce me. Why should she want to destroy me? I was so surprised I couldn't utter a word.

She got up and walked over to the mantelpiece, rested her elbows on it and her chin on her linked fingers, and gazed tragically at herself – a trick I had seen her play before. I could see the reflection of her pale face, and the great eyes gazing at herself with mournful delectation. It looked as if she were acting a Pinero scene to herself, and it irritated me. Did she expect me to comfort her by making love to her? I deliberately turned my back and poured myself a drink.

'Why don't you say something?' she said over her shoulder, still keeping her elbows on the mantelpiece.

'Because there's nothing to say,' I replied crossly. 'I'm sorry, I simply don't understand you.'

She gazed at herself in the mirror again, looking very tragic-lovely, and then turned away.

'Life's an awful hell, Bob,' she said. 'I haven't slept for three nights and I can't face another. Do you know that René committed suicide yesterday?'

'No!' I exclaimed, shocked. 'Are you sure?'

'I had a letter from him this morning, a beautiful letter,

like a Rimbaud poem, saying he was going to do it. And Solange sent me a telegram this afternoon to tell me he was dead. I must have known he was thinking about it, I've been feeling so miserable and bored. Do you think he meant to show me the way out?'

This struck me as a gratuitous piece of false sentiment. If she had really cared for René, there were plenty of ways in which she could have shown it. For instance, she need not have flattered his French bourgeois vanity and avarice by suddenly picking him up and whirling him into a life of cosmopolitan extravagance, and then as suddenly have wounded both vanity and avarice by kicking him out with brutal energy when Boris turned up. However, I didn't say so, but my sick annoyance expressed itself with a certain brutality.

'Look here, Constance,' I said, 'I haven't much sympathy with these erotic suicides, especially when they're complicated by bits of bad Rimbaud. It's all too remote from reality to move me. If they take themselves off violently, it's probably the best thing for everybody. René was no good, anyway.'

'I know,' she said thoughtfully, 'but he was a divahn creature. If only I'd known how he was suffering.'

It was on the tip of my tongue to retort: 'Well, you ought to have known, since you caused it,' but for some reason I began to lecture her.

'You'll have to pull yourself together, Constance. You can't go on like this. You're an international scandal. I can't pretend to be very sorry about René – he was a worthless little gigolo, anyway. But he's dead, so that's that. And you've broken with Boris apparently. Why don't you go right away by yourself somewhere? Go to Pekin or New York. All this talk about drugs and suicide is rot ...'

She laughed and I stopped dead. I couldn't help it. I had been talking as one comrade to another, and then she laughed in that London hostess way. You might really have thought she was a lady resenting an impertinence. Then she said in the most friendly way:

'Shall we go out and have a drink before the pubs shut and then go and dance somewhere? I shan't be able to sleep to-night, so you'll have to amuse me. You know how I hate to be alone.'

I did know. It was one of the sinister things about her, that inability ever to be alone happily. I guessed that the Narcissus-worship and talk about suicide and drugs and what not had no more tragical basis than the prospect of spending an evening alone. My mouth was half open to reply, when my bell rang with unnecessary violence and duration. To my complete amazement, I found Boris at the door, rather drunk.

'Hullo!' he said. 'Is Constance here? I'm afraid I'm a bit late.'

'What makes you think she's here?' I asked cautiously, scenting the possibility of a row if they met.

'She told me she'd probably be here. Hasn't she turned up yet? She's generally so punctual.'

This was almost too much for my sanity – especially after I had been assuming that everything was over with Boris. I felt I couldn't stand this mess another minute.

'She's in there,' I said. 'Go in, and for God's sake get her away. I'm sick to death of you all.'

Characters all of a piece rarely exist in Nature. French comedy of the seventeenth century is a convention, contradicted by all the memoirs of the period, which is why, as we grow older, we exchange Molière for Saint-Simon. Conventional etiquette is much more rigid in public-houses than in the halls of those who wear evening dress. Yet, even on the sunny side of the great divide of evening dress, there is a good deal of conventional behaviour and far more convention of manner – both very useful things with so many idiots going about. Perhaps one reason why Constance seemed so incoherent was that, although frequently in evening dress, she had none of the evening dress mannerisms, except in the rare moments when it suited her book to play the lady. Yet I can't help thinking that she abused the bohemian conventions of irregularity and incoherence. It's a fatal thing to take literature and art too seriously if you lack judgment. Lautréamont and Dostoievsky, Joyce and Brancusi, Dada and jazz – what an extraordinary potion she had brewed for them! And what an intoxication of unhappy extravagances resulted! But, no doubt, every effort to educate the upper classes is bound to be disastrous. Constance had been educated beyond her station in life. The humble Etonians and Guardsmen with whom she was born to consort no longer satisfied her, and she became an intellectual climber, prodigal of *gaffes*. The grave festival of the Muses became with her a Mad Hatter's tea-party, and she refused to listen to the warning cries of 'No room! No room!'

The utterly absurd scene at my flat, which I have just related, is typical of many such performances. At first I was taken in by these displays of temperamental virtuosity, but in time I came to see that they bore very little relation to realities. They were a kind of emotional magic-lantern show, an attempt to enliven a very unconvincing life-performance with dramatic images. With no defined aim in life, no standard of conduct, no points of reference, no genuine culture, no sense of individual or collective responsibility, Constance desired to cut a figure in the world. Unfortunately for her, she chose the wrong world to impress. You cannot persuade an analytical chemist to vouch for a formula he knows is wrong; you cannot dazzle a classical scholar into interpolating the text of Josephus; and in the little world where Constance tried to shine you cannot hope to be esteemed except for what you are in yourself. And Constance was not such great shakes. In her own world, with her beauty, her money, her social standing, her 'queerness', she could almost have married royalty and have got away with it. But she couldn't deceive shabby men who clung to the ideal of trying to see things and people as they are. That made her wild.

Constance was energetic and obstinate, and she had a considerable amount of sex appeal, on which she made prodigal overdrafts. But if you waved that aside and observed her with detachment, you gradually became aware that this extraordinary flamboyant creature was essentially ordinary, rather less than ordinary. Her intellect would have been less than mediocre but for her impressionability, her capacity for absorbing – and then exuding as her own – the most contradictory and extreme influences. A cocktail Aspasia. She had no disinterested aims, and no feelings which were not personal and vulgar. Her 'romances' were so essentially sordid that they made one yearn for the decorum and discipline of monastic life. They arose from a kind of inverted snobbery, a corrupted sense of social values, and not from passion or tenderness. (How Constance would have smiled at such gaga sentiments!) She had an innate love of cads. She hadn't the splendid crapulousness of Messalina in Subura, for she never competed openly with professionals. She specialised in being the temporary wife of a series of *faux grands hommes*, almost anybody who was remarkable for false pretensions which brought him humiliation. She liked unread poets, painters who never sold a canvas, musicians who had to play in restaurants, boxers who were always knocked out, remittance men, jockeys who had been warned off the course, drawing-room anarchists who got into trouble with the police, unofficial representatives of oppressed national minorities, fraudulent solicitors and unfrocked priests. Nor was this charity, an offering of the ample and consoling loins of Venus Pandemos. On the contrary, there was a kind of ghoul in her which fed on the man's weakness and made it fatal. She loved cads, because she could destroy them utterly. But they must not be common gigolos – any woman with five thousand a year could destroy *them*. Her prey must have had the hope of better things, must have slid down the ladder and be trying madly to struggle up again. Then, under pretext of espousing their cause, she settled on them like a lecherous octopus, and flicked the husk of a man to contempt and despair. Not a female Don Juan – one would applaud that legitimate *revanche* of the sex – but a kind of erotic boa-constrictor. She swallowed men whole. You could almost see their feet sticking out of her mouth.

Such, roughly, were my harsh reflections when Boris had restored tranquillity to my flat by taking Constance off to supper and a night-club. Perhaps I was too harsh, for I was angry. Why play such silly tricks with life? Why pretend to me that she was wrecked by a great sorrowful memory, when her whole life life rose up and vowed by the Styx that she was incapable of such a passion? Why flaunt René's suicide like a gutter-press journalist out for a sensation? I had no great compassion for René. Who would want to pretend that he is afflicted by the death of a completely worthless and pretentious parasite? Still, if Constance had left him alone, he might have enjoyed his little worm's life. Why go out of your way to squash a worm? Still less could I feel sorrow for Boris. His vague, senseless Slav emotionalism made him an ideal victim; I could imagine the preposterous and violent scenes they had together. Constance would be quite thrilled, and feel that she had got into a Chekov play in real life at last. I could only hope that he was enough of a Russian gentleman to beat her occasionally. How she would love that, and what a destructive revenge she would take!

I wondered what Nemesis would avenge this Hybris.

II

I had reached that point in my reflections when my bell rang again. Hastily I looked round to see what Constance had forgotten – she usually shed gold objects about the place – but I couldn't see so much as a powder-puff. Had they come back to make my flat the battleground for another Idiot scene? It was no good sporting the oak with the lights in my windows. I opened the door with extreme reluctance – and found Morton standing outside.

'Hullo! How are you?' he said. 'Busy? I'll go away if you are.'

'No. Come in. I'm really glad to see you.'

Morton is a good many years older than I am, and a good deal more tolerant – which may mean that he is wiser, or simply that he is older. At any rate, he has reached an age or state of serenity; things no longer irritate and bother him as they do me, perhaps because he long ago gave up any hope of altering them.

I went to get him some wine, accidentally smashed a glass, and damned it with more impatience than was necessary. He looked at me benevolently through his glasses and said:

'Anything wrong?'

'Nothing personal. Constance was here half an hour ago ...'

'Ah!'

'I gathered, perhaps wrongly, that she'd left Boris. Then he turned up, apparently by appointment, and they left. René has committed suicide.'

'That's bad. I'm sorry. I had hopes for that lad.'

I looked at him with amazement.

'That chap, I thought him an awful little scrounger. Why, I've seen him beg from Constance.'

'He was very poor, and she must have seemed fabulously rich to him. And very wasteful. He could live for a fortnight on what she spent in an evening. And he'd given her all he had. There was a streak of genuine feeling in him, and he was young. Was Constance much upset?'

'I don't know,' I said rather fretfully. 'I had a feeling she was dramatising, and that made me suspect her sincerity. I admit I don't understand her. I wish I did. I'm not interested in the *chronique scandaleuse* of her nights and days, which other people smack their lips over. Vice seems to me one of the most tedious of human activities. It's much the same with all people and in all ages, and inevitably narrows down to Dead Sea fruit and disgust. I suppose it's natural to cry "Vengeance upon Jenny's case, fie upon her," but I don't think it's very intelligent. I'd much rather try to understand how she came to be what she is from what she was. How do you explain it?'

Morton took a long Panatella from the round box on the table and lighted it carefully.

'She's an interesting case, isn't she?' he remarked, 'but there's no cut-and-dried explanation of these wavering and complex characters. For the matter of that, can we really "explain" any character? We can describe it like a biologist, which is perhaps as far as any one ought to venture in dealing with others. Or we can pass judgment in accordance with some preconceived idea of what human beings ought to be. A Freudian will have one explanation, a Roman Catholic another, a man about town yet another. You can see in a minute what each of them would say; and hopelessly at variance their explanations would be. They're not valid. But what's your explanation?'

As briefly as possible I told him what I had been thinking between Constance's departure and his arrival. He listened carefully, occasionally shaking his head and smiling. When I had finished:

'You've got something,' he said, 'but you haven't got everything. You see the complexity of her, the contradictions

66

which puzzle us all. But you pass judgment. You've got an ideal Constance in your mind, a vague picture of what you think she ought to be, and you're annoyed with her for not being it. You've got all the ferocity of the disappointed idealist, Bob.'

'I'm annoyed with her for letting herself down, and for letting other people down too. I admit she may have any amount of gifts and fine qualities, but with her they all turn to insolence and poison. Look at the trail she's left behind her, ending up with this squalid little suicide. She's an abuse, and ought to be suppressed. She's got power – the power of money, of class, of her personality and sex, and she abuses it. Isn't it because she has such a degrading attitude to other people that she degrades herself? She hates every one who resists her, and degrades every one who yields to her.'

Morton smiled.

'That's all true enough, but aren't you taking the judgment seat rather loftily? Just now you said that you'd been wondering what would be the Nemesis to avenge this Hybris. Let's beware of Hybris in ourselves, and, above all, disclaim the part of Nemesis. We could go on all night being moral at poor Constance's expense, and we shouldn't have achieved anything, except to make prigs of ourselves. It might be worth while trying to find out why she is what she is ...'

'That's it,' I said. 'Why? I'm ready enough to cut out the moral rough stuff. And as to the Nemesis – well, good Lord, when you think of what she was potentially and what she now is and must inevitably go on being, that's Nemesis enough. Let's get down to the Why. I fancy it'll be a tough job.'

'The English upper classes,' said Morton reflectively, 'are not really an aristocracy. They're a wealthy and privileged *bourgeoisie*, with most of its prejudices and not all its virtues. Every privileged class tries at first to whitewash its black sheep; if they prove incorrigible, they're kicked out. Quite right. If you won't play the game you can't expect to score. But such a society has no more room for a Renaissance woman than it has for a great poet. How about Constance as the female *Byron de nos jours?*'

'Won't do,' I said decisively. 'Byron had genius. At her age he was recognised as a great European figure. I don't say Constance hasn't talents, but she hasn't done anything with them, and therefore I'm entitled to count them out. Hitherto the chief talent she has displayed is the uncommonly perverse one of getting herself and other people into confounded scrapes.'

'All right. Let me put it this way. Byron's class made life impossible for him, and he got out. Constance's class – pretty much the same – has done likewise with her. In both cases this society has judged without amenity and, I suggest, without intelligence. In doing so, hasn't it in fact passed judgment on itself?'

'I see. You mean that the exceptional person of their class can't and won't accept their values, and therefore is driven into flouting them? In other words, Constance is the victim of her environment?'

'That's a convenient formula,' said Morton, 'but I should prefer something a little less obvious. You can't classify human beings with any sort of accuracy. There are still a hundred and one superstitions in the way. And then people like Constance are really so highly developed, so differentiated, that each of them is almost a separate species. The biology of man hasn't got very far, if it's even started. What is known of the laws of human heredity? Very little. Yet the blood mixture is important. I never saw Constance's mother – she died nearly thirty years ago, but the father was a queer bird in his way. The country people still talk of him as the Mad Lord. We can't possibly know what curious or common traits Constance has inherited. I believe there's a streak of

Celt in her, and it doesn't always mix well with our Germanic stock. And there was big business in the family – that's bad. The descendants of millionaires often inherit rapacity and un-scrupulousness, without the drive and purpose. They may even have the drive, but no purpose except a kind of egotism.'

I thought this rather arid and general, a little off the point.

'That's all very well,' I retorted, 'but if we've got to wait for the founding of the science of human biology before we make up our minds about Constance, we may as well drop the matter at once. And your argument finally boils down to the old destiny and free-will dilemma. We've got to assume that, whatever the heritage and environment, a human being is free to make a right or a wrong use of himself – he can either be harmful or the reverse. A lot depends on how people manage their frustrations. We don't need to invoke Kant's moral law to protect ourselves from what is harmful to us or to decide that it should be discouraged. I come back to my Hybris and Nemesis.'

Here the conversation drifted off into one of those friendly wrangles about abstractions, which are the curse of our undisciplined talk. Naturally, we achieved nothing except the feeling that we had spent a pleasant evening. I couldn't help reflecting that Morton had not been very successful in his effort to play *advocatus Dei* on Constance's behalf. But some-thing of what he said influenced me. I saw that it wasn't much good taking Constance in the present as a sort of static unit. No human being is that, and all personality is a kind of flow from one state to another. What had to be explained was how the present Constance – talking about drugs and suicide, and making herself a nuisance to the world – had evolved from the earlier Constance, who had started life with everything in her favour. Perhaps that was one of the clues – because she was given everything which seems valuable without any trouble to herself she despised it all, and wanted to destroy it, as a spoiled child smashes expensive toys. Constance had spent a lifetime wanting toys – human ones – and smashing them. How long would the gods go on providing them, and what would happen when the supply ceased?

III

That was three years ago, and now that I and every one else know the squalid sequel to it all, I can't help wondering why I was so excited and what it was I expected. Of course, it was bound to end ignominiously and greyly. But there was a kind of Duchesse de Longueville dashing quality about Constance (when she wasn't too crapulous) which I suppose made me imagine she would go off in a grand Brock's display.

Outside it is still raining greyly, with a persistent dreariness. Every now and then the wind gives a melancholy howl, like a lost dog or the despairing lament of a bereaved negress. The long soak of the rain has taken all the tragic colouring from the autumn leaves, and left them dun and squalid. Only two days ago the edge of the wood was like a cliff of exotically-coloured rocks. Now it looks like khaki rags hanging from huge skeletons; one wishes it could be cleared up and the debris buried. I suppose my thoughts are influenced by these memories of Constance, but I have never before seen so rapid a transition from almost insolent brilliance to sordid decay. I had never thought that Nature could be sordid. There is no living thing in the garden but that most sordid of living objects, a moulting and bedraggled hen which has somehow lost itself from the farm. I haven't the heart or energy to want to chase it away. Let it try to shelter under those rain-smashed chrysanthemums, while I return to my memories ...

At eighteen, Constance was one of the most admired heiresses in an England which had not yet cut its own commercial throat like Coleridge's pig. There was even some tradition of grandeur, which in 1912 had not yet wholly collapsed, as it was destined, into a paroxysm of low fear and hatred and Lloyd Georgism. There was still some justification for the insolence of the English upper classes. True, Constance was not real gentry – there had been trade in the family. But the peerage, though only a latish nineteenth-century creation, had already rapidly skipped three generations. And there was plenty of money, which is always respectable. According to the gossip-columnists the Lechdales were '*kite* GOOD people', and social editors would always buy press photographs. This favourable prejudice seems to have been shared by the superior fiends who control the pomps and vanities of London. After the death of Constance's mother, Lord Lechdale married a lady of charm and limitless social ambitions; and, though she never succeeded in ousting the old-established firms, yet she could engineer meetings between a revolutionary writer, the Prime Minister and the Archbishop, under the guise of entertaining royalty. Thus Constance grew up among the grandeurs of the world, in familiarity with the great, whose essential nullity was soon patent to her critical intelligence.

Constance adored her father. There was a faint tang of vulgarity in all the Lechdales which passed as originality by contrast with the insipidity of mere good manners. It flavoured their good looks, their natural health and acquired insolence, their caprices and triumphs, their intrigues. While it distressed her stepmother, it fascinated Constance – deep calling to deep. She liked her father's disregard for other people's feelings, his almost *naïf* confidence that everybody must give way to him; and she liked him the more because he was inclined to suspend these rules in her favour. The energy and determination of his great-grandfather had been used to exploit a vast and solid Victorian business. He used the inheritance to get his own way on all occasions, reasonable and unreasonable. Along with the money, this was his most conspicuous legacy to Constance. But for the strain of commonness in it, Constance's lifelong surprise that people occasionally sacrifice their own inclinations for the sake of others would have been amusing, for it was so unfeigned. This egotism was displeasing because she hadn't the gifts or the grandeur to carry it off. Far from creating the illusion of a second Queen Elizabeth, she produced the somewhat unfortunate impression of a Bowery bester. She was a bit of a thug in her attitude to life.

No specific blame can be laid on her stepmother. The second Lady Lechdale was so determined not to play the typical wicked stepmother that she treated Constance very well, far too well. This was no tremendous sacrifice, since she had no children of her own and was absorbed in the complex task of retaining social prestige while gratifying an extra-marital passion. Nevertheless, she did her best for Constance. She saw that Constance went to the best schools, and met the best procurable people; and she placed an expert knowledge of clothes at her disposal as she grew up. Matters of conduct and discipline were left to the girl's father, and his method was to let her do as' she liked where other people were concerned. If she happened to defy him beyond the point where it was his whim to let her go, he scolded her savagely and boxed her ears; an agreeable little trait which Constance successfully acquired from him. Unfortunately, among her stepmother's 'best people' were a number of young intellectuals. Anxious to do something to pay their shot, they abounded in fulsome commendations of Constance's 'intelligence'; and she had little difficulty in believing them. Moreover, they were disinterestedly anxious that this brilliant heiress should be secured as a lavish patroness of the arts; and therefore secretly encouraged and even provoked rebellion against authority.

The one person who had any real influence over Constance was her father. She understood his stormings and ear-cuffings, and would have obeyed them when she merely took delight in perverse opposition to the most friendly warnings of others, and indeed to elementary common sense when it seemed to thwart her. Scorning commonplace people who want to be happy and if possible to make others happy, she concentrated on getting her own way. She got it. Six months after Constance came out, her father suddenly died of heart failure, leaving her far too much money and the example of a brilliantly selfish life.

This was in 1912. The next two years seem to me the very crux of Constance's life. In every life there are moments or periods where a decision must be made, and these secondary crises may go on occurring until the end. But there is often one supreme crisis, and on its resolution the whole of a future depends. The life-stage is set, all the conflicting influences are at a balance, the gods withdraw, even Fate is in suspense – the protagonist is (or seems) absolutely free to choose wisdom or unwisdom. The slightest decision alters the balance, and when we, knowing the ultimate catastrophe, look back, we see that from the moment of this decision everything that followed was inevitable. So it seems in Constance's case. She had to make the decision early, but if not mature – she never was really mature – she was grown-up, and not in the least afraid of taking the responsibility for her own life.

About two months after her father's death, Constance was living quietly in London with her stepmother. They never met before lunch, because Lady Lechdale had a large correspondence to deal with and a daily mask of beauty to create. Constance was not bored – she had discovered literature, and always read the books written by people she met. At lunch one day she remarked indifferently:

'Mary wants me to go to a party next Tuesday.'

This was said, not to hint for permission, but merely to make conversation. Constance had long ago asserted her right to go where she liked, when she liked, and her otherwise-occupied stepmother would have been the last person to try to interfere. And Constance had not the slightest wish to go to the party. She disliked Lady Mary's matinée-idol beauty and rather blatant sexual charm, unrelieved by any gleams of intelligence either in herself or her guests, who generally contrived to make parties drearily rowdy and drunken. In fact, Constance had already half-determined to refuse, and to go out to dinner with a young Guardsman who had aroused her sympathies because he wanted to write poetry and hated the Army. Unluckily, Lady Lechdale replied with placid indifference:

'I thought you didn't like Mary.'

'What makes you think that?' asked Constance, immediately on the alert against "interference".

'Well, dear, she's getting rather a bad reputation, isn't she?'

'Don't be silly,' said Constance sharply. 'Who cares about that sort of thing nowadays? Mary can do as she likes.'

'Yes, but she may have to pay for it. People are beginning to talk.'

'As if that mattered. Come to that, they talk about *you*.'

Lady Lechdale wilted slightly – she preferred not to be reminded of certain difficulties in life.

'I know your father didn't like your being intimate with Mary, especially after you had both left school,' she said a little tartly, rather stressing the insinuation that Constance was still not much more than an emancipated schoolgirl.

'Why bring in father and remind me that I've lost him?' Constance was already half in a rage. 'He never tried to thwart me in the namby-pamby way you always do. Why shouldn't I see Mary if I want? I'm going to her party!'

Lady Lechdale shrugged her shoulders and said nothing. She was not going to prolong the discussion – not only was it useless, but the servants had returned to serve another course. She changed the conversation.

Constance went to the party and got drunk, far more drunk than she had ever been. She was kissed by one young man about halfway through the dance, and sat out enjoyably with another, who cheerfully paid a three-pound taxi-fare to take her home by devious routes. The next day she had a headache, did no reading, and was bored. To get rid of her boredom she rang up several friends and gave an impromptu party in Soho, where again she drank rather too much and again was taken home in a taxi – by another young man. Within a very few weeks she was fairly launched on a hectic life of parties, rendezvous, night-clubs and strange meetings of all kinds.

This sounds like copy-book morality – 'If dear Constance had stayed at home with stepmamma and a nice book, she would never have gone to the bad. Let this be a warning, my dear.' But it's not that at all. Why on earth shouldn't she go to parties and meet young men? What are girls for, anyhow? But she deliberately chose to associate with the most futile and vicious young set in London because she wanted to defy her stepmother and her stepmother's friends; and not because she really liked it. If she had not been better than that lot, we shouldn't bother about her. But she was. As often as not she was completely bored by them, and drank more than she wanted in consequence. And this constant going out started the craving for vulgar exterior excitement which led her to the most deplorable experiments. Besides, she knew she could never rival Lady Lechdale in the *haut monde*, and that silly little devil of always having her own way made her prefer facile dominations to any acknowledgment of equality or superiority in others. She deliberately collected about her people whom she could dominate – by her money if they were poor, by her wits if they were rich. It was a kind of displaced snobbery; she became the Lady Lechdale of the *demi-monde*.

The gods are just. In their infinite compassion they sent a Great War to give Constance another chance. In the crash of falling cities and the smoke of bombardments, the ugly little whispers about her were obliterated to silence. There were forty ways in which she could have gained some touch with reality, broken out of her fool's world of incomes, and drink, and free love which was neither free nor love, and artistic flapdoodle. She could have scrubbed floors or held a bed-pan to her betters. Unluckily, Lady Lechdale was naturally an enthusiastic war-harpy, and therefore Constance was pacifist and defeatist. The only war-work her conscience would allow her to perform was the entertainment of officers on leave. Obviously, somebody had to do this, and it must be admitted that she did it very well, especially before the restrictions on hours and rations. In the case of officers proceeding for duty overseas, she carried patriotism to the extent of driving down by night to the port of embarkation with them. One officer drove, with his friend sitting beside him, but Constance invariably sat in the back with one or more other officers, carrying on.

Lady Lechdale was perturbed, fearing that Constance was overtaxing her strength – and perhaps the world's charity – by this enthusiastic devotion to her self-imposed task. The only hope left was that she would take a matrimonial rest-cure and as it were, demobilise herself into monogamy. Not yet was the question: 'Who on earth would marry Constance?' but 'Who would Constance marry?' There were still plenty of candidates, and Constance made quite a hobby of unofficial engagements. The difficulty was that nobody could live up – or down – to her standards for any length of time. The young Duke of Nethermere was really devoted to her, and rushed out to the Somme (with the inevitable consequence) because Constance broke off their engagement within a week.

'But, my dear,' said Lady Lechdale in mild distress, 'is it too late to straighten things out? What has he done?'

'He's a fool,' said Constance emphatically.

'Why? What did he do?'

'He didn't *do* anything,' Constance retorted with bitter scorn. 'He's got a mind like dog Toby. I asked him when he'd last seen Nijinski, and he giggled and asked if it was a Russian cocktail. The dank fool!'

Lady Lechdale tried to hint that she was being a little hard on an almost fatuously enamoured man for a stupid joke, but Constance only hardened. Another even more serious engagement – it lasted ten days – with the Italian Prince Monte-Carino was broken off by him on account of an absurd fit of southern jealousy. At a party Constance took off half her clothes and sat kissing on the knees of a hideous young Jew, who had written a book too obscene to be printed even in Dijon, and was therefore held by Constance to be a great persecuted genius. The Prince said Italian ladies never did such things at large parties, and retired. And since he was not familiar with the ways of English gentlemen, he went back to Italy at once, without telling any one – even Lady Lechdale – the reason for his abrupt decision.

These lightning engagements, more adapted for short than for long leave, gave Lady Lechdale some concern. Evidently they had their use in providing an education in human nature and allowing a young girl to make up her own mind, but might they not be abused? After the Duke and the Prince, she was careful not to announce engagements to the press, and left it to Constance to contradict rumours which were true when handed in to the composing-room, but false when sold for a penny in Fleet Street. Knowing her Constance, she schooled herself to the assumption of cordiality when the chosen partner was plainly preposterous, and to the nicest show of indifference when he seemed barely possible. The Jew genius didn't last three days, for Lady Lechdale promptly invited the whole family to a very private dinner, and the atmosphere of dominant philoprogenitive males revolted all Constance's higher instincts. But Lady Lechdale was startled out of her reserve, with fatal results, in the case of 'Horry' Townsend.

There was nothing preposterous about Horry, except the fact that he and Constance were most patently unsuited to each other. The family were the dullest of dull County, and Horry himself was a kind of half-witted Adonis. Polo and yachting were his only interests in life, and Constance had a peculiar horror of both. The attraction was the naval uniform – Constance was really very sick of khaki, even when relieved by red trimmings or those funny little strips of colour they wore in France. In every other respect he was exactly the kind of man Constance most detested, a blundering, self-satisfied, 'Oh, I say' fathead, who by all the rules should have married a barmaid or a clergyman's daughter. Lady Lechdale, who thought herself prepared for anything from Constance, was not prepared for this.

Constance, looking extremely beautiful in evening dress, came into her stepmother's room, buttoning her gloves.

'You're dining out?'

'Yes, with Horry.'

'Horry Townsend?' asked Lady Lechdale, with some surprise. 'I should never have thought you'd want to see him for five minutes.'

Constance ceased to button her gloves and looked crossly at this thwarting creature.

'Why not?' she asked, almost truculently.

'Oh,' replied Lady Lechdale, not noticing the battle signals, and never dreaming that her remark would be taken as anything but a compliment. 'He's the most ordinary young man I ever met, and you like extraordinary people, don't you, dear?'

'He's divahn!' Constance asserted angrily, 'It's just like you to criticise the man I'm engaged to, as well as sneering at my friends.'

Too late Lady Lechdale saw her error, but the most abject feigning of approval failed to placate Constance. She felt that the most elementary Wellsism demanded that she should make a stand against this quasi-parental tyranny. Was she, Constance, the most original and brilliant woman in London, to be for ever treated as a schoolgirl by a senile stepmother who hated her? Not to be thought of. The great all-important principle of having one's own way at all costs must be asserted. The engagement lasted a week, two weeks, a month. Lady Lechdale lost her head. She implored Constance not to ruin her life by marrying a man she would be weary of in a month and loathe in a year. Constance laughed at her. Lady Lechdale invoked the aid of every one she could think of, begging them to 'influence' Constance. The intellectuals were sadly annoyed – a pretty state of affairs if all this money were to go to sports, as usual, instead of to found a new renaissance. They remonstrated seriously, and thereby made the marriage a certainty. Whatever interior doubts Constance may have had, she could not lose the opportunity of asserting her own will against practically everybody, for naturally the County Townsends hated her, and by no means wanted Horry to link up with such a feminine volcano.

It was just like Constance to marry a compendium of the ordinary. In every other case – and, alas, such cases were frequent – she invariably demanded of a man some elements of genius, the falser the better. Perhaps that was partly a revolt from the overwhelming experience of Horry's ordinariness. But it does seem incredible that so restless and exacting a creature, who could never be sufficiently entertained, should have confided herself to a man who would bore the Bath Club – which is saying a good deal. However, she did it, and was wedded with all appropriate swagger. Needless to say, in less than three years she divorced. Lady Lechdale, stuttering like an agitated hen, was blamed by Constance for having forced the match on her. Henceforth, she was told, Constance intended to stand alone.

The early post-War world seemed to have been made for Constance. If she had made a Faustian compact with the devil she could not have been given a fairer run for her money on the road to damnation. The prince of darkness for once did things well. He gave Constance everything she wanted, and she took and broke her gifts with an avidity of destruction which must have been like cooling waters to the old gentleman's burning tongue. To the sound of ten thousand jazz bands, with the ominous tom-tom undertone beating on the nerves, those sinister years shuffled and shimmied their dance of death. When evening twilight sank with heart-shaking sadness over the million silent graves, already the taxis and cars crowded the streets, hurrying to restaurants and parties; all night the restless feet slid and stamped, and the niggers grinned over the drums, and the joyless rejoiced without joy; and at dawn, when the wind breathed an immense sigh over the cross-marred desolate fields, the feet still stamped, and voices still shouted for more drink, and paler cheeks more plainly showed the smears of reddened lips. A happy time. You could almost hear the rattle of the bones in this macabre pageant, dulling thought and feeling like a villainous drug, which had always to be renewed in larger and longer doses. Constance danced with the weariest, and out-laughed the most broken-hearted.

As if they had determined to make her the epitome and only

image of this now dead and disgraceful time, the gods afflicted Constance with the lust of gambling. It was not enough that she should be a parody of passion, simulating a promiscuous lust which was sterile, lugubrious and alcoholic. And it was not enough that her 'revolt' itself should be ridiculous, a parody of the flaccid snobbery of the age, as she played the part of a Lady Lechdale *déclassée* to her little mob of cocktail Communists and persecuted geniuses. She had an innate dislike for anything healthy and useful. While she haggled skilfully over a taxi-fare and the wages of her domestic slaves, she scarcely glanced at a night-club bill, and could not be dragged from the gambling table so long as she had five shillings left in her bag. If she had had them, she would have staked her virtue at *roulette* and hazarded her reputation at *petits chevaux*. What did it matter, so long as the Honourable Constance was amused and excited? Was it not for her, the very symbol of delicate and leisured civilisation, that the bleeding and dwindling barrier of men's bodies had been reinforced and reinforced and reinforced? And if ten thousand men must labour to maintain this gutter goddess, had they not the consolation of service in a great ideal?

On with the dance, let joy be unconfined.

And what a dance it was, and what a joy! If Constance danced it was not because she liked dancing, but because you cannot sit and drink all night, and you must have some exercise to maintain that tapeworm figure. And she would have thought it unintelligent, not to say low, to admit that she had ever hoped to be happy. Why, then, go on with it all? Obviously, the thought must have struck Constance, since she had staged her little drugs-or-suicide scene. But, after all, that was only part of the game. True to the sporting instincts of the race, Constance continued to play the game, although she was much too intelligent not to know that it wasn't worth playing. There was a kind of competition about it – who could keep going longest, waste most and destroy most. The male or quasi-male victims of Constance's will (one must not pollute the word 'desire') were not of such a quality as to cause any vivid regret for their disappearance in her whirlpool. The Jews and Japanese resisted best, but the Americans and Latins went down like straws. Still, a human being is a human being, and there were times when it seemed a pity that the sacred cause of getting one's own way should demand such an extravagant consumption of alleged humanity.

IV

Boris didn't last very long. I forget what his number was in that arithmetical progression of bedfellows, but it was a lucky one. He got off lightly, and quite soon settled down to performing Cossack dances for the cultured *clientèle* of a Russian restaurant in Nice. Boris was a simple soul, with a Slav hankering for the impossible, which perhaps explains his escape. He was succeeded by an even more Herculean imbecile named Eddie, who was an almost perfect combination of low cunning and inefficiency. He had passed through an extraordinary variety of occupations, none of which he had been able to retain for long. He made a virtue of this.

'I'm an adventurer,' he would say. 'I love adventure, it's in my blood. As soon as I get tired of a job, I chuck it up and find another.'

He omitted to state that it was invariably the job which chucked him. When Constance first saw him, he was pretending to be a lion-tamer in a circus. Since the lions were old and heavily doped, Eddie was able to put his head in their mouths with complete immunity. This, added to the leopard-skin loincloth, the artificial bronze of his limbs, the curly hair and exquisitely stupid blue eyes, strangely fascinated Constance. She was not so much jealous of the lions, as convinced that if Eddie would only put his head in her mouth, she would pretty soon chump him up. Constance sent round a note to him from her box, and Eddie supped in paradise that night. Within a week he had abandoned lion-taming for the far more dangerous task of gallanting Constance. In a way, it was a bit of luck to get a new job so easily, for he was under notice when Constance spotted his genius.

Constance was not one of those wives who are jealous of their husband's talents. She always wanted to 'help' them. This was pure Lechdalism, the bounteous flow of patronage upon the artistic inferior; just as the obligatory choice of 'genius' for collaborations where genius is of no avail was an echo of Lechdale snobbery. We all create little conventions for superiority for ourselves and our associates, to decorate our nullity with a quiff, and to hide from ourselves the immense apathy of the stars. Constance, nothing if not original, had invented a very curious set to meet her curious circum- stances. Thus, it was sufficient for some one to be taken up in the bed-and-board line by Constance for him to become an epoch-making genius, hitherto unrecognised by the stupidity of the world. So it was with Eddie. Constance refused to see the palpable fact that Eddie's lion-taming was the merest accident in his career; his 'genius' was just as much fitted to be a shipbroker's clerk or a commissionaire. She hastily assumed the extraordinary faith, to which she had hitherto been a com- plete stranger, that lion-taming was one of the major fine arts. And, naturally, Eddie was the very top-notch in this difficult and exquisite art. He had to be given 'his chance', and when he had 'made good' by the aid of Constance, then he would be allowed as much of the joint glory as Constance didn't want for herself.

Eddie didn't like this at all. One glance at those slightly bulging blue eyes would have told any one but Constance that Eddie's true part in life was that of a gentleman of leisure, a squire to dames of large, independent means. He was one of the boys who make no noise. But Constance had her plan, which she revealed to the poor fellow over dinner very soon after she had abruptly whisked him from the sawdust ring to cosmopolitan luxury. Still feeling the glory of a new and excellently-cut suit, the reassurance of a gold cigarette case in one waistcoat pocket and of a gold lighter in the other, the solid comfort of a thick wad of notes in his pocket-book, and the perfect peace of not having to work, Eddie heard her with dismay and cursed the restlessness of the female nature. But he was too cunning to offer any opposition, having gauged his Constance with an accuracy impossible to more complex minds.

'Darling,' said Constance, neglecting a superb *sole cardinale* which Eddie was almost noisily appreciating, 'I want to talk to you seriously, because I don't want to be a hindrance to your Art.'

'Eh?' muttered Eddie rather thickly through a mouthful of prawn and mushrooms. Constance *adored* Eddie's manners – they were so natural.

'Don't you think you ought to have some animals to practise with? I'm afraid you'll be getting out of touch.'

Eddie bolted his mouthful in consternation – was she trying to get rid of him already? He seemed to have heard that Constance was a little fickle. He defended himself with a brave laugh.

'Well, y' see, Connie, it's like this. Lion taming's partly a gift and partly showmanship, if y' see what I mean. A chap's got the magnetism or 'e 'asn't. If 'e 'asn't, 'e might 's well shut up shop. If 'e 'as, it's all in the power of the heye. There's no practise about it; it's a gift.'

'I know, darling, but I can't bear to think of your wonderful gift being wasted. It was horrible for you to be among those ignorant fools who couldn't appreciate you.'

Eddie smiled modestly, and flashed a killing glance at her; but Constance for once was serious, and ignored it. She went on:

'I've been thinking it over and I've made our plans. I want you to be recognised, and you *shall* be. But you can't do anything with horrible mangy beasts like those you had to deal with. We'll go to Africa, darling, and form a little hunting expedition, and you shall capture a dozen or so of the very finest lions – really fierce and marvellous ones you can use your Art on.'

'Good Lord!' exclaimed Eddie in profound consternation; but added with swift tact, 'Well, you are a one, Connie. What the 'ell put that in y' little head?'

'And then,' Constance went on in her purest Mayfairese, 'we'll bring them back, and you shall star through all the capitals of Europe. I'm sure the Russians would appreciate you – we'll go to Moscow first.'

Eddie made rapid mental calculations – if Constance would come down handsome, there'd be plenty of pickings before the show went broke. As to the lions – well, get hold of some professional out of work – five quid a week – call him assistant – make him do the job.

'It'll cost a wad o' money,' he said with a leer which he mistook for a glance of exquisite intelligence, 'and then we'll have to advertise – plaster places with bills.'

'I've thought of that too,' said Constance, with a look of dreamy abstraction. 'I shall write a novel about the circus – you can give me details and colour – about our Love and your Art. I'll have it translated into every European language, and people will simply *flock* to see you.'

'Christ!' said Eddie with awed simplicity. He was extremely flattered at the thought of being the hero of a 'Society woman's' novel. As to the very real practical difficulties of the scheme – well, so long as she had money to burn ...

'Nice little bit o' stuff that,' said the junior waiter, after he and the Head Waiter had bowed to the wake of Constance and her Barnum Pheidias. 'I bet she knows what's what. Shouldn't mind half an hour meself. What's her name?'

'That,' replied the Head Waiter ponderously, with a sort of inclination of the mental spine, 'is the H-onourable Constance Townsend, *née* Lechdale.'

'Go on!' The junior was plainly astonished. 'Why, I thought she was a Maida Vale tart.'

'It's hard to tell the difference nowadays, very hard,' replied the Head Waiter, who was a family man and read the *Daily Herald*. 'If you ask me, the only difference between her and a professional is that she does it for nothing. But what can you expect, so long as the means of production, distribution and exchange are in the hands of a gang of boss robbers?'

'Garn, don't talk Bolshie. Who'd keep the races going if the bosses went? Not your psalm-smiting Heraldites. But who was the bloke with the Honourable lady?'

'Chap from a circus. She likes corrupting the workers ...'

'Corruption be blowed. I wish she'd try a little corrupting in the waiting profession. I know one brisk young feller who wouldn't have to be ast twice.'

'Here!' exclaimed the scandalised superior, 'none o' that! You get on with your work, young man. Number Five's calling for you, and there's no bread on Number Seven. Jump to it!'

Fortunately for Eddie, his imagination was not powerful. A distant and contingent danger did not disturb him, though he could be acutely distressed by an imminent one. The prospect of capturing lions in Central Africa by putting salt on their tails seemed to him so absurd and remote that he accepted Constance's proposal with the complete indifference of one humouring a madman. And this was fortunate for him, since the least opposition would have roused Constance so much that she might actually have dragged him into peril in Uganda. As it was, she prepared for the expedition with characteristic energy and vagueness. She gave two farewell parties, or rather she issued a great many telephone invitations to people who, in numerous cases, had unbreakable appointments for the same evenings, or were unexpectedly detained at the last moment. Constance commented on the fact to Eddie, who tactlessly remarked, with a class-conscious sense of inferiority, that no doubt her swagger friends didn't want to meet him. She was furious with him, as she was with anything and anybody seeming to contradict or to criticise her, however indirectly. During the next two days she did a record amount of quarrelling by telephone. Most of these disputes terminated with the lofty form of dismissal remembered from grander days: 'I hope I shall never see you again.' At the almost invariable retort, 'I hope not, indeed,' Constance slammed down the receiver with a tightening of the lips and a clenched fist. If she had been gifted with television to see the quiet smile at the other end of the line, saying as plainly as possible, 'Well, thank God I've finished with *her*,' she might have reflected on the consequences of always getting one's own way.

The plan was that they should drive to Marseilles in Constance's car, take ship 'somewhere or other', then drive on again until they came to lion-haunted country, where they would 'make up an expedition', Eddie would whistle the lions to heel and they would be shipped to Hamburg. Delightful and simple project. It seems a slight reflection on Constance's elegant finishing school that she forgot the existence of the Sahara (which is only about 2000 miles wide) and sundry other little difficulties such as roads, petrol stations, permits and the like. Constance was accustomed to her own way, and in Europe she almost invariably got it – by paying. If you live in the European Cloudcuckoodom of plutocracy, it is not difficult to fall into the belief that you can get anything by paying for it. No doubt Constance believed that roads would appear across the Sahara, and petrol-pumps emerge from the mirage at convenient intervals, if she condescended to remark that she was Constance Lechdale and was willing to pay. To meet all difficulties she provided herself with a letter of credit the amount of which made Eddie start, and with a large bundle of ten-pound notes which made him blink.

Constance drove the car herself. She did not like to worry Eddie with driving, any more than she wished to burden him with the responsibility of carrying the money. Artists, she felt, should be relieved of all such annoyances, and she was willing to sacrifice herself. So, to his chagrin, Eddie didn't even get one tenner to look after. Eddie was concerned, since his own wad of notes was now considerably thinner. He had yet to learn that after the first fortnight Constance invariably held the purse strings as closely as an over-anxious parent – you could *not* trust the artistic temperament with money. They drove out of London in silence. Conversation never flourished between them, and Eddie was a little sulky. Constance sat very upright at the wheel, haughtily damning policemen who had the cheek to hold her up at cross-streets and traffic which got in her way, and blasting very energetically an errand boy whose bicycle side-slipped off a tram-line just in front of her. She almost damaged her brakes and tyres in avoiding the brute. Under a proper Communism, with a dictatorship of the proletariat vested in Constance and her friends, such things would not be allowed. She communicated this great thought to Eddie, who grunted from behind a newspaper. Like many people who earn their livings in precarious ways, Eddie had no great opinion of Communism. There was too much work and too little pay about it. They drove on in silence.

About half an hour later, Eddie put down his paper and gazed carelessly at the ravishing rural prospect of Kent as visible from an arterial road.

88

'Any news in the paper?' asked Constance.

'No,' said Eddie. 'They haven't copped the chap that murdered the old woman. Sheffield United beat the Arsenal, and there's a big crash in America.'

'Crash?' enquired Constance, accelerating to pass a small car on a blind curve.

'Yes. On Wall Street. You know, stocks and shares.'

'Oh. Those brutes! I hope they lose every penny. Swine!'

It *was* unfortunate that Constance had no television. If she could have seen those frantically buzzing tickers in Wall Street and in and about Austin Friars, she might have noticed something. She might, for instance, have observed that she was growing poorer with incredible speed as wave after wave of frantic selling swept over a panic-stricken market. Seeing her there so upright, confident and insolent at the wheel, you wouldn't have thought power was crumbling in her fingers, that she was shedding hundreds of pounds a mile, and that when she drove haughtily on to the quay at Dover she was a tenth poorer than when she left London, with a menacing prospect for the afternoon and morrow. Constance never troubled about such things – she left them to solicitors, bankers and brokers, who were paid to see that her balance remained inexhaustible. The tape-machines ticked furiously and the din on the Bourses was like a mad Zoo ...

On their way through Paris Constance gave another party which was quite well attended; Constance was not so compromising on the Continent as in Virtue's peculiar home. One of the noisiest and thirstiest guests was a young man with ginger curls and a double-breasted waistcoat, who had just won some money on the *roulette* table at Dieppe.

'Fifteen thousand francs!' he kept saying. 'Fifteen thousand good old bloody francs! Money for nothing. Have another bottle on me.'

Constance was much attracted by the young man; she always

respected a man who could drink nearly level with herself, and luck in gambling seemed to her an equivalent of virtue.

'It's clever,' she said to Eddie. 'He started with a hundred-franc note and won fifteen thousand. It's really *clever*. Shall we run over to Dieppe to-morrow and try our luck?'

If Eddie's intellects had not been a little clouded with superfluous champagne, he would have jumped at the opportunity of postponing the lions; and by showing so much eagerness to escape would very likely have brought them on himself. But he had a fuddled delusion that it would look extremely well in company if he opposed Constance and made good his cocktail boast to one of the men that Constance was so much in love with him that she'd eat out of his hand. So he said:

'What d'we want to go back to Dieppe for? I don't want to go to Dieppe.'

The alcoholic tenderness in Constance's eyes went hard, and her thin lips were a fraction thinner as she retorted:

'Well, I do. And I'm going. You can stay here if you like.'

'Oh, I say, Connie,' protested Eddie.

'Don't call me "Connie" – it's sloppy. And don't imagine you can order me about. What next!'

And leaving a very disconcerted Eddie, she danced a little unrhythmically with the young man, who 'explained his system' with more good-will than lucidity. On the way back from the night-club Eddie tried to vindicate his wounded vanity, but only succeeded in provoking a flaring row and a series of snubs which he resented far more than he was able to retort. This was his first real experience of domestic bliss with Constance, and he was stunned and appalled by the violence of her invective and the cold hatred in her voice. The hatred seemed so much more genuine than any other emotion she had shown to him. It was exactly like the violent resentment felt by a man about town for a low woman who has

betrayed him into follies. In his dull, muddled way Eddie got
the feeling that her real emotion about him was this bitter
hatred, which was obscured rather than subdued by his attraction to her senses. He was startled and not a little perplexed
by this apparent anomaly. He had not yet made the discovery
that there are women who use their sex to hate with, that
there are love affairs in which desire is confounded with contempt and hatred. He especially failed to see that with Constance there was not, and could never be, any tenderness or
softness, that by nature or by habit she had come to use her
sex for domination, for gratification, even for the abasement
of herself and others, but never for love and exaltation. In
her life she had preferred to give money and crude luxuries to
forty *louches* males whom she could drag at her heels like grin-
ning lackeys and dismiss with contumely for disobedience or
for growing stale, rather than to give a particle of herself which
might have won the response of a flash of real tenderness.

They went to Dieppe after Constance had staged a repul-
sively erotic reconciliation. To compel Eddie's reluctance,
to dominate his resentment, to force the words and gestures
of desire from a man who was still raging from the humiliation of her insults – that was a pleasure not to be missed.
Having given her mouse a good sharp nip, a hint of the final
and mortal bite which was to come, she now played with him
with clawless velvet paws. She almost caressed the steering-
wheel as they drove along, and she would have been charmingly feline if she could have given any suppleness to that
rigid, dieted figure, which seemed like a Vogue pattern-figure
cut out and mounted. But Eddie failed to profit by these good
dispositions, owing to another clumsiness at Dieppe. On their
first visit to the Casino they both lost heavily. Constance was
annoyed; not that she minded losing the money, but because
she had not been 'clever' enough. Eddie was scandalised and
distressed. He calculated that in a single evening they had

lost very nearly half the amount for which you could get hold of a nice little country pub and be comfortable for the rest of your life. The economist and the philanthropist in him revolted. It was quite right for Constance to waste money on him, but immoral for her to waste it on herself.

Back in the hotel bedroom, he said:

'Well, I suppose we'll be getting off to-morrow. Shall I tell 'em downstairs?'

'What are you talking about? I've no intention of leaving. I'm going to play a different system to-morrow.'

Eddie protested:

'I say now, look 'ere, Connie ...'

Constance stamped her small gold-shod foot.

'I've told you before not to call me "Connie." I hate you when you're sentimental – as if you thought I was a creature in spangled tights ...'

'Well, Constance then,' said Eddie sulkily. 'Anyway, I'm trying to stop you making a fool of yourself. Let's B.O. to-morrow, first thing. This *roulette's* a mug's game.'

'A mug's game!' Constance raged. 'How dare you call me a mug, you filthy gigolo? How dare you!'

Standing half-undressed, with a face distorted by anger and hatred, she looked more like a Montmartre *buveuse d'absinthe* than an English lady. Unable to find words sufficiently expressive, she snatched up a heavy gold travelling clock and threw it at Eddie's face. He dodged, and it smashed against the wall. Desolate at this destruction of valuable property, he half turned round, and before he was aware of what was happening, Constance sprang at him and hit him twice in the face with her clenched fists. A heavily-jewelled ring cut his eye-socket, and partly blinded him. He clutched his hands to his face, believing he had lost an eye.

'You brute!' Constance cursed him, 'you foul **** of a brute – that'll teach you to insult me!'

Eddie collapsed into a chair, and what with pain, vexation of spirit and the artistic temperament, sobbed aloud. With complete indifference, Constance went into the bathroom and slammed the door.

They returned to the Casino, of course, and Constance won steadily. Eddie refused to play, since Constance refused to give him any extra money to play with; and he wandered feebly about, or stood with ignominious patience behind her chair. His one consolation was to see the money coming back. But Constance was not content to recoup her losses; she wanted to outdo the 'clever' young man. Presently her luck changed, and when the Casino shut down she had lost more than ever. She went back to the hotel in a cold rage, hardly speaking to Eddie, and thereafter spent every available hour, day after day, losing money to the croupier. In less than a week the large packet of notes had gone, the letter of credit was exhausted, Eddie was almost demented with chagrin and baffled avarice, and she had only a few thousand francs in her bag. Eddie was in a state of perpetual drunken bewilderment; he almost wished he had never taken up with the aristocracy.

The rage of gambling left Constance as abruptly as it had possessed her. She treated Eddie with a charming sweetness, which made him touch the half-healed scar on his face and wonder vaguely if this exquisite siren could be the same person as the hard-faced drunken fury who had scorned and smitten him.

'Darling,' she said, 'I think we'd better run over to London for a few days. I'm so sick of these beastly French and their foul cheating casinos. My dear, they simply *robbed* us. I want a few days' change, and then we can start again.'

'All right,' said Eddie compliantly. He was far too scared to oppose anything Constance intimated was her wish. By now he had spent all the money she had given him during the two-days' honeymoon – which was all Constance ever allowed herself for any marriage. And after recent events he was afraid to ask for any more.

'We'll start at once,' Constance decided. '*Dear* old London, it'll be quite nice to see it again.'

Dear old London did not treat Constance quite as affectionately as this condescension on her part merited. She had a row with her Bank Manager, who pointed out that she was exceeding her income, that the capital value of her investments was declining rapidly, and that the rather speculative industrials she owned were dangerous to hold. He counselled economy and an immediate transference to gilt-edged. For him to advise was sufficient reason for Constance to reject – as if she would be dictated to by a wretched little creature like that! Just to show him his place, she insisted on having a couple of thousand in hundred-pound notes, and signed haughtily, without reading them, the documents he put before her. Then she stalked out of the Bank, indifferent to the admiring gaze of fifty inferior animals behind the brass grill. *Comment!* A Lechdale is a Lechdale, we hope!

Outside, Constance was a little surprised to find Eddie talking very absorbedly to a rather flashily-dressed girl. Eddie appeared to be excusing himself. Neither noticed Constance until she stood beside Eddie saying :

'Here I am – forgive me for interrupting.'

They both started slightly, and Eddie said with a great affectation of heartiness and aplomb:

'Hullo, back a'ready? I was just 'aving a word with Elsie. You know about Elsie.'

Constance *did* know about Elsie. One of the minor joys of fostering Eddie's artistry had been the knowledge that Elsie very much disapproved, and had shed many tears at his leaving her. Elsie was part Sicilian, thin and dark, with black, rather frizzy hair and large emotional eyes. She shrank a little away from Constance's opulence and assured possessiveness of Eddie, and gazed at her with the timidity of a girl who has always been poor, but with a savage jealousy. Constance was amused. She was not one of those women who refuse to meet the former mistresses of their lovers or who, if they do, display signs of hysterical disapproval. On the contrary, Constance liked to torment them by showing how completely the male creature had become her possession. She held out her hand with easy patronage, and said with a sweetness surprising to Eddie's crude apprehension:

'But of course I know about Elsie! I've been *longing* to meet you, darling. How are you?'

Elsie took her hand suspiciously and unwillingly, as if she expected a dagger stab from the other hand. But the more she shrank from Constance, the more Constance was determined to charm and dazzle her, to make her admit that the better woman had won. Besides, Constance was fully aware of their embarrassment, which meant *lèse-majesté*, a confession that they still had some feelings contrary to her sovereign power over Eddie. She rattled on:

'I'm so glad you happened to see Eddie. I've asked him a score of times to bring you to see me, but he will keep all his best friends to himself. Eddie, get a taxi. Hurry up. You must come back and have a drink with us, Elsie. I'm longing to hear all about the days at the circus when you were with Eddie. You know, we're going to have a real show for Eddie soon, a tiptop affair. But it's a great secret. Ah, here's the taxi. Jump in, dear.'

Now Elsie did not in the least want to get into a taxi with Eddie and Constance; she wanted to go away and cry and hate Constance and think of impossible but terrific ways of being revenged on her. But she was powerless before Constance's grand imperious ways. And the more she tried to find excuses to get away, the more cleverly Constance contrived to keep her, having a very large portion of humble pie she was determined the girl should eat to the last crumb. It was torture to Elsie to be firmly guided into the large hotel bedroom, which was more luxurious and intimidating then anything she had seen, and to be plunged into all the evidence of their intimacy. She suffered when Eddie ostentatiously displayed the new expensive wrist-watch Constance had just given him, when he offered her a cigarette from the gold case, and lighted it for her from the gold lighter with its discreet monogram of an interlinked 'E' and 'C'. Eddie couldn't help showing off his parasitic opulence to impress her, and Constance cunningly encouraged the vulgarity. She was all sweetness and charm to Elsie, all assured dominion with Eddie. Constance mixed the cocktails herself in a large silver shaker, and talked gaily and made Eddie feel beautifully at ease so that he talked. Everything she said seemed kind and gracious and charming, and yet nearly every sentence was a stab in Elsie's heart. It was as if all this talk only meant: 'See how happy we are, you miserable little outcast; how rich and comfortable we are, you poor, ignominious wage-earner; how devoted and ensnared Eddie is by his Circe-princess, you unattractive little vulgarian. Don't you dare speak to him again without my permission, and don't imagine you can get a flicker of the eyelid from him unless I order it, you impudent bitch.'

Elsie tried again to get away, but Constance wasn't going to miss such an opportunity. Elsie had got to have her lesson, and learn that circus supernumeraries mustn't presume beyond their station, especially in such an enormity as still wanting a lover who was temporarily needed for more important purposes.

'I reely must go,' said poor Elsie, 'I'm on early this evening.'

'Nonsense!' cried Constance, 'you must dine with us, and then we'll all go and dance somewhere.'

'But I can't miss my turn – I'll get the sack.'

'Eddie,' said Constance, 'just ring up Elsie's manager and say I want to speak to him. My dear, I'll arrange it – you *must* have a holiday some time, and I want us to celebrate our meeting. I'm sure we shall be great friends.'

'But I can't go out with you in these clothes,' Elsie protested, looking at her cheap finery, which was so obviously tawdry beside Constance's Paris and Bond Street turn-out.

'Oh, that can easily be settled. I've got dozens of dresses, darling, and you're just about my size ... Are you through, Eddie?'

She took the telephone from his hand, and the two plebeians marvelled at her easy insolence to the tyrant before whom they had trembled.

'Hullo!' said Constance into the telephone, 'is that the Manager? Yes? How do you do, Mr Shorter. Constance Lechdale speaking. What? Yes, Lord Lechdale's daughter. What? I want to ask a little favour of you. Can you reserve me two boxes for next Monday – I shall be bringing a party of friends. Oh, thank you so much. How kind of you, I'll send you a cheque. And, oh, by the way, Mr Shorter – I want one of your artistes to dine with me to-night. You'll give her permission, won't you? It's Elsie. What? Yes, Elsie, you know Elsie. She wouldn't accept without your permission, Yes, she's here. Oh, thank you. How kind of you. Yes, I shall see you on Monday – you must dine with me some time. Good-bye.' Constance hooked up the receiver. 'Horrid little brute,' she remarked carelessly, 'but it's all right, Elsie, he said you may stay.'

Presently Constance sent Eddie off to his dressing-room and rang for her maid; and Elsie's torments redoubled. Constance insisted on giving her a set of new underclothes, and then stood over the maid while dress after dress was tried on the unresisting but raging victim. Each time Constance stepped back to look at her critically, Elsie felt as if she would spring at her throat; and each time she felt the touch of Constance's fingers as she pulled a dress this way and that, it gave her a thrill of hatred. Finally, Constance decided on a magnificent red silk, which was a little too majestic and dignified for Elsie to carry properly, and added a necklace which perfectly stressed the slight vulgarity of Elsie's face and frizzly hair. Then she sent out for yellow roses, and fastened them in herself. Constance contemplated her handiwork, and glanced at herself in the mirror. She was well pleased – any one could see who was the lady.

They dined at an exceedingly smart and expensive restaurant which Elsie had never heard of. Everybody was in evening dress, and though the place was full it was very quiet and softly lighted, with gentlemen waiters moving about noiselessly and swiftly. The waiters bowed to Constance as she came in, and the Head Waiter came and bowed as soon as she was seated, and the proprietor came and bowed, and listened most attentively to everything Constance said, and made respectful suggestions about wines and food, which Constance carelessly accepted or as carelessly rejected. And Elsie felt as if she would burst into tears and wished she could sink through the floor – it was so horrible sitting there beside *that woman*, with her gracious insolences Elsie didn't know how to parry or return, and people glancing over at them from other tables and then discreetly whispering with discreet contemptuous smiles. And there was Eddie, dear perfidious lost Eddie, sitting opposite them, just as well dressed as any of the other gentlemen, and Constance calling him 'darling,' and he calling her 'dear,' and obviously as pleased as Punch with himself, and nearly as patronising to her as Constance herself. And the pair of evening shoes Constance had lent her pinched her toes.

Elsie didn't much enjoy the food – it was too rich, she thought, and she would rather have had a Worthington or a nice double whisky instead of the wines. But they made her feel rather drunk, especially when Constance insisted on her drinking neat brandy afterwards out of huge great glasses, rather like a melon with one end cut off. Elsie had no patience with these upper-class fads – where was the sense in drinking a thimbleful of brandy out of a pint glass? It was just silly swank. But it made her warm and intoxicated, and the more intoxicated she got the more she hated Constance, and wished she could scrag her, the impudent wicked thing. And Eddie sitting there like a stuffed dummy, looking like a silly ponce. That's what he was – a silly ponce.

When the bill came, Elsie saw with a thrill of amazed horror that it was nearly ten pounds. For a moment her heart jumped at the thought that Constance mightn't have enough money to pay, and then what would happen to them? But Constance carelessly opened a large handbag with a strong flexible metal handle she kept round her wrist even when eating, and Elsie saw her rummage among some pound notes, and then turn to the other side where there was a huge awkward bundle of Bank of England notes. As Constance slid one of them between the folded bill Elsie saw with awed astonishment that it had '£100' printed on it. A queer glint came into her eyes, and she glanced at Eddie; he too was gazing at the note with a look of envy and cupidity on his face. Constance quietly enjoyed the sensation she had caused, and swept the change back into her great lucky-bag without counting it, leaving a tip which Elsie would have been very glad to earn in two days.

They went to a swagger music-hall and sat in the stalls. Elsie took a professional interest in the 'work' and longed to be on the real stage herself – even the chorus had such lovely dresses and sang so beautifully. But Constance yawned and said it was terribly dull and old-fashioned, so they had to go on to a night-club and dance and drink champagne. And then they went to another night-club and danced again and drank more champagne. Elsie wasn't tired – she was used to sitting up late – but she felt quite faint with her loathing for Constance. Later on Constance began to talk about going to a third place, and then Eddie, who was getting very drunk, said he knew a 'joint' down in the East End where all kinds of queer and dangerous characters went. Constance was delighted at this, and said they must go at once; and Elsie wondered why the gentry were so keen always on meeting criminals – it was as if they were all pals together.

The 'joint' was a sordid-looking place, with heavy curtains and clouds of tobacco smoke. They couldn't get in at first, but Eddie said to send for Bert, and when Bert came he remembered Eddie, and said they could come in. Eddie whispered something in Bert's ear, and Elsie *knew* he was whispering 'Honourable Constance Lechdale,' and hated him for it. They were given a table just by the door, and every one stared at seeing two ladies in evening dress, but especially at Constance. There was no champagne, but Bert himself brought them a half-full bottle of Johnnie Walker, which he left on the table after pouring out three drinks. Elsie had her back turned to the room and couldn't see what was going on, but suddenly a row began among some men near them. There was an uproar of shouts and curses and screams from women, a crash of breaking furniture, and then crack! crack! crack! from a revolver. Elsie looked at Constance, and saw her shrinking back with a look of coward terror on her face; and this abruptly destroyed the prestige with which she had held Elsie down and tortured her all evening. The dammed-up hatred in Elsie suddenly broke loose in a passion of murderous loathing. She seized the bottle and hit Constance's face with it twice – once with the whole bottle, and again with the broken part left in her hand – just as somebody switched out the lights. But she heard Constance scream.

When the police burst in and switched on the lights, they found the room in an empty confusion. Constance had fallen forward unconscious on the table with her face in a pool of blood. Eddie and Elsie had gone with the others, and the large handbag was no longer hanging on Constance's inert wrist.

V

It is now late at night, and I have spent many hours thinking and writing about Constance, setting down what I knew directly and trying to build up a probable and logical construction of what can only be conjectured. When I opened the window just now a draught of wet, cold air gushed into the room and sent my loose pages whirling. Yet the wind had sunk to a gentle soughing, and the heavy rain had diminished to a chill drizzle as the huge skirts of the storm swept northward. Looking from the lighted room into the darkness, I could see nothing and hear nothing but the muted wind. The darkness seemed to press close up to the house and to isolate it, as if there had been an unthinkable lapse of time and the earth were slowly turning in sunless and starless space where movement and non-movement are the same. I shivered; and shut and curtained the window.

Sitting afterwards by the fire, I remembered that it would soon be All Souls' Day, when people think about the dead and pathetically try to symbolise their memories with flowers which fade only a little more swiftly. The sense of injustice and of loss creates the need for ideal justice and compensation, and men – who certainly cannot be accused of a lack of self-importance – have imagined that all the forces of the universe are concerned with their motives and conduct. As if Betelgeuse were an interested witness of our tiny heroics and meannesses! We judge and are judged, and there is not one of us but takes a godlike survey of his fellows and rashly believes he knows them. As if any of us knows another! 'Then shall I know, even as I am known' – that was the cry of human loneliness, setting in an impossible other-world the hope it dared not place in this. But if human tragedies and comedies mean nothing to the indifferent forces, they are all-important to us; and what happens to another happens to us. We cannot be indifferent unless we become non-human; and, being human, we judge.

More than a year has passed since Constance met so violent a Nemesis to her Hybris, in the midst of the vulgar pleasures whose vulgarity she attempted vainly to conceal under the pretence of personal originality and patronage of 'genius'. Naturally 'the name' was kept out of the papers; and just as naturally there was a sea of wild talk, with currents and cross currents of rumour. I tried hard to find out where Constance was and what had happened to her; but the whole affair was surrounded in mystery, and I could discover nothing accurately. The talk was still at its height when I had to go to New York, where the newspapers had run Constance's disaster as a front-page display, and where talk was even wilder than in England. Of course I did not believe any of it; and when pressed for my own version, I contented myself with saying that a conspicuous personality like Constance was bound to be maligned.

Not until several months later, when I got back to London, was I able to piece together the mosaic and discover Constance's fate. The night after my return I went round to see Morton. After we had discussed a number of topics of more immediate personal interest, I said:

'And now I want you to tell me something, which has been puzzling me. What has happened to Constance since that ghastly attack in the East End? How is she, where is she, what is she doing?'

Morton stared at me.

'Good Lord! Don't you know? I thought everybody had been talking about it.'

'That's the difficulty. Everybody *has* been talking, and they've talked such an infinite variety of absurd and contradictory things that I haven't the faintest idea what has really been going on. I know or can guess for myself what went on between Constance, Eddie and Elsie up till the moment when poor Constance was knocked out so brutally – but what happened then? Was Constance badly hurt?'

'Very badly indeed, poor thing. Apparently, the first blow fractured her skull; and at the second, her face was horribly torn by the broken glass. For days, even weeks, it was thought she wouldn't recover, but that amazing tenacity of hers pulled her through.'

I felt a little shiver of horror run through me, and asked:

'And is she permanently marked?'

'I haven't seen her myself,' Morton replied, 'and I only have the report of Mrs Denningham, who saw Constance just before she left England. She said that most of the wounds had been wonderfully healed – war surgery, you know – but that one cheek was permanently disfigured and one eye gone.'

'O God!'

'It's very pitiful,' he said reflectively.

'It's also very sordid,' I answered. 'Imagine getting mixed up with such people! By the way, what happened to Elsie and Eddie?'

'They disappeared completely. Whether the police couldn't find them or whether it was thought best not to pursue the matter, I don't know. At any rate, they vanished. And, by the by, Constance's handbag, which apparently had a lot of money in it, vanished with them.'

'You think they stole it? Do you suppose they decoyed her down there to rob her?'

Morton shrugged.

'I don't know. I'm more inclined to believe in a *crime passionnel* – a revenge on the part of the jilted mistress. She was part Sicilian, you know.'

'I know. I suppose it's possible that the other fracas might have been staged independently in order to rob Constance, and that Elsie simply took her opportunity?'

'Quite likely. Anyway, they've gone, and Constance's money went too. You know she's poor now?'

'No!'

'That's quite certain. She had over-spent even her large income considerably, and mortgaged many of her securities to her Bank. The securities themselves were ill-chosen and depreciated enormously in value owing to the slump. Naturally, the Bank got frightened and insisted on realising. I'm afraid poor Constance has to starve on a beggarly thousand a year now.'

'Doesn't Lady Lechdale help her?'

'Not she. She was terrified of the scandal, and refused to have anything more to do with Constance. One can't really blame her. Constance had always treated her with contempt – why should she have wrecked what is left of her life for a prodigal stepdaughter?'

'It would have been generous,' I suggested.

'Quite. But that sort of generosity doesn't often occur in real life.'

'And where is Constance? What does she do with herself?'

'I believe she's much the same, except that there's more bad temper in her imperiousness. She's longing for a revolution, to avenge herself on the world. She wants to be a *tricoteuse* when the guillotine is erected in Pall Mall.'

'But where is she?'

'Nobody knows exactly, because the few letters she writes and receives all go through an agent. But the story is that she has a small house in one of the French Colonies in North Africa. The authorities know all about her, and leave her alone – a thousand a year is a lot in those parts. It's said that she lives with an Arab, and wears native women's costume so that she can hide her disfigurement with the veil.'

'Good Heavens,' I said, 'do you really mean it? What a come-down. It's the most humiliating fate I can imagine for her – compelled to counterfeit the costume and habits of women who are treated as slaves. Excess of freedom succeeded by its opposite. The gods may be just, but they are very stern in this case.'

'Your Nemesis and Hybris.'

I was silent, thinking of many things – of all that splendour and glitter and high-spirited insolence now glad to hide itself behind an ugly black Berber veil. I remembered how Constance had often seemed to me a symbolical figure, an embodiment of the post-war plutocracy and its jazz Dance of Death. Well, the plaster visage had fallen off the Death's Head in her case. Only it wasn't a complete death, any more than the dance had been a real dance. It was the kind of death where you remain sufficiently alive to know you are dead – the most horrible kind. It struck me that a similar fate had already descended on Constance's epoch and companions, the bored revellers who had caroused so drearily over the graves. No sudden catastrophe had overwhelmed them, no grand conflict in which they could at least die nobly. They had simply got drunk once too often and lost their money – the blood money of the dead legions. They had had their little day and danced their dance, and the world had grown weary of them. It hadn't even bothered to scratch them off, but left them to drop away one by one, like aged parasites. My feeling was one of serenity and hope, as if a sickness were ending, and health was in sight.

Morton interrupted my silence:

'Well? What do you think about it all?'

'I think,' I said, rising to fill my glass, and lifting it, 'I think we owe a cock to Aesculapius.'

Nobody's Baby

A MYSTERY STORY

Haveth childers everywhere.
JAMES JOYCE

I

IT was, it must have been in those pygmy days before the lustral flood of War that I stood talking with a young American between the acts of a fantastically amateur performance of The Florentine Tragedy. A bare room in Victoria Street made into a tank to hold earnest aquarium specimens from the artier suburbs, and the young American handing me a printed invitation card with the generous patronage of those in the know ...

'Good Heavens!' that far-off shadow of me exclaimed, 'Charlemagne Cox! What a name! Is it a joke?'

'Noh. It's a private misfortune or an unintentional parental advertise-ment. He's a verry talented young man from way out West. You oughta hear him.'

I read the card, an invitation to be present at Lady Medlington's drawing-room between the hours of three and five, when

MR CHARLEMAGNE COX

would play, price Two Guineas.

'But,' I said, 'I can't possibly accept a two-guinea ticket. It's a terrific amount of money ...'

'That's all right,' he interrupted genially, pointing to the word 'favour' printed in minuscules at the bottom of the card. 'You get into this particular menagerie gratis. The rich boobs pay two dollars and a bit for a place in the bread-line. Two guineas – that's Charlemagne. He's got a hunch it looks kinda swell and maybe'll raise his prices on some of the other guys.

You breeze in there and take a good look at Charlemagne; it'll put you wise to a't salesmanship. Charlemagne's a hell of a birrd for putting it over on Europeans. And Lily Medlington's a peach – she was the belle of Noo York until she married that goddam fool Englishman.'

In such terms did this genial savage refer to the Rt Honble the Earl of Medlington, Viscount Horseborough, Baron of Minsfield, Clappington and Stoke-Ravelswick, Lord Warden of the Cinque Ports and one of His Majesty's Principal Secretaries of State.

I accepted the ticket. I thought it would be nice to go to Park Lane and meet Lady Medlington, even if she was only a lily of New York and not one of the real gentry I had been brought up to respect. And I thought it would be very nice indeed to learn something about art salesmanship from Mr Charlemagne Cox, in spite of his funny name. All the same, if somebody had offered me five shillings for that ticket ...

The hall of Lady Medlington's house was inhabited by two anachronisms in pseudo-eighteenth-century costume, one of whom examined my entrance card with suspicious *hauteur* while the other accepted my hat with overwhelming condescension.

'Will your car be calling for you, Sir?'

'No,' I said. 'No. Probably not, *most* probably not.'

And I went up the stairs to the drawing-room, feeling their eyes directed at my back like searchlights, and almost convinced that there must be a hole in the seat of my trousers.

Lady Medlington's drawing-room was eighteenth-century – panels and portraits – for in those days even the upper classes still went in for period furnishing. Most of it was occupied by a miscellaneous collection of Chairs, from the chastest Sheraton to the curliest of Louis-Seize rococo, with a grand piano at the far end. I looked round for my nice American

friend. He was not there, and I began to feel the discomfort
of entering a house without knowing the hostess. My nervous-
ness made me dart into a chair almost in the front row, as far
as possible from the chattering groups of dowagers and young
men. On the seat of each chair was a large printed document.
I picked one up and obtained the following extraordinary
information:

By invitation of Lady Medlington (this in very small letters) MR
CHARLEMAGNE COX (in very large letters) will play:

(1) Renderings from a second-century papyrus, deciphered by the
late Professor Pzebzekovski, corrected and arranged for the piano by
CHARLEMAGNE COX.

(2) Fingolini's Quintette for strings and piano. The string motives
only, arranged for the piano by CHARLEMAGNE COX.

Interval

(3) Bantu tom-tom Symphony, arranged for the piano by CHARLE-
MAGNE COX.

(4) Harold Hardrada, an OPERA. Fragments of his great musical
work in progress, arranged for the piano by CHARLEMAGNE
COX.

NOTE.— MR CHARLEMAGNE COX *particularly* requests that he
shall not be annoyed by applause during the performance of Works
of Art.

The respectful hebetude induced by this modest programme
was dispersed for me by a sharp doglike laugh which went off
in a diminuendo of harsh, hiccupy chuckles. It was the least
spontaneous laugh I had ever heard. Beside the piano were
three large arm-chairs. I became aware of two legs in dark
trousers ending in white spats, which were crossed, uncrossed
and recrossed with spasmodic energy in about twenty seconds.
These led to a trunk couched very low in the deep arm-chair,
two hands with long twitching fingers and a very pale handsome face, rather like the Hermes of Praxiteles cut in cold
cream. This parody of a god uttered a remark, which was
incomprehensible to me, in a violent American accent which

seemed rather paraded than restrained. My bovine British intelligence abruptly registered the suspicion, the certainty that this was the great Mr Charlemagne Cox.

It was. In the arm-chair to his left sat a plump kindly-looking old body, who reminded me of a Sussex housekeeper we had at home. Mr Cox addressed her as 'Emelie', and I thought perhaps she was his nurse, brought to hear his concert in the generous American democratic way. Later I learned that 'Emelie' was the preposterously rich, aristocratic and benevolent Duchesse de Montigny-Bellegarde, whose ancestors had been Serene Highnesses of the Holy Roman Empire. She was slumming in London drawing-rooms. The other chair was occupied by a lovely slender creature with watchet-blue eyes and delicious coils of soft-looking gold hair, a really tiptop Ambrose McEvoy. She, I afterwards learned, was Betty Pencester, the daughter of a wealthy English baronet, who detested her class and *adored* everything that was really unpopular and *avant-garde*. She, poor thing, became a Communist after the War, and was murdered in the Avenue de Clichy by a Senegalese mulatress. But that is another story.

Mr Cox treated them both with the utmost familiarity, contradicted them flatly, laughed scornfully when they made a remark, and held Betty Pencester's hand. The ladies seemed to enjoy it all very much, and I thought wistfully of my own obscurity and of how wonderful it must be to arrive at the status of a Great Artist.

I shall not attempt to describe Mr Cox's concert, and I have been thus particular so far only because one's first meeting with Genius is naturally unforgettable, and because it reveals to some extent the grand-society side of Mr Cox's life. I must record, however, that before the execution of each *morceau* Mr Cox delivered an explanatory lecture, which was so obscure, to me at least, that I wished he would explain his explanation. Perhaps my attention was distracted because Mr Cox kept shutting the window behind him owing to the draught and smuts on the back of his neck, and then kept opening it since the room was too warm. A certain amount of discreet tittering outraged the performance of the Bantu tom-tom Symphony, which consisted in a rapid staccato hammering of middle C in a rhythm of tum-tum, tum-tum, tum-tum, gradually rising from pianissimo to fortissimo. Mr Cox had, perhaps, aroused too great an expectation in his audience by announcing that this Symphony would prove the basis of all future music. Betty and the Duchesse applauded loudly and loyally, however.

When this display of virtuosity ended, many of the audience departed with a haste I thought rather pointed. A number of women lingered and were introduced to Mr Cox. His manner of proceeding interested me. Before each lady he bowed low, ostentatiously low, shutting his eyes and clenching his lips as if he were performing some complicated athletic feat, while his long wispy hair fell tumultuously forward. Then suddenly, with a leonine gesture, he flung back his head until his chin stuck out with aggressive salesmanship, his hair flew back into position, and he thrust out a long bony paw with which he heartily shook the hand of his victim. At the same time he cackled insiduously, and said:

'Verry pleased to meet you. Hope you enjoyed the caancert.'

What songs his sirens sang in answer I shall never know, because Rendle, my American friend, appeared at my elbow.

'Well, Braithewaite,' he said. 'Well, what's your reaction?'

'A remarkable display,' I murmured. 'I think I can say it is the most remarkable and curious performance I've ever seen.'

'Yes,' he replied, cheered by what he thought was my enthusiasm. 'Charlemagne's got real salesmanship. He knows how to put it over on these goddam boobs. I wannu to meet

Charlemagne, because I gotta hunch there's something to you, and maybe Charlemagne'll give you a boost. That's where you Britishers all fall down – you've got no salesmanship. Now we've got salesmanship. We've got the goods, and we know how to put 'em across. I wannu to get in right with Charlemagne. I like you. There's no British high-hat about you. And Charlemagne's going to like you. We'll put you over. Shall I introdooce you?'

Seduced by his picturesque enthusiasm I nearly cried 'Sure thing,' but, remembering that my part was that of a Britisher who wasn't high-hat and needed putting over, I said:

'I should be grateful and honoured.'

And immediately the excellent Mr Rendle led me up to the high altar, where the inimitable Charlemagne was putting over salesmanship on half a dozen bewildered but flattered ladies.

'Mr Caax,' said Rendle, 'excuse me one moment, Mr Caax.'

'Verry pleased to meet you', said Mr Cox automatically.

'I wanna present to you my friend, Mr Braithewaite. He's a great admirer of yours and just crazy to know you.'

'Is he dong le mouvemong?' asked Mr Cox superciliously.

'He's a pote, Mr Caax, and does a weekly article on a'tistic London for *The Noo Bellman.*'

Mr Cox grasped my hand.

'Verry pleased to meet you, Mr Braithewaite.'

Here I felt acutely my lack of attistic salesmanship, for I did not quite know what to say to Mr Cox, and could only murmur something resembling 'Honoured, I'm sure'.

'Eh?' said Mr Cox, 'so you're a pote?'

I protested against the usurpation of that most honourable of names, but admitted I'd tried my hand at verse now and again.

'Potes have a helluva long furrow to plough in this world,' remarked Mr Cox, offering as the fruit of ripe wisdom and meditation what I later discovered was a Middle West commonplace.

'You betcher,' said Mr Rendle.

And they both exulted over the length of the furrow ploughed by the unfortunate pote in this world.

'Voltaire,' I ventured timidly, 'became a millionaire ...'

'You can't put that medieval dope over now,' asserted Mr Rendle confidently. 'It's pass-eh. Voltaire was a swell guy, but he'd have to use salesmanship if he lived in the twennieth century.'

Mr Cox seemed to lose interest in a conversation which had regrettably drifted away from the topic of himself. He turned his back on us rather abruptly, and returned to his titled muttons. But Mr Rendle was not so easily put off. As Mr Cox made a move for the door between two of the women, Mr Rendle rushed over and spoke to him again. I didn't hear what he said, but Mr Cox shook his hair, coughed in a consequential way, and said in a loud voice:

'Nao, I caan't. I'm driving back with the Doo-chesse. But you bring him round one evening. I'm at home on Fridays from nine.'

A few evenings later Rendle and I ate a very modest dinner together on the Dutch system, and then set forth to visit Mr Cox. Inexperience suggested to me that a man of Mr Cox's a'tistic salesmanship and aristocratic connections must live in genial comfort, if not in opulence. His address was unfamiliar to me, but in a 'good' district, one of those S.W. addresses which suggest solid upper middle-class wealth. I imagined a discreet butler and a large music-room with Whistlers and perhaps a couple of Outamaros ... From the bus-stop Rendle led me down a side street, from which he suddenly turned into a kind of alley, with a long blank wall on one side and on the other a row of lean-to shops, chiefly old clo', sweets, tobacco, and newspapers, and fish and chips. Distinctly proletarian.

'Good Lord,' I said, 'I didn't know there was a section like this out here.'

'Picturesque, isn't it? You can back Charlemagne to find the picturesque in any old European city.'

We came to a sort of paved court with small blackened houses of yellow brick, imperfectly lighted by one gas lamp with a broken mantle. Picturesque? I suppose the foreigner's picturesque is often the native's squalor. Rendle knocked at the door of one of these unsavoury dwellings, and it was eventually opened by a child who peered at us suspiciously in the darkness and said:

'Whadjer want?'

'Hello, Buddy,' said Rendle cheerily. 'Mr Caax at home?'

'Wipe yer boots afore yer go up them stairs,' said the child, and slammed the door behind us. An extraordinary odour gripped my nostrils and throat, an odour which I can only liken to the stale, acrid flavour of a very old and much-neglected chicken-run. It was an odour sufficient to disgust a saint with apostolic poverty – imperfect drainage, a slight escape of gas, years of insufficient cleaning with a damp rag tied on a broom-head and the memory of innumerable meals. A tiny yellow leaflet of light from a naked gas-bracket made the stairway just a little darker than it would have been with nothing. As we stumbled up, I clutched a handkerchief over my mouth and nose – I just had to. 'A'tistic salesmanship,' I murmured in bewilderment, 'a'tistic salesmanship?'

After we had scuffled about noisily on a small but Cimmerian landing, Rendle knocked at an invisible door. Immediately a loud but muffled voice shouted:

'Come IN!'

And the door was flung open with extraordinary violence, revealing Mr Cox himself, down to the white spats faintly gleaming in the hazy light from the room. Mr Cox grasped our hands in turn with real democratic heartiness, and waved us forward. At once I became aware that Mr Cox had been creating an a'tistic atmosphere by burning joss sticks – very welcome after the entrance hall. The room was not more than dimly lighted. In place of the gas, which Mr Cox evidently thought too garish, there were a couple of small candles on the mantelpiece and a large painted one on a fat wooden support at the other end of the room. The whole effect was faintly mystic, dilute Sar Péladan. I perceived that there were other people in the room. Mr Cox introduced us all with a mixture of warmth and embarrassment which did credit to his unspoiled nature.

'Mrs. Clifford Dawson.'

We bowed.

'Miss Ophelia Dawson.'

We bowed again.

'Mr Atherton Brindley, the famous a't critic.'

We shook hands with a'tistic limpness.

After a good deal of fussing I was accommodated with a bedroom chair, while Rendle democratically sat on the floor. Mr Cox's embarrassment was so genuine that he easily communicated it to me, so that at first I only noticed that Mrs Dawson was rather tall and fair and had been pretty, Miss Dawson shorter and darker and very pretty, and that Mr Brindley wore a very large black stock and a conspicuous signet ring. Mr Cox displayed a brown velvet coat. I was a bit nervous of talking in front of what I felt sure were advanced musical highbrows, since my own very imperfect musical education had been gathered in such commonplace resorts as Covent Garden, Queen's Hall and the Opéra. I had never been an Aeolian or Grotrian fiend. So I sat mum and examined the palace of a'tistic salesmanship.

With a shock I perceived that there was no piano, not even

an upright; but there was a bed, imperfectly camouflaged by a bit of Egyptian cotton stained with mystic symbols of old Nile. Evidently, Mr Cox had only the one room, for he would scarcely receive guests in his bedroom if he had two. But how, I wondered, could Mr Cox pursue his a't without the indispensable instrument of a piano? A great many books and papers were scattered on shelves, two small tables and the floor; and among them were an African drum, an oboe, a flute, a glockenspiel and a ukulele. It suddenly occurred to me that Mr Cox might be one of those greater geniuses who despise the mere practice of an art to specialise in Theory. Obviously, to know better than the best, to take the masters as your pupils (even when they remain strangely and obstinately deaf to your lessons) is the highest form of Art.

I made these observations under cover of a long anecdote (which I heard imperfectly) in which Rendle described with gusto how a guy of some sort had tried to double-cross him in some important matter I didn't quite grasp, and had been laughably defeated by his (Rendle's) superior wit and knowledge. Mr Cox seemed to listen with impatience, coughed a good deal, interrupted Rendle with witticisms I thought rather pointless, and at the end laughed in the 'huck-huck' manner I felt must be such a strain on his larynx. Feeling I ought to say something, I addressed one or two timid remarks to Miss Dawson, but received such discouraging monosyllables that I shut up, especially since the loud voice of Mr Cox cut my second sentence into fragments. Gradually my sluggish English wits tumbled to the fact that we were not there to talk to each other, but to act as audience – a select, docile, appreciative audience – to a continuation of Mr Cox's drawing-room performance.

'Mr Braithewaite,' he said pointedly, 'I'd just like to know your opinion of the Sacre.'

'The Sacre?' I said, in innocent bewilderment, 'what Sacre?'

This ignorance on my part was received with a gasp from the Dawsons and Mr Brindley. Mr Cox 'huck-hucked' in a derisive way which was painful to my young vanity. I must here point out that in 1912 the Sacre du Printemps had just been performed for the first time in Paris, while Stravinski was little known in London until the Russian Ballet season of 1914. Rendle came to my aid nobly.

'Braithewaite waddn't in Paris when it was aan. He's just mad he didn't make it.'

Waving aside this apology impatiently (what do We A'tists care about the ignorance of the *hoi polloi*?) Mr Cox immediately began a very wandering discourse about Stravinski, in which Stravinski occupied about one part to Mr Cox's nine. I gathered that Stravinski's 'sense of melody' was pretty bum and that his orchestration was generally feeble on account of his inability to make use of his harps. On the other hand there was some hope for him, since he had listened attentively to Mr Cox's advice (and Mr Cox gave an imitation of himself advising Stravinski in a French of peculiar syntax, vocabulary and pronunciation), but had been forced to hurry away to a social engagement, remarking in his dazzlement at Mr Cox: 'On ne cesse pas de s'instruire, nom de Dieu.'

I was probably the only person in Mr Cox's audience irreverent enough to wonder whether Stravinski had not been ironically quoting from a then fashionable humorous poem by Georges Fourest, the inventor of *La Négresse Blonde*. But Mr Cox evidently felt that he had made a deep impression. He then went on to discuss other composers, expressing deep contempt for those I had heard of, such as Mozart and Wagner and a mitigated appreciation of two or three I had never heard of and cannot remember – but I gathered that they were either Polish Jews or citizens of the U.S. Mr Cox illustrated his remarks (which certainly needed elucidation) on one or other of the instruments scattered round him. I felt his mastery of the flute and glockenspiel was inadequate, but he was certainly a vigorous performer on the African drum, for he brought down a lot of dingy plaster from the ceiling. His ukulele rendering of a Rimsky-Korsakov symphony struck me as ingenious but a bit rag-timey.

It is quite possible that I did not give Mr Cox's performance all the attention it deserved. My feelings were composed of a sad wonder why the Fates should so afflict me and an impatient desire that the affliction should cease – a mood I subsequently endured, but with more intensity, during bombardments on the western front. On the pre-war scale of values, Mr Cox's prolonged whizz-banging on the African drum was enough to ruffle any one's nerves. The difficulty was that I couldn't leave without Rendle, and he seemed to be deeply impressed, and even anxious for more. My only distraction was to observe the others, particularly the Dawsons, and to dally with the problem of why they were there and what were their relations with Mr Cox. What with his 'huck-hucking' and unintelligible explanations and cacophonous musical 'experiments', Mr Cox did not leave his guests much time for conversation. And Miss Dawson took very little advantage of the small intervals he did permit. Her remarks had that strained banality of the nervous person who feels something must be said, who would like to make a good impression, and is aware that the effort has failed before the remark is half uttered. It seemed to form an un-intentional bond with Mr Cox, who also made prodigious efforts to say something striking. But whereas he failed in an atmosphere of contempt and annoyance at his cheek, she aroused a pity that was almost tender.

In the end we were dismissed by Mr Cox, instead of being allowed to leave on our own. There came a moment when he abandoned noise-production (perhaps on account of the irritated knockings on his ceiling and party walls) and sat gloomily silent, with folded arms, apparently paying no attention to our spasmodic efforts at talk. He tilted back his chair with his chin stuck well out, looking a very greasy Hermes, and said:

'Waal?'

The excessive American accent was, I think, meant to be funny.

Instinctively we all got up, and Mr Cox shepherded us to the front door with alacrity and a candle. He took Rendle and me first. With social hypocrisy, I said:

'Thank you, Mr Cox, for a most pleasant and instructive evening.'

Said he:

'Did you get all the dope you want?'

'I beg your pardon?'

'If you want more daacumentation, come around at four to-morrow.'

'Thanks, I ...'

My invention lamentably failed me. I was still thinking of an excuse not to come when Mr Cox 'huck-hucked', and said:

'A'right. Four o'clock then. 'Night.'

And we were alone in the unsavoury court.

As we walked home, having missed the last bus, I said to Rendle:

'What the devil did Cox mean about dope and documentation? What's he want me for to-morrow?'

'Oh,' said Rendle, 'to fix you up about your article on him in *The Noo Bellman*.'

'Oh,' said I.

And I reflected bitterly on how one does let oneself in for things. Obviously, a'tistic salesmanship had found an easy victim in me.

'Who are the Dawsons?' I said, to change the subject.

'They're members of the highest British aristocracy,' said

Rendle proudly. 'The old man's bin a general or nabob or some darn thing in India. Gee, he hates Charlemagne. Won't have him in the house. But I guess Ophelia's pretty sweet on Charlemagne,'

'And he is in love with her?'

'She inspires his a't, and when a woman inspires Charlemagne's a't, he just has to have her. He's a hell of a Lothario is Charlemagne.'

'I see. And I suppose Brindley is the evicted but hated rival?'

'Sure. The old man wouldn't have Brindley at first, but when Charlemagne came along he got mad as hell, and said anyway Brindley had been to a public school and didn't have long hair. I guess he'd let her marry Brindley right now, just to spite Charlemagne.'

'Did it strike you,' I said, 'that in an oblique way the mother was trying to make the girl see ...' (I was going to add 'what a fool and a charlatan Cox is,' but remembered in time that he was Rendle's hero) '... make her see Cox in a rather unfavourable light?'

'No,' said Rendle stoutly, 'it did naat.'

'I thought she did it very cleverly,' I persisted, 'and Brindley backed her up.'

'She hates Brindley. I don't mind telling you that she's a bit sweet on Charlemagne herself. Maybe she'd like him for herself. I wouldn't put it past her.'

'Maybe,' I said reflectively, 'maybe.'

After I left Rendle, I could not help meditating a little on the rather odd situation I had got an inkling of that evening. By now it was evident to me that Charlemagne was one of those vain, self-seeking humbugs and *ratés* which America very wisely excretes upon Europe. I had seen his kind before, but never such a ripe and impudent specimen. How the devil had he got Lady Medlington – a great London hostess – to take him up? Through wire-pulling by the Dawson woman? Very likely. But what about the Dawsons? I had seen at a glance that they were not 'Bohemians', even of the revolting University sort. On the other hand, I was very doubtful about Rendle's 'highest British aristocracy'. Aristocracy might ask Cox to their houses as a kind of parasite butt; they certainly wouldn't go to his smelly room. Voices, clothes, manners all shouted that the Dawsons were moderately comfortable middle-class. If they were Anglo-Indians that explained the touch of insolence which Rendle mistook for breeding. But what in the Mogul's name were such people doing with Cox? I laughed aloud to myself at the thought of Anglo-India going arty, and picking up a Cox instead of phoenix. Obviously the girl was in love with that lanoline Hermes profile, and couldn't see the fool for the god. But the mother? Was she trying to put the girl off, to save her from an utterly foolish match? Or, improbably, was she, as Rendle suggested, trying to snaffle him for herself? Why didn't the nabob simply forbid them to see this 'hell of a Lothario'? Doubtless, like other autocrats, he only played ineffectual cricket on his own hearth ...

I decided I *would* call on Mr Cox.

Once more I affronted the approaches to Mr Cox's den, whose 'atmosphere' seemed to me even more lamentable by day than by night. As I climbed his dingy stairs I thought – I don't know why – of those young lairds in the Waverley Novels who always get into dismal lodgings just before they achieve the heiress and a fortune.

Our interview at first was not a success. Mr Cox 'sensed' my reluctance to put into print anything laudatory about him. Nevertheless, he put me through a course of documentation. I was shown portfolios of photographs of Mr Cox, with a piano, with a book, with a cigarette, with a tennis racquet, and even with a Duchess – the last being a press snapshot. Two portfolios of press-cuttings exposed convincing evidence of Mr Cox's genius and social connections. There was no hesitation in the tone with which they proclaimed his immediate achievements and dazzling future. Indeed, why should there have been, since those which had not been written by Mr Cox himself had been composed by indulgent friends in the world of journalism. I could only wonder why a man with all these press-cuttings wasn't both famous and rich. Finally I was permitted to feast my eyes on Mr Cox's acknowledged but unpublished compositions. They included surprisingly little music, nothing in fact beyond those masterpieces which had already been given to an enthusiastic world in Lady Medlington's drawing-room but a great deal of written manuscript. I glanced at some of the titles: 'Modern Music and the Cosmic Urge'; 'Mozart, Beethoven, and Other Waning Classics'; 'How to acquire Perfect Piano Technique'; 'The Opera of the Future', which, as I surmised, turned out to be Mr Cox's opera. And so on. It occurred to me that Mr Cox's a'tistic salesmanship was a bit too transparent. He boldly assumed that he possessed what he hadn't got; that he'd achieved what he hadn't done; that since he was right every one else must be wrong; and, especially, that the future of music was Mr Cox.

When I had expressed my admiration with more politeness than accuracy, I spoke of the delightful *soirée* Mr Cox had given us all, and then endeavoured to turn the conversation on to the subject of the Dawsons. But here I was baffled. Mr Cox was as reticent about them as he had been expansive about himself – and that is saying a good deal. My tentative enquiries seemed to fill him with suspicion, as if he thought I was plotting to abduct both ladies, or at the very least to prejudice them violently against him. And he created such a feeling of mystery about these two ordinary and respectable women that I felt as if I ought to go about on tiptoe, and immediately search the room for listening members of a murder gang. All I obtained was Mr Cox's expressed opinion that Miss Dawson was 'praabably' the reincarnation of an Egyptian priestess of the Fourteenth Dynasty, on account of her profound skill in the weird and subtle science of palmistry.

'She remembers her life in Egypt perfectly,' said Mr Cox with awed solemnity, 'and her mummy's in the Egyptian room of the Metropolitan in Noo York.'

Dismissing immediately the wild surmise that the 'mummy' in question was Mrs Dawson, I found myself scratching my head in stunned amazement. Mr Cox seemed pleased at the effect created, and gave me some valuable but alas forgotten information about occult mysteries. From there, as sometimes happens among young unmarried men, the conversation somehow drifted on to the subject of erotics. I had forgotten that Rendle had given Mr Cox the character of a Lothario, so that I was again surprised by the abundance of his information and the (alleged) extent of his conquests. Apparently it was impossible for any woman to resist a siege by Mr Cox. He couldn't understand the difficulty some fellows seemed to have ('huck-huck'), for his part he was positively worn out by the pursuit of numerous wealthy and lovely females belonging to the best American and European society. Not that he didn't sometimes take pity on them ('huck-huck'), but he had his a't to consider. A't must come first. So long as a woman was a stimulus to his a't, he didn't mind obliging – otherwise, he cut it out. But when you saw most women's husbands ('huck-huck') you couldn't help feeling sorry for the poor little creatures.

'But,' Mr Cox went on, suddenly grave, 'I do realise that I'm in an exceptionally privileged position. A man of exceptional potency is always pursooed, and the other guys get left.'

And Mr Cox illustrated the theme of his potency with divers anecdotes which I felt were both unsavoury and improbable. I couldn't help wondering if the science of a'tistic salesmanship had not been imported into his erotic life, with possibly similar results. However, I did not mention this, for Mr Cox most graciously outlined a theory of seduction for the use of weaker brethren. He had never found it necessary to use the method himself ('huck-huck'), but several of his friends had expressed themselves as delighted with the results and deeply grateful for information derived from Mr Cox's incomparable experience of the other sex. He warmly invited me to consult him in any sort of marital or amatory difficulty, and promised special attention to my case. As a preliminary introduction to the Cox improved method of seduction, he offered to lend me Stendhal's *De l'Amour*, which I declined on the ground that I had read it. He then repeated his offer of skilled assistance in circumstances of whatever difficulty and danger, adding negligently that his one annoyance was that women were usually so infatuated with him that he could never induce them to take precautions. In fact, he led me to assume that while he was fast overhauling Solomon's record in one direction, he was becoming a dangerous rival to Abraham in the other. I had a vision of a world inhabited by profiles practising a'tistic salesmanship on the few remaining Gentiles.

For some weeks, indeed months, I saw and heard nothing more of Mr Cox, and thought very little about him. Rendle had gone to Germany; I had not written the required article; so Mr Cox and I gyrated in our separate systems without ever meeting. But Fate or some obscure law of celestial dynamics insisted that this flaming comet of genius should from time to time blaze across my path in space. Once he dashed up in the columns of an evening paper during the silly season. The article, which was unsigned, congratulated the world on possessing a genius who would undoubtedly cause the twentieth century to be regarded as a turning point in the history of Art and Humanity. I recognised many of the phrases as peculiar to Mr Cox, while a whole paragraph seemed to have come from his 'Modern Music and the Cosmic Urge'. Without applying any of the tests demanded by a serious exegesis, I decided that in this case Mr Cox had written his own gospel. The word was illustrated by a new profile portrait of the master, a little blurred in reproduction. I observed that Mr Cox had adopted Brindley's stock, and that he looked more like a degenerate Praxiteles than ever. And then the comet disappeared in the wastepaper basket.

The next appearance was less expected and more sensational in the news it brought. I was talking to a woman friend at a studio party and she said something about 'Mrs Dawson'.

'Do you mean Mrs Clifford Dawson?' I asked.

'Yes, do you know her?'

'No, but I met her once with her daughter. They're Anglo-Indians, aren't they?'

She laughed.

'What made you think that? Mr Dawson was a planter in Ceylon. He had some losses and sold his estate in disgust. He's a nice old thing.'

'Then they're not wealthy?'

'Oh no! They have enough to live on decently, but that's all. By the way, did you know the girl is engaged?'

'No, really? Who to?'

'What *was* his name – I've forgotten – but it appears he's an *extraordinary* genius ...'

'Cox?' I suggested.

'Of course! Cox! How silly of me to forget. But what made you think of him?'

'I met the Dawsons at Mr Cox's West-end residence,' I said.

'Oh, then he's wealthy? I'm so glad for the girl's sake.'

'Well,' I said, 'wealthy perhaps is too strong a term. In fact, if I were a policeman I think I should describe Mr Cox as being without visible means of support.'

'You're joking!'

'Honest. If the girl has a few hundred a year of her own, it'll be opulence for Mr Cox.'

'How *extraordinary!* I wonder whatever made her want to marry him?'

'That's exactly what I hoped you'd be able to tell me. Cox is good-looking in a rather obvious flash way. I liken him to a bad and rather greasy copy of the Hermes of Praxiteles. But he'll go soggy. In five years he'll look like a meek Nero, and in fifteen like an abashed Vitellius.'

'You talk of women being catty, but you men are positively cruel to each other!'

'Sober truth, I assure you. He also gave me to understand that he had exceptional physical advantages, which no woman is able to resist.'

'What nonsense!'

'I'm only repeating what he told me himself. I spare you the details.'

'You really mean that Ophelia is going to marry a penniless creature for his good looks?'

'Partly yes, but not entirely. Mind you, I'm only conjecturing, because I've only met the Dawsons once and Cox twice. My impression was that the girl is fascinated by him. That profile is certainly printed on her heart. But that isn't the whole story. I should say that she's dead bored by an over-sheltered, utterly uninteresting life, and yearns to get away from it. Cox seems to her the great genius struggling against hostility and indifference, which she thinks he will eventually conquer in a blaze of glory. She know little about art and less about human nature. Just as she mistakes the charlatan for a genius, so she believes the adventurer in him is a bold pioneer character. She's marrying a dream – not the first time a girl's done that! I'm sorry for her. She's in for a stiff course of disillusionment. But if she has courage and common sense it may turn out to be the starting point for a better life. If she finds a better man and runs off with him in, say, a couple of years, Cox will have done her a good turn.'

'She won't do that. The family tradition of respectability is too strong.'

'Then I'm sorry, but I'm afraid she's cooked her own goose nicely.'

'Poor girl!'

'Poor girl indeed. But there's a lot we don't know. What puzzles me most is the attitude of the mother. She struck me as a reasonably cultivated and sensible woman. She must see through Cox. In fact, I'm sure she does, from one or two remarks she made. Why does she encourage the marriage? She must have had terrible rows with the old man, who, I'm told, detests Cox. Is she jealous of the daughter and anxious to palm her off into obscurity, or is she in love with Cox herself? It's a genuine mystery.'

My friend protested against such 'scandalous notions', and our conversation petered out into nothing, leaving the problem as far from solution as ever. I could scarcely believe that Mr Cox would get away with this marriage. Somebody, I felt, would blow the gaff. And yet, a day or two later the Court Page of the *Morning Post* informed me that:

The marriage arranged between Mr Charlemagne Cox of New York and Miss Ophelia Dawson will take place ...

I was not invited to Mr Cox's wedding, an oversight I did not resent very bitterly. Yet I should have been glad to witness this important event, and to observe the countenance and behaviour of the various parties involved. I had to content myself with a cutting, sent me by Rendle, from the Continental edition of an American newspaper, which I carefully preserved among a lot of other useless papers. It read oddly then, and reads still more oddly to-day:

American Beats the Band in Fashionable London.
Charlemagne Cox, Famous Ohio Musician and Art
Leader, Weds Blooming British Bride.
'Proud to be U.S. Citizen. My Husband is a
Cosmic Force,' says Mrs Cox.

Considerable stir has been evoked in the most select circles of fashionable London by the marriage, which took place yesterday, of Mr Charlemagne Cox of Ohio with the famous British society girl and beauty, Ophelia Dawson, daughter of a proud and ancient military family. It is rumoured that many young British aristocrats are sore that yet another of their famed beauties has yielded her hand and fortune to a scion of the New World. Mrs Cox, who looked radiant, was interviewed by our London representative yesterday as she boarded the train for an unknown destination on the Continent, where the couple will spend a quiet honeymoon in ideal surroundings. Asked if there was not considerable resentment among London fashionables at her abandonment of British citizenship, Mrs Cox replied: 'That is all nonsense; I am proud to be an American citizen, because my husband is American, and I am proud of him. I feel sure his genius will one day be recognised as a world force'.

Mr Charlemagne Cox is better known in Europe than at home, where musical criticism has not yet awakened to the fact that in Charlemagne Cox America has a musical genius who can vie on equal terms with the most renowned European composers. Last year Mr Cox performed fragments of his great opera, before a large and enthusiastic London audience, who unanimously acclaimed his vigorous and original personality. Mr Charlemagne Cox has all the versatility which marks the highest type of genius. In addition to his remarkable musical works, he has written on the history and future of music, and is now at work on a book of the highest importance which will revolutionise the whole conception of the arts and open up a new era of progressive culture. Mr Charlemagne Cox is twenty-six, and came to Europe from Ohio two years ago, after a brief sojourn in New York. In apearance Mr Cox resembles a College athlete rather than the conventional musical type. He is tall, good-looking, and carries a cane. Mr Charlemagne Cox ...

II

'Your Division's somewhere on the Somme,' said the R.T.O. patiently. 'They were in yesterday's show, so God knows where they are now. Railhead is back at Bapaume, so you'd better go there and ask again. The R.T.O. there will know.'

'Right you are,' I said. 'Thanks.'

The platform was crowded – returning leave men, a biggish draft of officers and a large draft of returned wounded. Suddenly a hand slapped heavily on my shoulder and a very cheery voice said:

'Hello, Braithewaite, old cock!'

I looked round, and immediately recognised Rendle, metamorphosed – greatly to his advantage – into an American infantry officer.

'Hul-lo,' I said. 'I never expected to see you here.'

'Where you going?'

'Up the bloody line again,' I said gloomily. 'What are you doing here?'

'We've bin on a tour of instruction with British imperial troops in the Bethune sector. Gee, they're swell guys. Treated us like brothers, and took fifty-five dallers off me at poker. We're going to Bapaume.'

'So am I.'

'Come along with us, buddy, come right along!'

A second later I was being introduced to a group of young American officers, very spick and span in their neat uniforms, and as full of buck as our fellows had been before the Somme. I don't know whether it was reciprocity, but they certainly treated *me* like a brother, shook my hand cordially, said nice things about the British Army, hustled me into a carriage labelled 'American Officers Only', offered me half a dozen flasks simultaneously and stuffed my pockets with chocolate. The R.T.O. looked in the window.

'You've no business to be in there. American officers only.'

'Hell,' said Rendle, 'he's my cousin I haven't seen for two years. You're from Missouri, aren't you, buddy?'

'Sure,' I said.

'Give him some Scotch,' said a voice.

'It's on your own responsibility,' the R.T.O. threw at me over his shoulder.

'Ach, to hell!' said Rendle disgustedly.

It was very stimulating to be with these fresh young men, still full of agreeable illusions about war, which I was careful not to tarnish. Nor did I find a trace of the brag and condescension I had been led to expect. On the contrary, they were boundlessly cordial, and treated me with embarrassing deference as a war-scarred veteran. Presently they dropped off to sleep one by one, and Rendle and I were left to talk. After we had decided that the War would last another three years (it was September 1918), and had established a just and lasting peace on the basis of the Fourteen Points, we talked about London and the people we had known in those immensely remote times. Finally I said:

'And what's happened to our old pal Cox? I haven't heard anything about him for years. Is he in your lot?'

'The hell he is,' said Rendle. 'The last I heard of him he was still bumming around London trying to put over some goddam fool notion about the Future of Art.'

From his tone of voice I gathered that Rendle had revised his opinion about the genius of Mr Cox.

'Good luck to him,' I said. 'I take off my hat to any one who has the wits to keep out of this mess. He's pretty plucky to imagine there's a future for anything, especially for Art.'

'He gets my goat,' said Rendle decisively.

Remembering Mr Cox's intimate revelations, I said in all innocence:

'I s'pose he's got quite a large family by now?'

Rendle stared at me.

'Who're you kidding?'

'I'm not kidding. Cox told me himself that he had great trouble in his affairs because he was so prodigiously fertile You yourself told me he was a Lothario.'

Rendle chuckled gleefully.

'Oh, boy! That's the biggest bluff ever pulled on us suckers. Gee, we were mutts in those days. When Heine gets us, I guess we can leave the future of Art to Charlemagne, but if the future of the human race was left to his loins the world'd mighty soon be an uninhabited desert.'

'No!' I said, 'do you really mean? ...'

'Take it from me, kid,' said Rendle solemnly, 'the Caax family is doomed to extinction with this generation.'

'Well I'm blowed!' I said; and we talked of other things.

The most intense comb-out of memory fails to reveal any further relation between Mr Cox and the Great War. Doubtless he too fought splendidly on his own front for The Cause – making the world safe for a'tistic salesmanship. I have to confess that the space occupied in my thoughts by Mr Cox was for some years insultingly small; in fact I never thought about him at all. But the comet was only far out in space; it was doomed to flame once more across the sky of my petty planet, years after the War.

There was a young fellow named Frank Marston, just down from the University. His parents, old friends of my family, were legitimately worried because he had gone Bloomsbury, or so they believed. They asked me to see the lad and 'to use my influence' – whatever that meant – 'to make him see common sense', which in this case meant entering the Civil Service. While I firmly declined to have anything to do with his morals, I said I was quite willing to examine his intellectual principles. And though I soon found that he had acquired plenty of Bloomsbury mannerisms, I also discovered that he wore his green carnation with a difference. He had, it appeared, made the acquaintance of a great unrecognised genius, a man of eccentric appearance but extraordinary powers, who was kept in obscurity by the jealousy and stupidity of his *confrères*. I said I thought that was extremely probable, if he really *was* a genius, and young Frank with a great deal of mystery offered to lead me to worship at the fane. Judge of my amazement when Frank revealed that the god in question was no other than Mr Charlemagne Cox.

'But,' I cried unguardedly, 'the man's a rank charlatan!'

'What do you know about him?' asked Frank with pained and superior contempt.

By this time I had reflected that Frank was not in a fit state to hear the truth about Mr Cox, and that unless I dissembled a little I should be ranked lower in the scale of intelligence than his own family. So I said:

'I saw something of him before the War. But I've no doubt he's made tremendous strides since then. I'd love to meet him again if you'll take me.'

We found Mr Cox in surroundings which may have been less picturesque than his pre-War haunt, but I for one was grateful to find them deodorised. Quite a neat little flat, rather on the small and dark side, and considerably encumbered by the baggage-train of Mr Cox's genius, but a tremendous improvement on his old squalor. Mr Cox had not changed much; indeed I heard the familiar 'huck-huck' through the panels of the door as Frank rang the bell. Naturally he had entirely forgotten me, and I was careful not to remind him. His appearance had evolved more rapidly than I had prophesied, for he was already in the Vitellius stage, and, having acquired at least an extra couple of stone, was now a fine figure of a man. He received us in the *négligé* of a man of genius, viz. a pair of trousers with large checks supported by a leather belt, an open-collared blue shirt, also marked with large checks the colour of heather flowers, a tie of gold brocade and no jacket. He looked like a degenerate Roman Emperor disguised as a barbarian clown for some unavowable purpose. I was rather pleased by his air of bravura, a sort of dammee-I-will-NOT-be-good determination.

As soon as we entered the little sitting-room, my attention was distracted from Mr Cox by the spectacle of Miss Dawson, who (I had to remind myself) was now Mrs Cox. I was startled and shocked, not so much at the thought of a nice girl pigging out life with Cox as by her appearance. Where he had waxed fat she had shrunk. Hers was not merely the fashionable skeleton silhouette. It was a kind of premature withering, like an apple left too long on a fruit-dish. There was a virginal pathos in her fragility, in the thin hands and wrists, and the legs which seemed too long for so tiny a trunk. Her clothes made me think of those eighteenth-century costumes you see on lay figures in museums, which leave you wondering whether the fabric has shrunk with time or whether it is just possible that women were once so bodiless. Her good looks had vanished helter-skelter. There were little wrinkles round her eyes, a sharp line on either side of her mouth, and she had cut her long dark hair to an Eton crop, which gave her the appearance of a prematurely-aged and nervous schoolboy. I noticed with pain that she repelled even the gentlest and most friendly approach with a neurasthenic hostility, and that she had unconsciously adopted some of Mr Cox's habits of speech, including a pathetic echo of his rasping laugh. So, I felt, might the ghost of Mr Cox laugh as he haunted the bed of some aesthete faithless to the principles of a'tistic salesmanship.

She seemed so emptied of life, so devoid of any interest or ambition. What could one say to this husk of a woman? My attention drifted back to Mr Cox, whose pallid double chin made me think of the fat German baker in De Quincey. Though I had long left behind me my temporary commission, I almost yearned to do a little tooling on that temptingly displayed gullet. I listened to the conversation between Mr Cox and Frank, which was carried on with such a wealth of abstract terms, private allusions and unfamiliar names that I had difficulty in understanding what they were talking about. Mr Cox 'huck-hucked' frequently at his own wit, which was often too Attic for my Boeotian understanding, and once or twice condescended to approve a particularly bright remark of Frank's with a single 'huck'. I noticed that Mr Cox had caught the English habit of referring to people by their Christian names in the presence of strangers, the assumption being that either the stranger is *au fait* and *dans le mouvement* and therefore an acceptable person, or, if he fails to understand is a bally intruder who had better take himself off, and not shove in among his betters. Thus Mr Cox more than once spoke of 'Osbert', which caused me surprise, for I could not by any effort imagine Charlemagne among Mr Sitwell's intimates. At best, I felt he could only prove a minor exhibit for Mr Lewis to vivisect. I noticed that Mr Cox frequently referred to the 'intelligence' and other virtues of one 'Maggie', whom I could not identify. I felt it could not be either Miss Bondfield or Lady Margaret Sackville, since 'Maggie' was apparently in the same line of cosmic energy as Mr Cox, and had indeed performed in public with him. 'Maggie says,' 'Maggie thinks,' 'Maggie told me' turned up constantly on Mr Cox's lips, and I had a vague feeling that Mrs Cox suffered a little from this undisguised homage, which was never extended to herself.

The *galimatias* of Mr Cox's conversation had by now become so complicated as to defy all effort to comprehend it. One caught glimpses of a pale moon of meaning through a heavy drift of cloudy words. Through these glimpses I gradually became aware that Mr Cox had made a complete change of front, and this explained to me something that had been a great puzzle, i.e. why a sharp lad like Frank had been taken in by him. Thinking that I should please the lad by pleasing Cox, I gave that great genius an opportunity to discourse on a'tistic salesmanship by remarking:

'Surely one of the great difficulties of the independent artist is to know how to "put over" his work?'

Both Frank and Mr Cox looked at me suspiciously, and Mr Cox 'huck-hucked' very contemptuously.

'Personality,' said Mr Cox emphatically, 'is a goddam noosance. Maggie says personality is the thief of A't. I mean you don't want to work for yourself. What you've got to realise is impersonality, the lens, objectivity. A't is more exact than Science. The great A'tist is more anonymous than the great Scientist. What you've got to have is the lens.'

This was a bit too deep for me, so I said:

'But isn't an artist without personality a contradiction in terms? A great artist is intensely personal because he cannot be any one but himself. No one can fail to recognise, say, the manner of Rubens. And though Shakespeare says nothing directly about himself, we not only recognise his manner in every passage, but are introduced through his characters to the spiritual adventures of a great individual mind.'

Mr Cox 'huck-hucked'.

'Shakespeare,' he said, 'was a medievalist. He don't interest the moderns. Take me, for instance. My work is impersonal, anonymous, a benefit conferred on the human race without their knowledge. I mean they don't know who I am any more than they know who invented the internal combustion engine.'

'They might look you both up in the Encyclopaedia,' I ventured.

'The great A'tist,' said Mr Cox seriously, 'is always rejected. They've rejected me. But My Work, as Maggie says, is influencing the whole future of the world. If Wilson had listened to me ... The great A'tist personally is always an outcast. You've got to be a lens and let the light through for humanity.'

'I see,' I murmured, though in point of fact the light of Mr Cox's lens was strangely obscure to me. I thought of the portfolios of photographs and press-cuttings belonging to the pre-War Cox.

'Charlemagne is the only living artist who is disinterested,' said Frank proudly. 'His devotion is absolutely unselfish.'

I couldn't help looking at Mrs Cox.

'Here,' said Cox, who had been rummaging through an untidy table, 'have a look at these.'

'These' were half a dozen periodicals with curious names, published in out of the way corners of the United States or in Paris or in Florence. The relevant articles were marked in red pencil, and were headed 'Charlemagne Cox on Anonymity' or 'Impersonality, By Charlemagne Cox.' Two were illustrated by photographs. I confess I merely glanced through them, but it occurred to me that Mr Cox was now courting publicity by denouncing it, and, so to speak, boosting personalities by pretending to reject them. However, I made no remark in this sense; and fairly soon we departed.

In the street, I said to Frank:

'Who is Maggie?'

'Haven't you heard of Margaret Bellington Shoemaker?' he exclaimed.

'No,' I said humbly.

'She's a great musician,' he said enthusiastically. 'She makes it her life work to interpret Cox's ideas. A marvellous woman.'

'I see,' I replied. 'Er ... an American?'

'Yes, I believe so, but she's simply *devoted* to Charlemagne '

'I see,' I said thoughtfully, 'I begin to see.'

Perhaps I did begin to see at that moment, but it is quite certain I did not see everything. There was, as they say, more to come; and that 'more' was involved in a mystery which really ought to be dealt with by my eminent *confrère*, Mr Edgar Wallace. Mr and Mrs Cox at last interested me, not as the Great Seer and his helpmeet, but as common human beings trapped in a relationship. It seemed to me that Mrs Cox had the worse end of the stick, though possibly Mr Cox would have felt differently. There was something in the poor lady's withered droop which I found hard to forget. I am not one of those who believe that the childless wife is necessarily unhappy or vice versa. When I considered her carefully, I did not think she was the kind of woman who ought to have children. She was too wispy and melancholy, likely enough in a moment of aberrant distraction to give the baby prussic acid instead of its Well of Loneliness.

Obviously, Mr Cox on his side was not completely satisfied. Those frequent and almost unconscious references to 'Maggie' were significant. Even the most guarded and reticent people are very apt to give away the secret of their amorous interest of the moment, simply because they cannot help thinking about the subject. And Mr Cox was neither guarded nor reticent. Yet, if Rendle had been right in his estimate of Mr Cox, there was no reason why his wife should feel any physical jealousy. And, in fact, the impression she gave was not that of a woman who is offended and hurt by infidelity, but simply a pathetic *quelle morne soirée* feeling. Why should she object, merely because her husband had found the only trained musician in the world who would take his ridiculous vapourings and caperings seriously? Doubtless, only Luv could explain this dementia on the part of Miss Shoemaker. But with her Luv might be Pure; and, if Rendle was right, would have to be so. Mrs Cox, far from being jealous, might take a sardonic joy in watching the repeated failures of her rival from a distance. There was, of course, the faint possibility that Miss Shoemaker might succeed where Mrs Cox had presumably failed ...

I decided that the melancholy of Mrs Cox was not due to jealousy, that she might even be grateful to Miss Shoemaker if that lady succeeded in loosening Mr Cox's Gordian knot. Always assuming that the Rendle Hypothesis was the correct one, then was there not sufficient basis for quite a respectable green and yellow melancholy in the fact that Mrs Cox was 'Mrs' only in the sight of the Registrar and not of Nature? A dismal dilemma. But I also decided that Mrs Cox must have suffered other, if less intimate, disillusionment. The exultant mood of confidence in Mr Cox's genius which had marked her (possibly exaggerated) communication to the press at the time of their marriage, had completely disappeared. No doubt, from a distance Mr Cox had actually seemed the colossal figure he represented himself so unblushingly to be, and she had felt it would be a grand thing to use her little fortune to smooth material difficulties away from the path of Genius. But eight or ten years of intimacy with Genius had very probably opened her eyes to a thing or two. Was it too monstrous to suggest that she had discovered that Humbug and Pretence are two cunning devils who often disguise themselves as the angel of Neglected Genius? Just think of being fed for years on Cox's prime tripe!

And then it seemed probable that before her marriage Mrs Cox had looked forward to a life of thrilling interest as the wife of a Great (if Neglected) Genius. She had no doubt seen herself as comforting him when his courage flagged, and rejoicing as he slowly forged a majestic way through opposition to the Recognition which was his due. And what a change this breathless struggle of the A'tist would be to the stagnant vacuum of middle-class retired gentility! Other men of talent would instinctively gyrate towards the great Charle magne, and she would live almost ecstatically, a gracious and comely Muse of the intellectuals. And I felt pretty sure that none of this dream could possibly have come true. Her life was almost certainly more restricted than ever, and whenever Charlemagne did catch a sucker, she had to sit back and say nothing. Doubtless, by this time she had also discovered that the 'intellectuals' are just as dirty dogs as every one else, if not a bit more so. *Quelle morne soirée* of a life!

Strange as it may appear, my sympathy with Mrs Cox concealed no plot against her virtue. Not that I had any great respect for Mr Cox's honour, but I just didn't want her. My feeling about her was not unlike one's natural compassion for an underfed but uncomplaining child. I have always had an intense dislike for pimping, but if Mrs Cox had asked me to connive at her intimacy with some stout and devoted young fellow, I don't know how I could have refused her. Fortunately she didn't ask me; and whenever Frank dragged me down to the temple of Charlemagne I could do nothing but watch her gentle timid droop with compassion. I must say I wondered why she didn't react against Cox's oppressive conceit, and run off with somebody else. I couldn't help wishing she would do it, even now when the *morne soirée* had lasted so long and turned the blue sky of life to a permanent twilight for her. But my woman friend of before the War had been right – the family traditions of respectability and honour had been too strong for her. Yet another victim of gammon ...

About this time I went to live in Paris, where I was lucky enough to come across Rendle again. Like many good Americans who get the poison of Europe in their systems, he was devilish restless. When he was in Europe he longed for the energy and human tumult of his native land, the stimulating climate of New York; and yet no sooner was he back home than he began to yearn for a seat in a café and a grey cathedral brooding over crooked streets and the chit-chat of Europe. This time, he said, he was in Europe 'for good and all.' I rather doubted it, though I noticed he had shed a number of American prejudices, and that he now tried to avoid the slang which he had previously rather flaunted as a kind of defiance to decadent Europe. All the same, he professed to be – and I have no doubt was – loyal to what he called 'Americanism', whatever that may be.

During our talks I told Rendle all I had seen and surmised about the Coxes since our meeting during the War. Since my interpretation was largely founded on what we now called 'the Rendle Hypothesis', he did not find much difficulty in agreeing with me.

'Caax,' he said, frowning, and unconsciously repeating a former judgment, 'gets my goat. He's the kind of American who gets us in wrong with Europeans. They see a goddam boob like that blahing around, and they conclude that all Americans are – what d'you call 'em in England?'

'Twirps,' I suggested.

'Um,' he said, 'that isn't a bad word. I guess you got it from us. But it makes me sore when people judge the U.S. by a rancid specimen like Caax.'

'What do you think will happen to the Coxes?' I asked.

'Jesus! What d'you think can happen to 'em? I guess they'll go on as they are until they fade out, and the local British mortician gets another job.'

'What about Miss Shoemaker? Isn't she likely to make trouble? Suppose she decides she wants the great Charlemagne all to herself?'

'I've met Maggie Shoemaker,' said Rendle. 'She's got a little apartment some place near the Luxembourg, and she gives piano recitals. Nice little thing. She's what we call the school-marm type – you know, canned culture and "idealism." I couldn't think who the hell she reminded me of until she started talking about Caax. Then I realised she'd gotten hold of some of his fool phrases and intonations and even that goop's giggle of his. Just as you say his wife has.'

'In spite of his praise of anonymity Cox must have a sort of personality, if he can impress two women like that.'

'Hell! He's the kind that want women to be an echo of themselves. But Maggie Shoemaker won't make trouble. She isn't that sort of American girl. No, sir. She don't give a damn whether Caax is a two-fisted he-man or not. In fact, I guess she'd be scared stiff if he was. She's just about as sexless as that British girl he married – that's what they call "idealism." All Maggie Shoemaker wants is to be carried up to heaven in the chariot of Mr Charlemagne Caax's fame.'

'What hopes,' I said.

Having thus decided that the Cox saga would peter out in ignominious wise, or rather that there would be no saga at all, we were more than a little surprised one morning to find paragraphs about Mr Cox in the Continental English and American dailies, announcing that he had determined to leave England and to establish himself in Paris. Mr Cox had evidently arranged his press with care and forethought. He announced that the British Empire was dead, and London a morgue. He said that Paris was the centre of the intellectual world, if only because it attracted the best American talent. He declared that no Englishman was capable of understanding modern experimental Art. His arrival in Paris (he added) had no political significance, but he hoped that his presence in The Quarter would prove a rallying-centre for all that was best in American and Continental Music, Literature and Art. 'Quarterites,' the paper commented, 'will be interested and flattered to know that this famous American has finally turned London down, and now admits that The Quarter is the real centre of Modernism. Mr Charlemagne Cox is not so well

known to Paris Americans as he ought to be and will be.
Apart from his work as a modernist musician, Mr Charlemagne Cox has investigated the whole of ancient music, about
which he has published valuable monographs. Mr Cox in-
tends to contribute actively to all the *avant-garde* periodicals
and hopes to publish in Paris an important book on the future
of literature and music. We are not at liberty to say more than
that this book poses the interesting thesis that poetry and the
novel are now dead, and that their place must inevitably be
taken by modern dynamic opera.'

'Well,' I said to Rendle, after he had read this valuable
paragraph. 'What do you say to that?'

'Caax has caught another sucker,' he said crisply.

'Evidently,' I replied. 'But what about the Cox saga? It
looks as if there might be another fytte after all.'

'He won't stay here long.'

'I wouldn't be too sure. Do you know, as I came along I
was told that the Coxes have taken a flat – in the same building
as Maggie Shoemaker?'

'The hell they have!' Rendle whistled. 'Oh, boy!'

'I think we may see some fun,' I ventured.

'See here!' exclaimed Rendle, 'it doesn't amuse me to see an
American citizen making a goddam fool of himself. He ought
to quit and go back home some place in Dakota and talk to the
hicks. He's making Amerrica ridiculous.'

'Get away with you!' I said. 'Forty thousand Coxes won't
take an inch off the stature of the Woolworth building.
Besides, didn't God create fools *pour nos menus plaisirs?*'

For some time we watched from a distance the pleasing
antics of Mr Cox in Paris. Somehow or other he had persuaded
the waiter at one of the cafés to reserve for him the table
which had once been reserved for Moréas, and there Mr Cox
and his double chin played the part of *Cher maître* to half a

dozen young suckers, as Rendle called them. I pointed out
that Cox might be considered the sucker, since he carried the
Cher-maître pose so far as invariably to pay for their drinks.
Mr Cox gave himself great airs, sticking out his chin, sprawl-
ing on his seat, and 'huck-hucking' to attract attention until
his throat must have been very sore. I suggested to Rendle
that we ought to present him with a large box of throat
pastilles, because if he lost his voice or got laryngitis we should
lose some of our fun. Meanwhile, the press 'sucker' continued
to boom Mr Cox with pathetic devotion, and to agitate the
world by dark prophesying about the wonderful things Mr
Cox would do when at last he took his coat off and got busy.
I admit I was for a long time more ardent than Rendle in
pursuing this new sport of Cox-hunting. I cut out most of
these press paragraphs, and pasted them in a book, which was
most unfortunately stolen by a third party whom we incautiously
initiated into the game. Yet it was Rendle who observed and
called my attention to the fact that Mr Cox never appeared in
cafés with either his wife or Miss Shoemaker – a little thing to
which I paid no attention at the time – and later the additional,
more interesting fact that Mrs Cox had never been in Paris at
all, but had remained in England.

'This looks serious,' I said, when Rendle passed on this
piece of information. 'Cox's discretion now has every appearance of what the Judge would call guilty behaviour. The call
of race has been too strong for Mr Cox. Evidently he has
abandoned the British lady for the American. We're seeing
life, my dear Rendle.'

But Rendle wouldn't have this. He maintained that it was
infinitely more probable that 'she' had left 'him', and supported his view by a picturesque but unfortunately unquotable
restatement of the Rendle Hypothesis.

'You can bet your life,' he added, 'she's through with that
guy. I guess she's found some decent British boy and pen-

sioned Caax off. That's why he's come over here, blahing about the future of everything.'

This aroused all my feelings of patriotism on behalf of British womanhood, and I wrote to friends in London asking for their version of the saga and for exact particulars of Mrs Cox. All the replies agreed. There had been no separation, formal or informal. Mr Cox had wanted to spend the summer in Paris, and Mrs Cox had preferred to remain for a time in England before rejoining him. Meanwhile, she was living quietly and most respectably in the country with relatives. My correspondents appeared to know nothing about Miss Shoemaker, or at least to attach no importance to her.

And, sure enough, later on Mrs Cox arrived in Paris. So we were told, for she never went out; or, at least, we never saw her.

'This beats the band,' said Rendle in deep perplexity. 'Say, we want a whole detective agency on this job. What in hell do they think they're doing?'

Nothing further happened for some time, and we were regretfully resigning ourselves to the inevitable fact that Cox-hunting had lost its savour, when we were electrified by a paragraph from the faithful sucker on the press. It ran something like this:

Quarterites will not fail to be excited by the news that an interesting event is awaited in the family of one of the Quarter's most famous figures. For some days it has been an open secret among the inner circle of Cox intimates that a new heir is daily expected. Mr Charlemagne Cox ...'

And there followed the usual blurb about the genius and plans of Mr Cox.

Rendle was as much staggered by those few lines of print as he would have been if Vesuvius had suddenly opened an annexe in the rue de Rivoli.

'What do you know about that!' he kept exclaiming. 'Gee, what do you know about that!'

'I don't know anything about it,' I said at last, rather impatiently, 'and neither do you. But it seems to me that the Rendle Hypothesis collapses ignominiously.'

'It's a can-ard,' he declared.

'How can it be?' I said. 'Even Cox wouldn't be such a fool as to announce an event which time must inevitably prove or disprove.'

Rendle shook his head.

'Get wise, buddy,' he said. 'Caax has been spending so much money entertaining his Court that he's got to raise a few dollars some place. Old folks get kinda excited about a grandchild. I guess Caax is handing this to his British relations to get a remittance. There isn't a baby, and there won't be a baby.'

'But,' I said, 'forgive me; both Mrs Cox's parents are now dead. There's nobody who'd be interested to stump up for an heir.'

'Then there's a rich, long-lost uncle turned up from the U.S. I bet you ten dollars there never is a Caax baby.'

'Ten dollars,' I said cautiously. 'That's a lot of money. But I'll bet you an even ten francs.'

'I'm on,' he said, 'though it's taking candy from children. You may as well hand it over now.'

'Not so fast,' I said. 'If you don't mind, I'll stand by the tradition of my country, and wait and see.'

Only two or three days later the Paris newspapers duly announced the birth of a Cox daughter, and among the usual babble the faithful sucker declared that the child was to be called Juliette Isolda. I felt that this was too good to be true, but the helpless infant was in due course crushed under those illustrious and tragical names. Meanwhile, I set out to find

Rendle to get my ten francs and to bury the Rendle Hypo-thesis for ever. But Rendle was nowhere to be found, and it was not until after ten at night that he turned up at the café, looking both tired and cross.

'Hullo,' I said, waving a newspaper at him, 'I've been looking for you all day. What about those ten francs?'

'Cut it out,' he said wearily, and then bawled, '*Garçon, un formidable!*'

I knew that Rendle must be in a grave state of annoyance and perplexity if he was going to try to drink that amount of beer, so I did not press the matter of the ten francs. He took a terrific A.E.F. swig at the beer, and then announced:

'Caax has been bumming around town to-day.'

'Celebrating the happy event?'

'Mrs Caax isn't around any place.'

'What the devil do you expect? She may be very ill, poor thing.'

'Neether is Maggie in town,' Rendle pursued.

'What are you getting at?' I asked.

'Listen here,' said Rendle, with a solemnity I thought very comic. 'There's an all-fired mystery about this. Caax wasn't grease-colour this morning, he was grass-colour. He looked scared to hell.'

'Been up all night, I expect, and worried about his wife.'

'Hell!' said Rendle, with infinite scorn, 'he worries some about her. See here, I've bin around to all the Amerrican noospapers in Paris to-day. They don't give a goddam about Caax, except all that sucker. I tried to pump him, said I was an old friend of the family way home, and wanted to send flowers. Gee, he may be a sucker, but he can keep his mouth shut if he wants. Wouldn't give me any add-ress and shooed me out. None of the other guys knoo where Mrs Caax is, but one of 'em let slip that Maggie Shoemaker's been out of town for months. What do you know about that?'

'Look here, old boy,' I said, 'Cox-hunting's got on your brain. What are you trying to insinuate? It's only natural that Cox should look worried. Damn it, his wife must be thirty-five. And with all this stupid publicity he can't resist, it's most natural that she should insist on her address being kept quiet. She doesn't want American reporters butting in to ask her opinion on the future of maternity. And if there has been anything between Cox and Maggie, isn't it only decent that she should clear out for a time under the circumstances?'

'She quit Paris weeks before Ophelia arrived,' Rendle objected.

'What of it?' I retorted. 'She must have known through Cox what was pending. It was natural that Mrs Cox should go to the country, and natural that she should be with her husband when the child was born.'

Rendel took another enormous swig of beer, and then shook his head.

'That isn't all,' he said. 'What do you think one of those noospaper guys told me?'

'Hearsay evidence,' I retorted. 'You're trying to save that ten francs.'

Rendle took a perfectly new ten-franc note from his wallet and held it firmly on the table with his right hand.

'If you've got the neck to think you've won that bet you're welcome to it. But listen here. That noospaper man told me there's a British philanthropist going around handing out dollars to people to have kids. One day he was drunk as an owl and told Charlemagne he'd give five thousand dollars to see a little Caax. Charlemagne thought he meant it, but I guess the Britisher knew all about the Rendle Hypothesis, and thought his money was safe. Oh, boy! Charlemagne just hated to lose those dollars. They hurt so much he stayed awake nights. So he staged this little drama.'

'Well,' I said, 'what of it? Suppose it's true? I don't see why the Coxes shouldn't have a child if they can get it endowed at birth.'

'Oh yeah?' said Rendle sarcastically. 'Well, Caax won't get a dime. That Britisher's got more grey matter than we have. He wanted to see Mrs Caax and be present at the birth. Charlemagne let on he was a gentleman from old Virginia, and told the Britisher to go to.'

'And quite right!' I said emphatically. 'They took his word that he'd pay up. He ought to have taken their word.'

Rendle handed over the ten francs.

'It's a goddam friendless world,' he said pathetically, 'where one old soldier'll rob another.'

'Look here,' I said, taking the note. 'Do you mean to insinuate that Cox, with the privity of Mrs Cox and the connivance of Maggie, went in for baby-snatching for the sake of a thousand pounds?'

'Let's drop it,' said Rendle wearily, 'cut it out. But listen here, Leonard Braithewaite, I guess we're the two bummest detectives that ever investigated a crime mystery.'

III

It is now over five years since Rendle reluctantly paid me the ten francs, which was a symbol of his admission that the Rendle Hypothesis had to be abandoned. At that time I felt convinced that the matter was definitely settled, and that my Cox-hunting days were over. The humours of Mr Cox, very limited in their range and operation, ceased to divert me; and I felt that the grave state of paternity *must* emancipate him from the status of perpetual sophomore in which he had wasted about twenty years of his life. I felt he could not go on for ever announcing that he was going to begin, and excusing his now inevitable failure as the persecution of the great artist by mediocrity. For a long time I had observed that Mr

Cox deliberately *provoked* (or tried to provoke) opposition by a senseless aggressiveness about trifles. True, the obstinacy of *raté* is inexhaustible, but I felt that Mr Cox at forty had ceased to be a figure of fun. He was either pathetic or a confounded nuisance. And most certainly a bore. Now that he had the responsibility of a child, I felt he had a chance of recovering from his lifelong attack of greatmanitis and of doing a job of work. R.I.P.

But in both cases I was wrong. From time to time, the comet of Mr Cox – ever diminishing in splendour and only visible through strong telescopes – still appears above the horizon. And every time I hear something about him, the mystery of the infant becomes more complicated and perturbing. I don't know whether I am influenced by Rendle's extreme reluctance to abandon his Hypothesis or whether the cumulative weight of evidence really tells in its favour, but I must confess there are times when I feel I ought to return the ten francs – or at any rate five of them. And the whole business is such an extraordinary muddle that I can only think of the unfortunate Juliette Isolda as nobody's baby. On the evidence she can't have any parents at all, but must have been found under a gooseberry bush or miraculously dropped like manna from Heaven. I myself no longer have an opinion one way or the other. I feel we are in the presence of an inscrutable historical mystery, like that of the Man in the Iron Mask.

And in the mystery of nobody's baby there is not even a Joanna Southcott's box to be opened by posterity for its disillusionment.

I must go back to the period just after this strange nativity, when I was called back to England, and Rendle decided to come with me on his way to America. I had plenty of things to think about besides Mr Cox, and it was Rendle who heard from Paris that the Coxes had abruptly left Paris for Germany, and that Maggie had taken the child and put it in an institution in England! Why Maggie? we kept asking each other. Why Maggie? Could it be that the Rendle Hypothesis had gained support in a totally unexpected way? Was it possible that the child was really Ophelia's but not Charlemagne's, and that all the curious hanky-panky in Paris which had perplexed us so much was simply a clumsy but generous plot on the part of Charlemagne and Maggie to shield the erring but repentant wife? Rendle jumped at this because it supported his theory, and kept clamouring for the return of his ten francs right up to the moment when I said good-bye to him at Liverpool. Rendle maintained that the precipitate flight from Paris was because Cox had registered the child as his, and the French police had found out that it wasn't. But I pointed out that this was purely gratuitous assumption, and that under English law a husband is always guilty of his wife's child unless he can prove himself innocent. Rendle produced a document which he said proved his case. This was an article contributed by Mr Cox to a small left-bank periodical in which he set out to explain why he had left Paris. Like most of Mr Cox's contributions to literature, this article was not remarkable for lucidity, but after a short rigmarole about Paris being dead (as poor old England had been when Cox removed to Paris) and Berlin being the centre of European culture, Mr Cox launched out into an extremely violent attack on French bureaucracy and the police force.

'There you are,' said Rendle triumphantly. 'The French cops were after him.'

'Rot,' I said. 'If you'd ever tried to buy a *carte d'identité*, instead of dodging it like most other Americans, you'd have plenty to say about French bureaucratic methods.'

And there we left it. Yet I must confess that there was one little uncertainty still in my mind – why did Mrs Cox never have the child with her, and why had Maggie taken it to

England? The only explanation was that the modern 'Bohemian' mother often does dump her child, and that the Cox-smitten Maggie was willing to perform any service. But 'Why Maggie?' stuck in my mind as a small question.

Two years later it became a very big query indeed, for the unfortunate Maggie suddenly died of appendicitis, leaving all her small fortune 'in trust to Juliette Isolda Cox!'

This was a staggerer. Could it be? It must be that Rendle and I had overlooked important clues, because we had started out with preconceived theories. We had never thought of Maggie. But it all fitted in perfectly. The child wasn't Mr and Mrs Cox's, it wasn't Mrs Cox's by another man, it was Maggie's and Charlemagne's! I remembered how Rendle had discovered Maggie had been away from Paris for some months previous to the nativity. Obviously, Mrs Cox had been the goat, and had generously offered to pretend to be the mother. Then she had found the situation too difficult and unpleasant, which explained the sudden departure from Paris. Naturally, Maggie had taken her own child to England (though it still passed as the Coxes'), and naturally she had left all her money to it. Q.E.D.

This seemed to me so complete an explanation that I immediately sat down and wrote to Rendle, calling on him to abandon all claim to the ten francs. Two days later I received from him a letter which crossed mine. In it he said:

Apropos our old pal Cox, you'd better send me back that ten francs of mine. Last night I met the wife of a young professor, who met the Coxes in Berlin. And what do you think she told me? Having a kid of her own, she began talking baby shop to Mrs C., who shut her up by saying: 'I don't know anything about babies. I never had one'. What do you know about that!!! I guess Cox found that daughter of his at the Enfants Trouvés. You'd better ship me that ten francs in gold.

But, as I immediately wrote him, this disclaimer on the part of Mrs Cox (if genuine) put the finishing touch of probability on my Maggie theory. And Rendle must have thought so too, because he didn't answer my letter. The whole problem again seemed solved.

And yet ... It surged up again as a staggering mystery about a year ago when I met at a freak party the very philanthropist whose subsidy Charlemagne had failed to obtain. He was a funny, open-hearted little man, with scraggly red hair and beard and a North Country accent. Apparently he had made a large fortune during the War, and then, having maddened his brain by reading an infinite number of books by modernist sex-quacks and eugenists, devoted the larger part of an almost princely income to endowing children of parents he considered either geniuses or eugenically sound. He was in high spirits, having arranged at this party for two babies to be produced by people who had never seen each other before. They had struck him as likely to produce 'interesting results'. He then described to me with great relish a sort of mixed maternity home and *crèche* he ran in the South of France, where the expectant mothers of his schemes were supported in luxury, and the 'results' educated in accordance with some further crank theory of his own.

I rather liked this warm-hearted little crank, and, finding him so extremely communicative, I ventured to ask if he had ever had any dealings with a man named Charlemagne Cox.

'Cox?' he said, looking at me sharply. 'Of course I have. Is he a friend of yours?'

'No,' I said, 'but I've somehow kept running across him all my life, and I heard a lot about him in Paris.'

'He's a charlatan,' said the little man vehemently, 'a-a-a most undesirable person. A-a-a eunuch!'

'You don't say so!' I exclaimed, feigning surprise.

The philanthropist tugged so violently at his beard that I saw even the memory of Mr Cox still made him angry.

'He came to me and said he was a musical genius, and that he was going to have a child with a Miss Somebody or other, who was also a musical genius, and would I give a subsidy to the child. He was a well-made feller, bit fat, but not bad looking. Seemed to me eugenically sound. I told him I should like to see the mother, and he said that could be arranged, so I promised my support. Then I heard from a very well-known eugenist that this confounded chap was incapable of having a child. I was indignant at being imposed upon, and I employed a private detective to get me the exact story.'

'And what was his report?' I asked, with intense curiosity.

'Why – perfectly disgraceful – the feller Cox had nothing to do with the child.'

'Nothing to do with it!' I exclaimed.

'Nothing whatever. He'd had some sort of petty flirtation with the girl, and thought he could establish his reputation as a man and at the same time draw a subsidy from me by pretending to be the father. A most disgraceful proceeding. The girl was pregnant by another man all the time.'

'Good heavens!' I exclaimed, 'I've lost that ten francs!'

'Eh?'

'Nothing,' I said. 'Only your explanation surprises me. I have always understood that the child was Mr and Mrs Cox's.

'I don't know anything about that. I know the facts of the case are as I tell you.'

'Do you happen to remember the name of the musical lady?'

'No.'

'Was it Shoemaker?'

'Shoemaker? Shoemaker? Yes, it was, I believe it was. Do you know her?'

'I never met her,' I replied, 'and the poor girl's dead. She left all her money to the Coxes' child.'

'You can take my word for it,' he said emphatically, 'it was hers. But I'm sorry she's dead. I don't like people to die. They oughtn't to die. Have you read Shaw's play? ...'

The philanthropist was so convincing that I very nearly sent Rendle back his ten francs at once. And yet the story was so extraordinary and ridiculous I couldn't quite believe it. If it were true, Maggie must either have deceived Cox or he must have conspired with her to deceive his wife for very ignominious motives. I couldn't believe it. And yet the philanthropist's tale was so circumstantial and he so obviously believed it himself ... I felt that the mystery was still·unsolved and that the children of the future would not ask each other 'Who was the father of Zebedee's children?' but 'Who were the parents of nobody's baby?'

I communicated the whole episode by letter to Rendle in New York, asking him if he honestly thought I should repay the ten francs. He replied:

Of course you ought to send back the ten francs – I always told you so. Cox isn't a proposition. But I don't believe the story of the British philanthropist. I've looked up two or three of poor Maggie's friends – including a girl who saw her constantly all the time she was in Europe – and they all swear that the story is ridiculous. They all say she was a very timid and 'virtuous' girl, and that her affair with Cox was a sort of mild hero-worship. She lived such a restricted, schoolmarm sort of life, she thought that fool guy was a genius. As for her having a baby – they simply scoff at the idea, and say she couldn't possibly have had one without their knowing. So the baby isn't Cox's, and it isn't Maggie's, and according to you it isn't Mrs Cox's, so it must be the devil's or the first case of parthenogenesis since A.D. I. Or maybe there isn't a baby. None of us has ever seen it, anyway.

And that last remark was only too true – none of us *had* ever seen the baby. I actually got to the point of asking myself whether it wasn't all a hoax, whether Charlemagne hadn't invented the history of the baby as a desperate expedient for publicity. The mystery now presented itself to me in different terms. It was no longer the question of finding parents for the baby, but of finding a baby for any number of hypothetical parents ...

So I thought until about a month ago. A warm spring afternoon tempted me into Hyde Park, and I walked along looking at the flowers which the gardeners had just bedded out or which had sprung up from bulbs. I was examining a very lovely bed of pheasant-eye narcissus, when something made me look round. On the broad asphalt path I saw some-body rather like Mrs Cox, but more drooping, more withered, more virginal-blasted-in-the-bud than ever, leading a little girl by the hand.

'Mummy,' said the child, 'you *will* buy me a Mickey Mouse, won't you?'

'Yes, dear.'

And that child was an exact female miniature of Charlemagne Cox.

A Gentleman of England

A SPECULATION

*How unjust when Nature gives something
wonderful, and Fortune spoils it !*

MENANDER

I

WE accuse Nature unjustly when we say that she never
creates a perfect human being. If Mr Harold Formby-Pett was
not perfect, it was not for lack of thinking so. After several
years' experience of himself as an adult, he had no fault to find
with himself – at least, he never found one. A wonderful thing,
the harmony of Mr Formby-Pett with himself. And a wonderful fate. Never to suffer doubt or humiliation, except through
or on behalf of others. Never to spend the midnight hours in
anything but well-earned sleep. Imagine! He was a Formby,
one of *the* Formbys, the Formbys of Formby, you know, fine
old house, picked up cheap too. And he was a Pett as well.
Everybody knows that the Petts had a great-grandfather who
was a personal friend of Palmerston's. With confident
prophecy he had been named Harold after his famous Uncle
Harold, who had been a blue and a half (cricket and billiards)
and had marched with Roberts to Simla. A great Imperialist,
Uncle Harold, who had unfortunately died insolvent, owing
to being as keen as mustard on the form of the Empire's
horses and the forms of the Empire's barmaids.

Even as a boy, young Harold had realised the advantages
and responsibilities of The Name. Blood and Breeding were
implied by the Name, which he inscribed with deliberate
beauty in all his school books:

HAROLD FORMBY-PETT
    School House
    Oldmixon School
    Oldmixon
    Salop
    England
    Europe
    The World

He was furious when some infernal little cad altered the last entry in all his books to 'The World's Pett Ass.' It looked so bad when the form-master happened to spot it. Rotten bad taste, too.

Amazingly, by one of those despicable tricks of hers, Fortune had refused to back Nature and Blood – the Formby-Petts were hard up, and old F.-P. had a devil of a job to keep up decent appearances. Had to give up his hunters and take to golf. Harold of course went to the old school – you can only get into Oldmixon if your father has been there – but he couldn't proceed to the old College. At nineteen – just imagine a mere child! – he had to start earning his living in the City; and at twenty-six he was still there, having performed the astonishing imbecility of marrying and begetting a baby.

An old pal of the great Uncle Harold had found Harold his City job – a sort of drop in a bucket-shop. Seven years later, when he dawns majestically upon our horizon, he was still only a drop, but a drop with position. Considerations of Blood and an odd thousand or two scraped together on mortgage by old F.-P. had spared Harold the indignity of being a mere employee. His position was rather ambiguous. He wasn't exactly a partner and he wasn't a clerk and he wasn't precisely a tout. He was a kind of financial Siren, or perhaps a mug-hunter. His job was to get hold of people with more money than sense, more cupidity than judgment, and put them on to good things which the bucket-shop was desperately anxious to be rid of. Harold had little or nothing to do with the business side, except to know prospectuses so well that he could exercise his gifts of persuasion without referring to the documents – have every detail at his finger-tips, as great financiers always do. As old Rosengrab, the senior partner, once said to him:

'You find the mugth, old man, and we'll find the thkeemth and thare the thwag.'

Harold worked on a small salary and a ten per cent commission on the thwag. But this frankness on the part of the old man was a shocking exception, a lamentable slide into bad taste. Harold was deeply pained and shocked by it, and had a long discussion with his wife, Esther, as to whether a gentleman could conscientiously remain in a firm which even jokingly could utter such disreputable sentiments. Esther was perfectly willing for him to resign and save his honour, but considerations of Home and Name kept Harold firmly to the only job with pickings he was ever likely to get. Old Rosengrab saw his mistake like a shot, and thereafter kept up an elaborate farce of gravity and solid worth, with much harping on the theme of the highness of their class of business and the good old English integrity which has made the City what it is. Harold found this reassuring. Honesty the best policy. When you know that's the motto of your city and firm – well, it gives you confidence, you know you can't go wrong.

The pleasing knowledge of his personal perfection did not prevent Harold from feeling a grudge against life and even the society of which he was a delicious if inconspicuous ornament.

'I never had a fair chance,' he used to complain to Esther, 'and I've had a hard life, a very hard life. I've had to make my way by sheer brains and integrity.'

By not having a fair chance he meant that he had not been given £50,000 on his twenty-first birthday; and by a hard life he meant that he had to earn his own living. And the living was not very brilliant, even for pre-War days. The limitation of income meant very serious hardships to Harold. Esther had everything a woman could want – her home and a baby, plenty of housework and opportunities to develop her brains by economical house-keeping, and always the return of her wonderful husband to brighten the end of the day. It was an extraordinary thing, Harold often reflected, that Esther seemed discontented and fretty, complained that she never saw any one and hardly ever went where she wanted to go, and was sometimes quite languid instead of ecstatic when he returned home. And that was particularly difficult to endure when he came back tired and discouraged.

The first serious autumn fog and the escape of a wealthy potential client too zealously pursued brought Harold home late one evening in a very tired and discouraged mood. The Underground was very crowded – everybody had dashed down out of the fog – and he had stood the whole way, in spite of the fact that he wore morning clothes and a top hat, and carried a perfectly-rolled umbrella. The bright station lights were fuzzy and the street lamps a yellow blur, while Harold's own select square with the six tennis courts in the middle was in rustic darkness. He had to feel his way from one dim lamp to the next, and was nearly knocked down by some rough individual whose only apology was a rude request to be informed why Harold couldn't keep his ruddy eyes peeled. The soft waves of fog entering his lungs had a sulphurous flavour, with a kind of grittiness under the softness which made him cough. When he recovered his top hat and umbrella, he could feel in the darkness that they were covered with slimy mud. Harold could have stamped with annoyance; he hated not to look well groomed.

The fog had got on Esther's nerves too. At the moment when she heard Harold's latchkey in the door, followed by his invariable enquiry: 'Where's my little lamb?' (meaning

Esther), she was lying on the bed, not far from tears of bore-dom and depression. She sprang up, dabbed her face with powder, and went downstairs with an obstinate languor which somehow could not translate itself into alacrity and radiant welcome. It was a capital crime in the Formby-Pett household if Esther were not waiting for her dear husband with a bright smile by the bright drawing-room fire, with Harold's slippers cosily warming in the fender. Harold was very keen on domestic bliss, and firmly believed in getting his money's worth out of his female helpmeet. She entered the small room, always uncomfortably crowded by her grand piano, bravely but guiltily, hoping against hope that Harold might have done something even more wonderful than usual that day, and hence be in one of his very rare good moods. One glance showed her error. He was standing at the slipperless fender before a black smoking fire which had just been hastily re-coaled, gazing at the enormous litter of small useless ob-jects he insisted should occupy the mantelpiece. His trimmed yellow moustache was pulled down at the ends by a sulky pout, his eyes were puckered with annoyance, and there were wet mud splashes on his shiny boots, spats and creased trouser legs. He did not look up when she came in, and almost refused the perfunctory kiss she tried hard to make less perfunctory. Automatically she uttered the accepted replique to the hall cue of 'Where's my little lamb?' by asking:

'Has my darling had a good day? Not *too* tired, I hope?'

But for once Harold departed from the frame of this daily domestic *commedia dell' arte*, where all the forms of a cloying sentimental affection were kept up, though the feeling had long ago subsided in a mixture of uneasy tolerance, tyranny and subjection. He said:

'Why isn't there a proper fire?'

Esther shrank a little from the petulant, domineering tone of whining complaint she knew only too well. She answered

with an almost craven tranquillity which surprised herself: by
its cravenness – how she shrank from these nagging rows! and
by its tranquillity – how used she was getting to them! She
said:

'I'm so sorry, darling. Annie must have forgotten it until
the last moment. You're late in to-night.'

'Late in!' Harold sneered indignantly. 'Is that any reason
why you shouldn't see things are done properly in the home?
Why aren't my slippers here?'

'I forgot those, I'm afraid.'

'Yes, you forgot them. I should like to know, Esther, why
it is you can never remember those little affectionate acts a
husband looks for? *I* don't forget to go to the office and work
and slave for you all day in all sorts of weather. You've got
nothing to do here except look after the home and amuse
yourself, and you can't even remember to put out my slippers.
Go and get them.'

The crudity of her husband's sensibilities hurt Esther more
than the foolish *naïveté* of his vanity and love of petty bullying.
There is no service too great or too abject to give a lover who
is too delicate to hint for it. She revolted helplessly against
Harold's cloying-sweet sentimentality which veered so
swiftly into cruelty. There were tears in her eyes as she returned with the worn slippers, symbols of her under-doggery.
She bolstered her pride by telling herself that the contempt of
ironic submission was more cutting than revolt – weakness
excusing itself.

Harold had taken off his muddy boots and spats, and sat in
the arm-chair wriggling his cold toes in socks which had gone
hard and wrinkled.

Esther held out the slippers, saying:

'Here they are, *darling*.'

She thought the ironic stress of her voice would sting him
to compunction, but he did not even notice it. He grunted:

'Hold them to the fire. They're stone cold. A nice welcome home. It's impossible to get back to the West End for a show on a night like this. Fog's thicker than ever. And when I was looking forward to a nice cosy evening over the fire ...'

'Dinner's served, Ma'am,' said the parlourmaid in the doorway.

Esther sighed relief gently. When the creature was fed perhaps he would be more tractable. The dinner let her down with devilish ingenuity. The cook had put the *croûtons* in the soup too early, so that they were sodden instead of crisp; the fish was over-boiled to shreds and the sauce treacle-thick through standing in the oven; the joint was burned and like tinder to the palate. The unexpected success of a good sweet came too late to save the meal, and did little towards seducing Harold into amiability. Housewives always admit candidly that the unfed or ill-fed male is a dangerous and unpleasant animal eager to display its resentment. The methods vary. In some cases there will be a display of sulky injured silence; in others a violent throwing down of table napkins and slamming of doors. Harold merely complained in a petulant and nagging way, calling Esther's attention to every lapse (of which she was only too much aware) and expatiating on his own misfortune in having to endure such things. Some women would have been glad to take up the challenge, and to talk about *their* disabilities; but Esther wasn't like that. Conscience-stricken at every real or imagined lapse of her own (which Harold deftly exaggerated), she was entirely tongue-tied when it came to defending or explaining herself.

All through the dismal meal she sat almost silent, trying to hide the tears in her eyes and unable to eat. It was worse when she had to follow him into the drawing-room and he discovered that his dirty boots and spats had not been removed. There was another scene, where Esther utterly failed to make her point that the drawing-room is not the place to take off one's boots, and Harold triumphantly established his point that nothing in the house was ever done for him and that his comfort was never considered. Esther essayed a feeble defence:

'But, darling, I do all I can for you. I hardly ever go out, except when you want me in the evening. I have to do the housekeeping and look after baby, who isn't at all well in this dreadful weather and ...'

'I never heard such nonsense and ingratitude!' Harold interrupted. 'There are thousands of women who'd give their very eyes to be in your place. Why, what more d'you want? You've got a nice home and servants to work for you – if you'd only use a little common sense and learn how to manage them – and a dear little child, and a husband I think you needn't be ashamed of!'

Esther sighed. It is hard to formulate a grievance when the grievance is that life is monotonous and tasteless. She sighed again. Harold talked on.

'Now look at me, for instance. I daresay you think I have nothing to complain of, but just imagine a man of my up-bringing and descent having to work, as I work, without proper capital. Such a thing has never happened in the family before. And with all the money I have to pay to keep up this establishment, I haven't a penny left for myself. I haven't even got a car, and I'm forced to live in a hovel in a wretched su-burb, instead of having a decent West-end house. And then I come home to an uneatable dinner. Suppose I'd brought an important client back? What would he have thought? What are my recreations? I can never afford to go to Cowes, or to Scot-land for the grouse-shooting, and it's three years since I was at Monte Carlo ...'

Esther listened with a patience which was gradually wear-ing down to exasperation.

II

The spirit of modern scepticism had not corroded Harold. On the contrary, he had Faith; and what he believed in was Money. In 1912 this was not so idealistic a faith as it is now. After all, at that time, you could still hold a sovereign in your hand, and the military guard at the Bank had something to look after in the vaults. But Harold's faith had certain mystic elements. Personal merit, of which his own was exceptional and indeed unique, should be acknowledged by the possession of money. Logically, this should have meant that Harold ought to be the richest man in the world; but the sporting spirit and the love of fair play coupled with the natural modesty of a gentleman made him confess that he would be quite content to be merely rich, though just how rich he never specified. If you hadn't money it looked very bad, not in good taste. Since a man with ten thousand a year was exactly a hundred times better than a man with only a hundred, all Harold's better feelings and finer nature clamoured for him to make money, and thus demonstrate his merit to the world.

Need it be said that this central mystic faith in omnipotent and all-beneficent Money implied faith in the two lesser gods of Patriotism and Morality, thus completing the trinity of respectable worship? Harold had no use for the effete if established religion of his country. Parsons hadn't much money, even though they might respect it, which Harold felt was their proper function. His youthful memories of pulpit oratory convinced him that you would never get a useful tip by listening to sermons. Naturally, if the Church had been livened up a bit and modernised, Harold would have been fervent. If there had been lessons on how to get rich, commandments such as 'Thou shalt underpay thy servants' and 'Thou shalt not give something for nothing', and communion with a consecrated cheque – well, Harold would have been there. As it was, he preferred money the father, patriotism the son, and morality the holy ghost. That was something a chap could take seriously.

Not until the Great War did Harold have an opportunity of demonstrating his merit and proving the efficacy of his faith. Then, by Jingo, Money, Patriotism and Morality came into their own. And then, by Saint Joan, the Harolds of England poured forth the last full measure of devotion, as their idealism prompted. Harold's patriotism was a beautiful and touching spectacle, which, if beheld, would have moistened the eyelids of many a warm-hearted lover of his country's wealth. There were some misguided fellows (ignorant of the True Faith) who identified their interests with their country's. Harold improved on this by a neat reversal. Instead of fighting for his country's interests, he saw with rare disinterestedness that justice and the sanctity of paper money demanded that his country should fight for him. As for Morality – well we all know what that is, don't we, Messieurs les maîtres du monde? If a fellow has been brought up decently and kept away from lower-class cads, he feels these things instinctively; you know, that sense of honour which feels a stain like a wound. Morality is Sex, and Sex is morality. A fellow's female relations, being related to Caesar, are naturally beneath suspicion; and a bounder who 'tampers' with them is a cad and a blackguard and a swine, especially if Caesar's ladies happen to make the first advances. When it isn't a question of Caesar's relatives, then of course Caesar's standards don't apply; it's simply a question of dodging the other fellow's sense of honour. And it is always a matter for debate whether lower-class women are 'women' at all in the Caesarian sense. Almost certainly not, if they are dependent employees. But there you are, I mean to say, so long as a fellow keeps his standards and his sense of honour, he *can't* go wrong.

The religion of Money enjoins on the faithful a peculiar

reverence for profits. 'Profits,' says the Gospel according to
Saint Denarius, 'make glad the heart of man. Profits are pure
and lovely as a virgin undefiled, as an English primrose by an
English river brim. Put profits in thy purse.' To Harold's ever-
lasting credit, be it said, he had conscientiously endeavoured
to practise this precept from the moment he entered the City.
For years the face of the God was averted from him, and he
had to scratch along miserably on not much more than five
hundred a year – almost an insult of the divinity to a man of
such merit. Yet who can fail to recognise that the God of
Money is a just and a zealous God, for though He trieth His
people (sometimes) in the Court of the King's Bench, yet
maketh He His paper to rain on the just and the unjust alike.
Whether it was entirely due to Harold's merits, or whether it
was a spontaneous exercise of divine benevolence, cannot be
known; but certain it is that God sent the profiteers' War for
the comfort of His people, and for Harold to do Work of
National Importance.

Never was such a time as that of the War and the Profits.
Feed the guns. There was the Government, borrowing Money
like mad, spending Money more madly. *Feed the guns.* They
needed cannon, shells, fuses, rifles, bayonets, bullets, machine
guns, bombs, trench mortars, Verey lights, gas. *Feed the guns.*
There were millions of boobs to be clothed, fed, washed and
shaved for the perfect oblation. *Feed the guns.* They needed
stretchers, bandages, hospital trains, surgical instruments,
beds, bedding, coffins. *Feed the guns.* They needed ships, tanks,
transport, petrol, coal, horses, mules and money. They lost
the ships, they lost the men, they lost the money too. *Feed the
guns.*

In such circumstances a religious man like Harold would
indeed have been a mutt if he had failed to 'make money', i.e.
to secure to himself a share of the purchasing power created
by the orderly habits of the community greatly in excess of the

average. And Harold made money. Almost every week he banked cheques whose amounts would have made him blink a couple of years earlier. He realised how Just God is, and that true merit (Formby-Pett merit) does not always go un-rewarded. He bought a large car, and patriotically lent it every afternoon to take disabled soldiers for an airing. Harold felt he owed it to them, for he had an idea they had something to do with this splendid boom. Then, finding it inconvenient to be without a car every afternoon, he bought another for himself and gave the first one to Esther on condition that it was permanently loaned for War Work. He bought an enormous fur coat, which made him look like a pompous and plethoric opossum, a bit mangy about the head. He bought a house. He bought objects of inartistic interest, clothes and animals, and had his portrait painted. He lived in a paroxysm of getting and spending, a series of financial orgasms. He could seldom resist the pleasure of going into a shop to purchase something which was of no use to him except as further evidence that he had become a controller of the King-dom of Heaven, and saying:

'Just put that down to my account – I'm Formby-Pett, the financier.'

And the respectful inclination of the shopkeeper's neck was unto Harold even as jam.

A late Victorian poet informs us that 'He who has once been happy is for aye out of misfortune's reach'; a statement which might be questioned if it came from a less august authority. Since the adequate discharge of religious duties is held to be the foundation of happiness, Harold ought to have been supremely happy, and therefore 'out of misfortune's reach' once for all. It is rather puzzling (optimistic philoso-phies *do* involve one in puzzles), but Harold didn't appear to be happy. In fact the more religious (i.e. the richer) he became, the more peevish his utterance and the more unbearable his domestic bliss. It may have been that he ate and drank rather too lavishly, and hence developed insomnia and a bit of a liver. Or perhaps it was the air raids, of which Harold took a serious view. All very well to drop explosives on the military – what on earth were they paid for? – but it was perfectly monstrous to attack the lives of innocent financiers and company promoters, who were the life-blood of the Country. So Harold bought another house in Buckinghamshire and called it Pett Towers. And that, of course, meant he had to have a bigger and swifter car, 'to get about'.

Naturally, Esther was the chief victim of Harold's merit and happiness. As the supernatural acknowledgment of his merit became more and more marked, he exacted from her a greater tribute of human respect.

'A woman's best friend is her husband,' he remarked frequently. 'If she doesn't cherish him as she has vowed before God, she's a-a-a public disgrace!'

So Esther entered upon a course of cherishing, and found it a remarkably tough job. It wasn't everybody who could cherish Harold up to the standard he demanded. Harold was so busy being a financier that he had no time to attend to the practical side of life. Esther had to run two houses at a time when food was getting rarer and servants difficult to keep. She had to look after the animals he bought, because he soon forgot about them. The more peevish Harold became, the more sweetly compliant she was expected to be. The slightest trace of rebellion on her part was ruthlessly put down, for Harold had some skill in making the worse appear the better cause. She had to meet and to entertain women, and pretend not to know that Harold was after them. True, Harold bought her clothes and jewels, but always indicated very plainly that the jewels were a loan, which might at any time have to be repaid, while a current interest of obsequiousness and meekness was charged.

As for the dresses – Harold frequently charged them to the firm's entertainment expenses. The logic of this may seem obscure, but it is sound. Harold discovered that Esther had an inexplicable attraction for many of his clients, very often for those who were richest and least amenable to his own wiles. Now Harold was the very soul of male honour; and, on the Caesarian thesis, Esther was the paragon of female honour. If a rich man developed an interest in Harold because that was the only way he could see Esther, and if he 'put a bit of business' in Harold's way in order to continue seeing Esther – well, I ask you, where is the harm? Business is business, and a woman who can't back her husband up is a public disgrace. It was necessary that Esther should be expensively clothed for this chaste pimping, and since it was all for the honour of the firm, why shouldn't the firm pay?

III

Towards the middle of 1918, old Rosengrab grew pensive and studied carefully the daily reports which came to him from Holland and Switzerland. On the 9th August he began to liquidate all his 'War Interests' with speed and caution. By the beginning of September nearly all the firm's assets were in cash and gilt-edged securities. Thereafter he waited, studying his reports, occasionally biting his finger-nails and praying that our unexampled prosperity might last. Harold was staggered, and wondered if old Rosengrab were not losing grip. He was still more staggered when the old man gave him a number of draft prospectuses, told him to put them into shape and to start sounding for likely supporters. He couldn't imagine what old Rosengrab was up to – with a heaven-sent War still in full blast and unimaginable profits being made. And when he read the titles of the new companies, Harold could only open and shut his mouth like a carp trying to suck down a crust too big for its gullet. There were, for instance, Reaping Hooks Limited, a company for turning tanks into agricultural tractors; War Gratuities Investments Limited, whose philanthropic intentions are obvious; and Imperial Supplies Services Limited, which proposed to adapt surplus War stores for civilian purposes.

In a few weeks Harold perceived the wisdom of the old man's foresight, and in a few months he was as enthusiastic a pacifist as he had been meritorious a War-dog. Esther found herself dining out very frequently, with a baffling number of gentlemen (accompanied by their ladies) with commodities to sell or money to lose. She became quite an expert at the soft answer which turneth away the wine-flushed suitor without losing his custom. If Esther was bored, often rather ashamed, sometimes mutely rebellious, everybody else seemed highly delighted. A most brilliant season. Never had there been such a boom, and profits were higher than ever. A glorious peace. Harold seemed dilated with his merit, and he and his associates hopped clumsily about with women on dance floors like swollen carrion crows on a succulent corpse.

Things being thus, Esther was not in the least surprised when Harold said one evening:

'We're dining out to-morrow with a rather important client' (all Harold's business associates were 'rather important'), 'and I want you to look your best. Wear those diamonds I lent you.'

Esther's mechanical and rather drooping, very indifferent 'Yes, darling' exasperated Harold.

'Why can't you be a little more lively and interested?' he complained. 'Other women are. Here you have a chance to help me with important schemes and to mix in the best society and to enjoy everything money can buy, and you mumble out *yes, darling*, as if I'd asked you to go to a funeral.'

'Who else is coming?' asked Esther, tactfully trying to be lively and interested.

Harold hesitated a moment, and then said:

'I asked Nancy to make a fourth. This chap's a Lord, Lord Blenthrop, and I want to make a good impression. Nancy knows how to deal with fellows like that – she's awfully well connected, you know.'

It was now Esther's turn to hesitate. She flushed slightly. Nancy was one of Harold's numerous Egerias, who made a point of being particularly patronising and sweetly offensive to her. Esther asked herself, as she'd done fifty times, why on earth she put up with it. She turned on him, meaning to protest, but found herself saying submissively:

'All right, darling.'

There was no use in protesting. It only meant a row, and rows made her ill, while Harold seemed to flourish on them. He enjoyed a verbal battle with Esther and, when he had made her cry with vexation and humiliation, almost invariably became very amorous. She submitted, as the weak must, but with an inner spirit which never quite surrendered.

For some tutelary observator, invisible but in the know, that dinner would have been a pleasant little farce, with a dash of pathos and tragedy – for Esther fell in love. There was Harold, pinkish pallid and flabby, real pearl studs and signet ring, a fraction too well dressed, slightly too hospitable, heaping lobster on caviare and game upon game, and mixing his wines like false metaphors. There was Nancy Thorndike, a little too pretty in the come-hither mode, a trifle too nobly gowned for one whose sole charm was accessibility. And there was Blenthrop, wearing a Staff uniform and a double row of ribbons, with slacks. He looked extremely distinguished and handsome, and the War was still near enough for people at other tables to whisper about him – a flattery of which Nancy and Harold were exquisitely aware, for Harold thought they were whispering 'Formby-Pett, the great financier, you know.' Both Nancy and Harold were super-amiable to a guest who added to the prestige of a peer the solid advantages of an influential and wealthy client-in-posse. Esther sat almost silent, noticing or thinking she noticed how Blenthrop's reticences and delicacies of good breeding exposed the vulgarity of the others. She would have liked to talk, but shyness and Harold's almost brutal interruptions made her feel ineffective and humiliated.

Blenthrop had come to be bored, and found himself amused and interested, 'intrigued' as the stylists say. Though he concealed it perfectly, he could not help feeling the soldier's contempt for the priest of paper money and the gentleman's dislike for the well-camouflaged bounder, as he so unjustly considered the meritorious Harold. He was not a professional soldier, only a 1914 volunteer; and had some knowledge of the world, though not of Harold's world. He thought Esther pretty, very pretty, and very attractive. In a few minutes he had guessed the situation – the mistress to his right, the bored but, alas, not neglected wife to his left, and the conceited little coxcomb opposite. He saw he had made an impression on Esther, but he applied himself so skilfully to flattering Harold and Nancy that all three thought he had barely noticed Esther. He was polite and no more. But the moment he began to dance, he said:

'I'm sure you like Chopin.'

'What makes you sure?'

'Well, you do, don't you? Do you remember that lovely Nocturne ...'

And he hummed the opening phrase through the narrow-bones-and-cleaver din of jazz.

'Yes,' said Esther, 'yes, I do. It is lovely, but why ...'

'I thought from the suppleness of your fingers you must be a pianist, and there's a look in your eyes – someone who is haunted by unattainable beauty. You would just *have* to like Chopin.'

'It sounds like detective work.'

'Doesn't it? But when people interest me – they very rarely do – I can't help trying to find out what they are. I don't mean in ordinary life, but in themselves. I should say you have great capabilities never developed, great sensitiveness which recoils on itself, a capacity for devotion which has been tried rather than exercised.'

Esther stiffened a little, and tried to laugh:

'I'm afraid your detective work has gone a little wrong there.'

'Has it? I wonder?'

Harold and Nancy, absorbed and yet observant, bobbed near them, and they were silent until Religion in the arms of Love had bobbed away again. Said Esther:

'I should never have thought you would care about Chopin.'

'Wouldn't you? I used to play him a lot before the War. And read poetry. And, which is even more scandalous, try to write it.'

'Oh! Do you like Dowson?'

' "And I was desolate, and sick of an old passion
    When I awoke and found the dawn was grey."
Yes, I liked him enormously then. After Swinburne, of course. Recently I've been reading Sassoon and Brooke, and a man named Lawrence.'

'Lawrence?' said Esther vaguely. 'I haven't read him. I thought he was brutal and anti-feminist?'

'I'll send some of his books to you to-morrow ...'

The dance ended. As they moved back to the table, Esther whispered hurriedly:

'Don't say anything about music or poetry to Harold and Nancy. They simply hate it.'

'As if I should!'

Already there was the charm of an innocent-guilty secret between them.

All the way home in the car Harold talked, a blissful coke-wold in fancy, if not yet in fact. There was a kind of flood-lighting effect in the car, for it was one of the innumerable minor rewards of merit to show the world how merit is rewarded. This flaccid Austin Friars Heliogabalus could not have the ways strewn with gold-dust for his auspicious pass-age, but he could at least show off his top hat and his wife's diamonds to an indifferent or hostile populace. Esther wanted the light out – if only Harold would be silent and let her sit there quietly with her eyes shut in the dark, she felt he would be less repulsive. Strange how repulsive he had become in a few hours. She said plaintively:

'Can't we have the light out? It hurts my eyes.'

'Nonsense. It can't hurt your eyes. I had it specially designed myself,' Harold dismissed her complaint with this unanswer-able argument, and proceeded. 'Now, do try and pay attention to what I'm saying, Esther. I don't expect you to understand the serious things of life; women haven't the brains to grasp them. But you can back me up. Try to realise that this is the biggest scheme I've ever floated, and that Lord Blenthrop's name and capital are quite *essential*. His name's extremely well known among the right people and carries weight. I had great difficulty in persuading him even to consider the scheme, and it's too aggravating to have you letting me down.'

'What do you mean?' asked Esther, with a slight strain of anxiety in her voice. Had Harold noticed the pressure of hands and the warm conspiratorial glance at the end of her last fox-trot with Blenthrop?

'You needn't have repelled Lord Blenthrop's advances quite so obviously.'

'He made no advances.'

'Good God, Esther,' said Harold peevishly, 'don't be so silly. Any one could see he was interested in you, and you sat there like a stuffed dummy, didn't open your lips, and left me and Nancy to keep things lively. You openly showed you were bored.'

Harold did not see the slight smile which Esther could not quite conceal – she was thinking how little she was bored at dinner and how much she was bored by this conversation. She said with calm dissimulation:

'I'm very sorry.'

'Now look here, I've got to invite him again soon, and next time for *God's* sake play up to him.'

'Do you mean,' asked Esther, just managing to control the laughter which suddenly surged in her, 'that I'm to let him make love to me?'

('Because I might,' she added to herself, 'if it's so important, and he was very urgent.')

'My God!' Harold exclaimed, scandalised, 'what a filthy mind you have, Esther. Can't you see the difference? This is a matter of *business* ...'

The car stopped, and Esther ran into the house quickly. The one thing she wanted on earth was to be alone and in darkness, to brood on her feelings. To be almost in love at first sight and to imagine delicious possibilities ...

With horror she perceived that Harold was speaking to her in the half-wheedling, half-commanding voice which showed that he intended to be amorous. In a kind of desperation she tried to huddle back the clothes on to her half-naked body. She implored him:

'Oh please, Harold, not to-night! I'm too tired.'

He came over and put his arms round her, and she heard the cooing but implacable voice:

'What nonsense my little lamb talks! Of course she's not tired!'

With a shudder she tried to thrust him away.

'Oh please, *please*, not to-night!'

With a bitter repulsion horrifyingly mingled with sensuality Esther endured the honour of conjugal rights.

IV

No man succeeds in an enterprise without some quality. Harold and Blenthrop were alike in possessing a quality of seduction. The gift which Blenthrop abused in merely human relationships, chiefly with women, Harold preserved for the service of the deity to whom he was dedicated. Harold kept himself in water-tight compartments. Business was business, and life was life; or rather business was life, and the rest of existence got along as best it could. Harold had one standard for himself and another for his wife. Similarly, he never thought of squandering on his family or dependents the treasures of insinuation, persuasion and seduction he spent so lavishly in the Great Cause. Perhaps he felt the strain, and had to make up for being too amiable to people who were in the exacting and triumphant position of possessing money he wanted, by being more than peevish with those from whom he had no financial expectations. The divine law of compensation. Not that Harold was competent to play a leading part in the financial-seduction line; without his cunning old bawd, Rosengrab, he was more or less helpless. As it was, he made a great deal of money.

While it is pleasant to be able to record that Harold's devotion to the True Faith was thus appropriately rewarded, it is also true that such single-eyed devotion had its inconveniences. Among them was a total ignorance of Esther's feelings and an obtuse lack of interest in her actions. Not that ignorance mattered to Harold – he was always ready to tell a jockey how he should ride a horse, or a portrait painter how to compose a picture. Seek ye first the Kingdom of Money and all these things shall be added unto ye. Yet those (and they must be many) who will admire this great and good man will certainly forget that his preoccupation with good works entirely prevented his noticing that Esther had fallen in love with Blenthrop. He also failed to perceive any difference when she became Blenthrop's mistress. The charitable will attribute this oversight to his ardent devotion to Business; and the uncharitable to the fact that he was at that very moment swapping his Nancy for a Maude. Nancy was a slim blonde and Maude a plump brunette, which only goes to show that financial gentlemen can prefer both.

The remorse which Esther had expected to feel after her fall when confronting her injured husband and innocent little child utterly failed to materialise. Her chief feelings were triumph and satisfaction. Where marriage has become a violation, adultery may restore self-respect. For nearly three months she lived in that febrile mood of intensity which comes from a secret passion which cannot be confessed, and can only be gratified by stealth at rare and often inconvenient moments. It might be too much to say that she was happy; but she was certainly absorbed. The self-control and dissimulation of faithless women in love made her task of deceiving Harold superlatively easy. Yet she needed both these qualities one evening about three months after her first meeting with Blenthrop.

Harold came back from his service to God and humanity in a more than usually pestilential mood. He began to bully Esther from the moment he entered the house, and kept it up with unflagging nastiness. She bore it all with the cool poise of one whose sin is worth the price. After the customary fault-finding in the matter of slippers, wifely demonstrations of affection and the menu, Harold suddenly burst forth:

'And that isn't the only thing I've got to complain about with you, Esther. I've found out to-day that you're not to be trusted.'

Esther's heart gave a little guilty jump, but she said quite coolly:

'What do you mean?'

'Why, you've let me down with Lord Blenthrop.'

Esther could feel her face flushing, and chided herself for lack of self-control. How on earth had Harold found out? Well, the only thing was to bluff it out to the end, and then face the inevitable. At the worst Harold could divorce her, and then – why, then, would it be such a disaster to become Lady Blenthrop? Almost superb in her faith in her lover, she said calmly:

'I really don't know what you're talking about.'

'Don't you?' asked Harold, with an attempt at sarcasm which was merely pettish. 'Well, I'll tell you. I introduced you to Blenthrop for business purposes, didn't I?'

'So you said.'

'And I told you to play up to him, didn't I?'

'And you think I took your instructions too literally?'

It was now Harold's turn to stare, but he ignored this cryptic remark, and rambled on querulously:

'Of course, you would go and spoil the most important piece of business I've ever had in my hands. Do you know I stood to make thirty or forty thousand pounds out of that scheme?'

'I didn't know,' Esther answered with distaste. 'How should I? You never tell me anything.'

'What's the good of telling you? How could you possibly understand important and difficult schemes, when you can't even carry out simple instructions? I might possibly have got the capital together from other sources, but without Blenthrop's name, the whole thing collapses. "Major Lord Blenthrop, C.B., D.S.O., M.C.", that was exactly what we wanted. It'd have reassured people, everybody's heard about what he did at Hulluch. Just the very thing – a War hero's name for a damned good post-War scheme. And then you go and spoil it all.'

'You mean he has refused? ...'

'Refused? He's not only refused, but gone away to prevent me getting at him. Accepted some military post in the West Indies ... What's the matter with you?'

Esther was very pale. She nipped the flesh of her left hand hard between the nails of her fingers to prevent herself from fainting. Harold gazed at her with angry, stupid eyes. She said:

'Nothing. Go on. To the West Indies?'

'Yes. This morning I got a letter from him saying he had to go, and that he couldn't go on to the board of directors, since he wouldn't be here to overlook matters. Such nonsense! As if we wanted him to *do* anything! All the better for us to have him abroad once we'd got his name. And he's gone without letting us have it. And it's your fault. You must have put him off, offended him somehow – he didn't even mention you in his letter. I'm sure I've played up to him enough. God! The hours I've wasted on that fool, pretending to be interested in his polo stories and his beastly intrigues with women ... What's the matter now?'

Esther stood up, quickly but shakily. She could feel her knees violently trembling, and a sharp migraine had suddenly caught her eyes and forehead. She put her fingers to her temples and felt the distended nerves twitching.

'I'm sorry. I don't feel well,' she said unhappily. 'Please let me go to bed. I'm ... I'm sorry I let you down, Harold.'

Harold stared at the empty doorway with some astonishment and more annoyance. What the devil was the matter with the woman? He was not at all pleased with this sudden headache and departure; he had planned a nice long scene of nagging, to be followed by one of his sticky reconciliations and mentally sadistic love scenes. He meditated angrily on the injustice of having to keep a woman who could never be depended on. As if it wasn't enough that she had failed to captivate Blenthrop until after his signature had been secured! Little fool! And just when Harold needed a little consolation, she must needs fail him by having a headache. A slight qualm of conscience suggested that he ought perhaps to go upstairs and see how she was. He found her lying in bed half-undressed with a damp handkerchief on her head, and the curtains drawn. He groped his way across the darkened room, stumbling over Esther's shoes and dress which she had thrown on the floor, and sat down a little ponderously on the bed.

'How's my little lamb now? Come, come, this isn't the way to treat your dear little hubby, is it?'

Esther turned her head wearily to and fro on the pillow, but said nothing. Harold put his hand to her face, and felt it flushed and damp.

'What have you been crying for?'

'I haven't been crying – it's the water from the hanky.'

To herself she was saying over and over 'his beastly intrigues with women,' 'his beastly intrigues with women.'

Said Harold:

'There, there, it wasn't all your fault. I ought to have been smarter in bringing him to the point, but I didn't want to appear too eager. But, you see, I thought if we could have kept up the social-friendly bluff a bit longer, it would be all right. I thought he was a bit gone on you, and that if you'd keep him dangling just long enough ...'

Esther began to cry again, and in her animal distress clutched Harold's arms.

'Hysteria,' said Harold firmly, from his male eminence, 'pure hysteria. Control yourself, Esther, and don't be ridiculous. If any one ought to cry, it's me. Think what *I've* lost!'

She thrust him away so abruptly that he almost slipped, offended, from the bed.

'Don't talk to me any more, please, please. Oh, do *please* go. You don't know, you don't know ...'

'Hysteria,' said Harold complacently, 'hysteria ...'

V

Almost a year passed before Esther forgot Blenthrop – the shock had been a severe one. When vanity is wounded through the affections, the healing process is slow. Esther had kept her first adultery on a high moral plane, which had not been altogether sincere in her and certainly not in Blenthrop. True, with her it had been a passion genuinely enough, but scarcely a passion of the Musset-Chopin intensity at which she tried to maintain it. Since she was ready to run away with Blenthrop, she assumed he was equally ready. Some hint of this added to a warning about Harold's religious activities in the City had no doubt propelled Blenthrop to the West Indies without a word of farewell to her. From Blenthrop's point of view the whole situation looked like a very low and nasty game. Quite unjustly, for at most Harold had meant that Esther should be a bait to be gazed at and not swallowed, and Esther herself had been completely innocent of any sordid motive. But the suspicion that Blenthrop must have judged her in that way was a perpetual torment. Even when the memory of him had long ceased to move either her emotion or her senses, she still suffered when she thought about 'what he must think.' So vital a passion is vanity, preceding and out-living nearly all others.

It was quite different with Harold. He was very much

annoyed ('aggravated' he called it) at Blenthrop's escaping
him, but, as he would have said, 'a busy man has no time to
waste crying over spilt milk,' an ungrateful if common metaphor. Within a week he had ceased to nag Esther about her
supposed lack of tact and inability to 'play up'. And old
Rosengrab kept him very busy indeed. It was the top of the
1919–20 boom, and the old man was worried; he wanted to
unload before the slump came. In a few cases they were left
holding the baby, and dropped enough for Harold to be able
to swagger in Dogberry's vein – 'one that hath had losses, go
to!' But though Rosengrab rather encouraged Harold to make
these lamentations (it was then the fashion for the new rich to
pity themselves as the new poor, with a hint that they had been
forced to sell the lands granted by William the Conqueror and
the plate presented by Charles II to a female ancestor) the
'firm' came out uncommonly well.

There followed a period when Harold rather jog-trotted.
Old Rosengrab lay low, and nothing of much 'importance'
was attempted. But as time went on, and the bankruptcy of
the War was still staved off, more and more schemes were
attempted, and Harold was more deeply involved than ever
in the seduction branch. Esther attended many of these love
feasts of finance, with a languid air of tragic detachment
which rather put men off. Not until a year after the Blenthrop
catastrophe did she yield, with an indifference which was perhaps not wholly simulated, to the urgent attentions of one of
Harold's fellow priests, a well-preserved company promoter
with the gift of the gab. Thereafter Esther grew a little reckless. She had ceased to be faithful to Harold for some time –
that was a fact which could not be blinked even by feminine
logic. And it was no good remaining faithful to a distant and
apparently indifferent Blenthrop, who returned no answer to
her despairing and then reproachful letters. Had she but
known, there were women in the West Indies too. In any case,

after the financial gentleman had faded into cold respect, Esther became rather indiscriminate and reckless. It was the only revenge possible in a comfortless life; and, then, was not Harold always exhorting her to 'play up'? So, like Hubert, Esther often drew a good long bow at Brighton.

Harold grew more pursy and meritorious. Continuance of wealth gave him confidence, and, though his peevishness increased, he looked forward without a trace of doubt to a long future of growing ever richer and richer. He had long ago abandoned any thought of fixing the limit at which wealth would coincide with merit, and his favourite theme of domestic and social converse was a heart-felt lamentation for the cruel incidence of super-tax and the absurd short-sightedness of Government in not encouraging 'business.' £10,000 a year, £20,000 a year, £30,000 a year – king, Glamis, Cawdor, he had them all. What matter if he could not pluck from Esther a rooted sorrow, which drugged itself with adulteries? He was so deep in paper money that it was as easy to go on as to turn back, supposing he had ever thought of such a thing. Why, he was safe till Birnam wood should come to Dunsinane, and 'The Bank of England promise to pay' become a broken promise. Things impossible, for God is great.

In the beautiful symmetry of things, it was natural that this super-salesman of financial pups should have a passion for dogs. These abject carrion-eaters have solved the problem of survival by gross flattery of the bipeds who might otherwise have disputed their food supply. Like many dog-lovers, Harold adored himself in his dogs; he did not like those animals which retain some of their integrity and refuse to be slaves or at least rebel against slavery. Anybody can boss his dog: 'Down, you brute!' and it grovels on its belly and licks the boot: 'Up, you abject!' and it leaps with servile joy, yelping thanks for humiliation and wagging a (probably mutilated) tail of obsequiousness. Harold liked all this, which naturally

revolts any one with a sense of independence. And then if dogs
are sufficiently inbred and useless they are worth Money.
Harold was never weary of vaunting the virtues of the dog,
which he declared were his ideal – for other people, of course,
since obedience was as abhorrent to Harold as chastity and
poverty. Perhaps this explains his constant succession of com-
panionate second marriages on the sly; none of them was a
success, no doubt because he could never find a woman with
really dog-like virtues, although some of the poorer ones did
their best. Harold always complained that he never found any
one to love him for his own sake.

In 1922 old Rosengrab was ill. He returned to the office in
time to prevent Harold from involving the firm in a 'scheme'
of exceptional magnitude and stupidity. In 1923 he was again
ill, and, after a struggle to continue his lifelong services to
humanity, died in 1924. There followed a confused period of
about six months, with much lunching and dining, many
dresses for Esther, buying out of interests and the like, with
the result that eventually the firm became Harold, and Harold
became the firm, under the simple title of 'H. Formby-Pett,
Financier.' By a simple arithmetical calculation Harold easily
convinced himself that, without partners, he would be at
least three times as rich as he had been before. True, the whole
conduct of the 'schemes' would rest with him, but Harold was
prepared to do any amount of lunching, dining and playing
up. He joined two very expensive golf clubs and bought a
yacht, so that even week-ends need not be wasted.

Unluckily for Harold two of his biggest 'schemes' were just
about to 'mature' in the spring of 1926. Then, as every one
knows, the week-kneed meekness of Government permitted
the vile rabble to indulge in an orgy of sedition which had the
most deplorable effect on Business. Harold dropped a lot of
money, and grumbled ceaselessly to Esther about her extravagance. To economise, he discharged his servants, sold his

town house and rented a suite at the Ritz. Since his daughter was then sixteen, he took her away from school because he could no longer afford the fees. She would be such a companion to her mother, he said. Harold hadn't much patience with this modern fuss about education; the girl had Blood and Breeding, there was Money, and that ought to be enough to make her one of the best matches in the kingdom when the time came. Plenty of time for that. In about ten years, Harold thought, when he retired with a couple of millions or so. These early marriages are a mistake. Meanwhile, apart from the companionship to her mother, the girl would always be there to look after Daddy's little comforts.

Whether it was the absence of old Rosengrab's artfulness, or whether God had turned His face from the firm, cannot be known; but Harold on his own was certainly not a success. He had any amount of excuses for it, ranging from Esther's shortcomings to the toleration of obscene and seditious literature, from the greed of the United States to the British lack of interest in sport. Whatever the explanation, Harold lost money steadily. And when he suddenly lost £70,000 in a really marvellous 'scheme' which was to have retrieved everything, there was a wild and panic-stricken flight from the Ritz. Esther's jewels, the yacht, the country house, the cars, everything but Harold's own personal property had to be sold. He scurried them into a cheap hotel at thirty guineas a week, but that soon proved too expensive, and Esther after all this grandeur found herself mistress of a small suburban flat without a servant. Harold took his daughter into the office as shorthand typist, and still remained a Financier as well as a Gentleman.

In a small flat it is not so easy to hide one's life from a husband as in a large house. One day Harold came back earlier than usual while Esther was out, and found lying on the mat a letter addressed to her in the handwriting of a man who had profited considerably by the miscarriage of some of Harold's 'schemes.' There had been a time when Esther had been commanded to 'play up' to him, but that was before the crash. Why was she receiving letters from the blackguard? With conscious virtue Harold opened the letter and found therein one of the shocks of his life, for the letter openly referred to and indeed exulted over frequent misconduct with Esther and fixed a rendezvous for the offence to be repeated. At first Harold thought it must be a vile pleasantry, a trap designed to poison his perfect home life. Re-reading it convinced him that he had been betrayed by a creature on whom he had lavished every comfort and luxury, an unworthy wanton who repaid the love of a faithful (well, at any rate, he always came home after the week-end) husband, by a breach of her marriage vows. At her age! With a grown-up daughter! ...

The scratch of Esther's latchkey halted Harold in the midst of a leonine pacing up and down the room. He had worked himself up into a fine state of injured and virtuous husbandom. Esther knew something was up the moment she saw his angry red cheeks, tremulous chin and slightly pouched eyes. Still in her hat and coat, she gazed at him, wondering what was the matter. Oddly enough, she did not suspect the real cause, although at the beginning of many another row her heart had jumped apprehensively, thinking he had found out something about one of her lovers. Perhaps she was no longer apprehensive because she no longer cared.

'Well?' said Esther, after a pause she felt was becoming ridiculous. 'What on earth is the matter now? You look as if you'd had a fright. Have you lost the little money you had left?'

'How dare you! How dare you!' Harold was quite incoherent with rage. 'What do you mean by speaking to me like that? I won't have it. I ...'

'Oh, all right. I thought you wanted to say something. But I warn you, Harold, I'm utterly weary of your scenes, and I won't stand them much longer. I'll go and take my coat and hat off, and get dinner ready.'

'Stay where you are!' Harold tried to 'thunder', as he had read of injured husbands doing in novels, but somehow his voice sounded squeaky and ineffective, and he didn't know how to handle his part at all well. He fled to abuse: 'You! You wanton, you vile creature!'

Esther flushed a little, but kept quite calm.

'That is sufficient, Harold. If you can't control your temper and tongue, you'd better be silent.'

Harold clutched the letter which he was concealing in his pocket to produce at the appropriately dramatic moment. He had an unpleasant feeling that he was going all astray, or rather marking time.

'Do you deny that you're a wanton, vile creature?'

'Of course I do. Don't talk nonsense. I must go and peel the potatoes, or you'll be grumbling about that.'

Harold had to play his one trump card to take his first trick.

'Do you know what that is?' he shouted, waving the letter furiously.

Esther recognised the handwriting at once and guessed what had happened. To gain time she said coolly:

'I can't see it if you wave it about like a flag.'

'You know what it is well enough, a letter from your paramour, a vile seducer ...'

'My dear Harold! *You* talking of vile seducers and paramours! To my certain knowledge you've had twenty mistresses since we were married, and God knows how many more I haven't troubled to find out.'

'It's not the same thing. A man can do things a woman can't ...'

'He can't do that sort of thing without another woman ...'

Harold was rather knocked off his high horse by this piece of logic. He tried to be dignified.

'I'm not going to bandy words with you, Esther. You're in my power, and I'll make that rotter pay for it. I'll get damages ...'

Before he knew she had moved, Esther had leaped forward, snatched the letter from him, torn it twice and had thrown the pieces on the coal fire. She pushed him away as he tried to rush forward and snatch them out before they were burned, and in his futile rage he hit her twice on the face. Esther turned on him, angry herself now. The slowly gathered exasperations of nearly twenty years suddenly broke loose. The words which so often had failed her now presented themselves. Under her fury Harold collapsed, and sat in a chair gazing stupidly at her.

'Do you think I'd let you do that? Do you think I'd let you pose as the injured and heart-broken husband? Let you throw mud at me and ruin a man who at least has treated me kindly? He wanted my body, and I let him have what he wanted – why shouldn't I? My body's mine, not yours. At least he had some little tenderness. He didn't despise me for it, as you despise your women. You know you're despicable, and something in you makes you feel that if a woman yields to you, she's degraded, whether she's your wife or not. You don't really like women, do you know that? It isn't only that you don't love, you couldn't love anything, but you don't even desire. You only want women because it gratifies your vanity and your sense of power.'

'Esther! What ...'

'You flaunted your women, you encouraged them to humiliate me, you even brought them into the house. You thought I was too poor a worm to protest, you thought I was helpless, because I was poor and dependent on you. It wasn't enough that I left you free – you weren't so precious that one could be jealous – but you had to humiliate me.'

'Esther! ...'

'I stood it for years, and for years I was technically faithful to you. I'd long ceased to love you. You didn't want love; you wanted submission and to humiliate me. Then I fell in love with a man, and I was his mistress.'

'My God!'

'Only for three months. Then I lost him – through you. I believe he loved me, not as much as I loved him, but he at least desired me warmly, not like a vicious slug. I lost him because he thought, and I admit he'd every right to think, that I was acting as your decoy. ...'

'What a monstrous ...'

'Well, you did tell me to "play up" to him, didn't you? I agree it was monstrous. I suppose it never occurred to you that the supreme honour of being Mrs Formby-Pett might not compensate for a life of misery and mental humiliation and physical degradation? I don't care about him now; he's gone, he's forgotten me. But I can't forgive you for losing me Blenthrop.'

'Blenthrop! My God, Esther ...'

'Yes, Blenthrop. Does that surprise you so much? Shall I tell you something else? You won't expect much modesty from a wanton you've just hit, will you? Blenthrop was the first, but he wasn't the last. He wasn't the last ...'

'Esther!'

'Esther! Esther! Don't Esther me! Do you think I'm the only person in the world to be humiliated? Oh, I cared little enough for them, but it made life more amusing, and some of them at least were more or less men, even though they were your "friends". Your friends! Do you know what it is to have a friend? They were only your "friends" because you thought you could get something out of them, or they thought they could get something out of you. Some of them got your wife.'

'Are you mad, Esther? What do you mean by these lies? I ...'

'Mad? No! Lies? You're hearing the truth now, Harold.'

'Be quiet! I won't have you raving like this. Listen to me.'

'I'm not raving, and I've listened to you long enough. It's for you to listen to me, and hear what a sham, what a shameful nothing your life has been. You and your wonderful finance! Why, without Rosengrab you were as helpless and gullible as a child, or a woman – I suppose that's the lowest metaphor in your mind. You despised him because he was a Jew, and you were a gentleman with a school tie and an accent. But he had the Jew's suppleness and toughness and the Jew's intelligence. You hadn't. You were as weak as your Blood and as flabby as your Breeding. You hadn't a genuine thought or a genuine feeling in you. You were just a muddle of prospectuses and banking accounts and menus and futile amusements.'

'I made money, and I made it honestly.'

Esther laughed.

'That hit your vanity, did it? You made money? Your partners made it for you, and made use of you to get it. Honestly? Why, what did you do to earn money? Did you make anything, did you do anything? You were a voice to part fools from their money. You did nothing but handle paper and persuade people that if they lent you money, you'd make them rich. They made you rich for a time, but did you make them rich? You made money! Yes, you made money when men were suffering and being killed; you made money when other men were doing the work of the world to keep themselves and their women and children alive. You a gentleman? You're an animated fraud. And you're such a fool you don't even know you're a fraud. I didn't know it at first, but I know it now. I told you some of my lovers were decent men, and I've talked with them. Not every one in the City is like you, thank God. There are a million English graves across the Channel. And you made money! There are more than a million English men and women without work and almost without hope, existing on a pittance you'd like to take away from them. And you made money! Thank God you've lost it, for you never had it; it was never yours.'

Harold struggled to his feet, and made for the door. Esther stopped him.

'Where are you going?'

'I'm going to ring up two doctors and get you certified.'

Esther laughed once more.

'Ring up if you like. But they're more likely to certify you. In any case I shall go.'

'What do you mean?'

'I shall pack a suitcase and leave at once. I'll send for my other things to-morrow. I suppose you'll let me have my clothes?'

'What nonsense! How are you going to live? You've no money.'

'That's my affair. And, by the way ...'

She slipped off her wedding ring and laid it on the table.

'I'll leave you this. I don't want it.'

'You mean you're going to desert your husband and your child? Be careful, Esther, there's the law.'

'It would take more than the law to make me live another day with you. And as for Ellen, do you suppose I'd leave her in your sentimental clutches? She'll come with me.'

'She will not.'

Without replying, Esther went to her room and began to pack a suitcase. She was trembling after the strain of her scene with Harold, but determined and in a way exultant. She had thought so often of what she would do if she ever summoned up courage to leave Harold that she had a plan perfectly worked out. She could hear Harold walking about in the sitting-room, blundering against chairs and cursing. She noticed, with some relief but amusement, that he did not telephone to the doctors as he had threatened. Obviously, he was now afraid of her. When she had finished packing her own bag, she went to Ellen's room and began to arrange the girl's things. Ellen came into the flat just as Esther was shutting the second bag. She heard Ellen's voice say:

'Why, Daddy! What's the matter? You're crying!'

Esther entered the room, and found Harold clutching his daughter to his breast in a slightly melodramatic pose.

'It's your mother,' he said. 'Your wicked, wicked mother. I don't know if she's gone mad, but she says she's going to leave us.'

'Not "us", "you", ' Esther interposed quietly. 'I've packed your things, Ellen.'

The girl twisted herself free.

'Are you really going, Mother?'

'Yes, dear.'

'Why?'

'Because she's been wicked. She's not fit to be in the same house as an innocent, pure ...'

Esther's clear voice cut across his.

'There's no need for you to be worried with sordid details, Ellen. I've meant to go for a long time, and now we're going. Are you ready?'

'You'll stay and be a comfort to your poor broken-hearted Daddy who loves you so much, won't you, Ellen?'

The girl looked at him with the clear uncompromising gaze of youth; and what she saw repelled her.

'I'm sorry, Daddy,' she said in a hard little voice, 'but if Mummy goes I must go with her.'

'But you can't! You mustn't. I forbid you to. I'm your father and your legal guardian.'

'I'm eighteen, Daddy.'

'I won't have you go off with a degraded woman like that! Why, you'll starve in a week!'

'Not with Mummy – *she's* never let me down yet.'

A minute later the front door closed with a sharp click, and Harold was left gazing at the mat, where two hours earlier he had picked up the letter which had exploded so effectively. He felt rather lost and more than a little vague. The things that bitch of a woman had said to him! And the base ingratitude, the unfilial ingratitude of Ellen – to abandon her adoring father. Result of spoiling the child and not keeping a tight hand on Esther. To think that any woman, let alone a wife of his, should have deceived a husband like that! The little wooden bird ran out from the carved Swiss clock and twitched its beak:

'Cuckoo, cuckoo, cuckoo, cuckoo, cuckoo, cuckoo, cuckoo.'

Harold listened carefully and gravely. Seven o'clock. Soon be time for dinner. He wandered into the kitchen and switched on the light. There was food in the larder, and plates and cups stood motionless and rather unfriendly in a cupboard. A nuisance having nobody to get meals. But they'd be back in a week – less than a week. *Then* they'd have found out where they were well off and who was master. Yes, by Jove! The things that woman said! ... Obviously a little deranged ...

He decided that, upon the whole, he would not trouble to prepare a meal for himself that evening. Not worth it, really; besides, it was getting late. After seven. Have to see about getting in a woman to-morrow to clean up and cook and all that for a few days – until they came back. Engage her by the day – not worth paying for a week. See, Tuesday, Wednesday, Thursday ... Back on Friday or Saturday at latest. Rather pleasant to have a few days off by himself – bit of a holiday. Women are *really* about the blessed limit. Who could have imagined the woman would have said such things? Absurd, mad, inconsequential things, but insulting and painful to a man of sensitive feelings. Have to take them both in hand next week, and show them which side their bread's buttered.

Yet, after all, was it so necessary to have Esther back? Ellen could look after the place perfectly well. A man has his dignity to think of, and after Esther's confession ..

'Cuckoo.'

Quarter past seven.

Harold abandoned his perambulations about the silent flat and rang up for a taxi. He dined comfortably at Frascati's, went to a show with a little friend, and, to save the taxi-fare back, spent the night with her.

Oddly enough, neither Esther nor Ellen returned to Harold's stately home in Clapham. Once free from the Harold regime, Esther had a chance to use her own faculties in her own way, and surprised herself by her confidence and efficiency. And in spite of anxieties she found she enjoyed planning and achieving an independent life for Ellen and herself. On the night of the break they went to a small hotel. Before lunch next day Esther had arranged with a woman friend for them to have a room in her flat, and to share meals at a reasonable price. She still had a latchkey of Harold's home, and while he was away on financial doings, they went and got the remainder of their possessions. By pawning her few jewels and some of her showiest dresses, Esther collected nearly ninety pounds. She interviewed several of Harold's 'friends', who had also been her lovers. Some of them were insulting, some very chilly, two or three of them decent. She got together enough money to take a share in a shop for antiques, run by a woman she knew, who wanted some one to help. In six months she was able to move into a small flat, and within a year had paid off half the money advanced to her. Ellen found herself a job in Fleet Street.

Towards the end of 1930 Esther received a letter from Harold. It ran:

DEAR ESTHER, – I have been greatly surprised at not hearing from you, and it has been very painful for me to have to pick up news of you from third parties. Deeply as you have wronged me, and much as your conduct in leaving me and taking my child from me has hurt me, I am willing to forget and forgive. Will you not meet me somewhere and let us talk over matters in a spirit of reconciliation, and endeavour to build a happy home together once more? In the past I lavished every attention and comfort on you, and now that Business is so handicapped I feel that the least you can do to repay my past kindness is to fall in with this scheme. My heart bleeds to think of poor Ellen being forced to do work which is so much beneath her breeding and with such associates. The tales one hears of journalists are *not* pleasant.

In spite of everything you have done I yet sign myself – Your loving husband,   HAROLD

To which Esther replied:

DEAR HAROLD, – Your letter is like you, and you are like your letter.

Your proposal is absurd. I am happy for the first time in my life, and nothing on earth would persuade me to return to the hell of living with you.

Ellen is answering for herself in a postscript.   ESTHER

PS. – Dear Daddy, what funny ideas you must have about people who earn their livings. I'm quite happy, my work interests me, and we're all far too busy to indulge in the orgies you seem to imagine. With love,   ELLEN

Harold showed this letter, rather unwisely, to some of his 'friends', with plaintive lamentations over Esther's conduct and pathetic regrets that 'that woman' had 'poisoned the child's mind' against him. They condoled with him to his face, and laughed at him behind his back.

Esther thought this was the end of Harold, but she was mistaken. Early in 1931 she received another letter:

DEAR ESTHER, – Your cruel and bitter letter pained me so much that for some time I felt I could not reply. Yet my feelings as a father and a husband compel me to ask you yet again whether you will not reconsider your decision, which I think is both rash and unkind, both to me and to the child, who must *long* for the comfort of home life. Could we not meet at a round-table conference and discuss possible avenues?

Things are very quiet in the City just now, so quiet that I have thought it best to give up my office, which is a useless expense. I am looking round quietly for some opening where I can make full use of my talents as a financier. The Country needs its best brains at this juncture, and I am offering my services to some of the biggest firms. There cannot be the slightest doubt that I shall land something pretty big, for never was there such a dearth of financial genius, and never such need for it.

Meanwhile, as things are in such an unsettled state, I should be obliged if you could lend me a hundred or so to tide over this difficult period. – Your loving Husband,   HAROLD

Esther's first impulse was to throw the letter in the fire and make no reply. Then some obscure sense of duty – after all she had been silly enough to marry the man – led her to make enquiries. She learned that Harold was living in one room with a woman who had once been his secretary, and now bullied him unmercifully. He had no work, and picked up a sort of scavenger's living by various odd jobs in the City. He still wore a faded morning suit and an elderly topper, and desperately kept up the fictions of Formby-Pett family eminence and financial merit. Most of his old 'friends' despised him, few pitied him and 'lent' him small sums, all laughed at him.

To her surprise, Esther found herself thinking: 'Poor old Harold. He wasn't quite as bad as some of them, and it's a shame they should laugh at him.' She wrote him a gentler letter, and sent him ten pounds. In a few weeks he wrote again, and Esther found she was sending him ten or twelve pounds every month. He tried hard to persuade her to see him, obviously with the hope that Esther would rescue him from the termagant typist; but Esther had enough sense to limit her pity.

Nor did this cost her so much as she had expected. Harold collapsed and died of heart failure just a few yards from the office which had once proudly borne the plate of 'H. Formby-

Pett, Financier'. The news that the pound had crashed was too much for him. Loyal priest of the divinity of the Pound Sterling, he died most appropriately with the fetish he had worshipped, and to which he had sacrificed everything which gives human life dignity and savour.

Two women, not in black, were the only mourners at his funeral

Stepping Heavenward

A RECORD

Non nobis, Domine, sed tibi gloriam.

I

NATURALLY the careers of great men are differently interpreted, and estimates of their characters vary surprisingly. Various, indeed, have been the portraits recently offered by a fecund tribe of biographers, professing to give adequate accounts and explanations of the life of the late Jeremy Pratt Sybba, afterwards Father Cibber, O.S.B., recently beatified by the Roman Curia. A critical analysis of the many biographies of this eminent and beautiful soul will form no part of the present work, whose object is to present a cool unbiased account of this celebrated life in its private rather than public aspects, paying chief regard to the earlier formative years, while merely summarising the great public events which are still fresh in every memory. But at the outset the writer feels it desirable to dissociate himself emphatically from the small but virulent band of militant atheists who have not hesitated to explain Cibber and his life as a case of chronic constipation.

This distressing and well-nigh universal complaint (as the advertisements of patent medicines so admirably phrase it) undoubtedly afflicted Cibber, as it afflicts many of his countrymen. So much may be conceded to malignity and the fashionable spirit of belittlement. But nothing but envy and a kind of secular bigotry would claim that the WHOLE of Cibber's career can be explained in terms of constipation. It is a pleasure to be able to refute this calumny at the very outset of an attempt at impartial and dispassionate judgment. The Superior of the Monastery in which Father Cibber spent the last, and perhaps most valuable, years of his earthly existence has placed at the disposal of the learned world a fact of the highest importance. At the advice, or rather command, of his Superior Father Cibber daily consumed a quarter of a pound of the finest quince jelly. The beneficent effects of this fruit at once made themselves manifest, and it is a fact of the highest significance that Father Cibber's first experience of Divine Visions occurred (it is said) three weeks after the beginning of the experiment. Thereafter, the appearance of the Visions was exactly regulated by the quantities of the remedy consumed. So much for the school of constipationists, whose pseudo-science has undoubtedly harmed them more than the noble spirit they sought to defame.

Jeremy Pratt Sybba (or Cibber) was born in the eighth decade of the last century in a flourishing and rapidly expanding town of the United States. Colonsville is situated in the rich but flat country between the Ohio and the Mississippi. It is an important railway junction, one of the centres of a rising agricultural district; and, in addition, manufactures felt hats, motor tyres, hardware, agricultural implements and chemicals. The proximity of oil-wells to the west, and of a small but exceedingly valuable coal-field to the east, facilitates commerce, and adds to its importance and economic splendour.

The Sybbas – or Cibbers, as the name is more generally spelled in England – were not among the earliest settlers of Colonsville. They belonged to an older and more romantic American aristocracy – the stern settlers of New England who attempted, not always with success, to subdue a barren and rocky country to the plough. Their estates in Maine were extensive but unprofitable, and some years before the birth of Jeremy, his father John Elias Sybba went West in the hope of finding lands more fertile and a less arduous existence. But, at the lowest ebb of their fortunes, John E. Sybba and Martha his wife never forgot that they were of purer blood and finer traditions than their neighbours; and this important truth was impressed upon Jeremy from his earliest youth. Chained to the Middle West as they were by economic necessity, they always cherished the bluer traditions of their ancestors.

The infancy of Jeremy Sybba was, apparently, undistinguished. Indeed, his behaviour in the first three years of his life induced superficial observers to believe that he was little better than a cretin. His progress in the accomplishments of infancy was distressingly slow. He was over two years of age before he could be induced to stand on his hind legs and raise his countenance to the stars. Up till that time he had preferred a locomotion of his own devising – with his left leg extended and his right leg curled inwards, he shuffled over the floor on his posteriors with amazing speed and pertinacity. Only the imposition of irons on legs which threatened to become permanently bandy rescued him from the fate of a *cul-de-jatte*. As if this were not sufficient worry for a hard-working American mother, he added to this peculiar habit a frigid indisposition for speech. Fearing he was congenitally dumb, Martha Sybba took her infant to doctor after doctor, but in spite of their enlightened efforts (based on all the latest discoveries of American science) the infant refused to speak. Need we wonder? Like the Blessed Virgin, young Jeremy was pondering many things in his soul.

Legend, as always, distorted and still distorts the interesting and valuable episode of Jeremy's first words. Critical research and much patient enquiry now make possible an authentic if sober version of the facts, already so gravely modified by pious followers. It is absolutely untrue to say that he spoke Latin spontaneously or through a miraculous gift of the Holy Spirit.

A work which unfortunately bears the imprimatur of a Cardinal Archbishop asserts that the child was rapt in contemplation, and said, to the amazement of the bystanders: '*America me genuit; Gallia me docebit; Anglia me fovebit; Roma me tenebit.*' Obviously an *ex-post-facto* invention. And we may also dismiss the more vulgar versions of the same legend. Here are the facts.

Jeremy was going on for three, and still had not uttered a coherent syllable. One exceedingly hot summer afternoon, he was sitting on the kitchen floor in his favourite posture, while his mother, like many American aristocrats of the old school, attended to the cooking. An old-fashioned type of ice-chest or refrigerator was within the line of his vision, and owing to the intense heat was leaking rather badly. Even as a child Jeremy's mind was exact and logical. Unable to explain this (for him) extraordinary phenomenon, the child tottered to his feet and clanked in his leg-irons to Mrs Sybba, who was heatedly trying to raise a pie-crust. He tugged at her apron, and she looked down at his eager face.

'Go away, Jeremy,' she said; 'can't you see Mother's busy?'

'Mother,' said the child in clear tones, 'why *precisely* does the refrigerator drip?'

Mrs Sybba clapped her hands together with a shrill cry of amazement and delight, and clasped the child in her arms, uttering many of those little endearments which would naturally rise to the lips of a mother whose apparently dumb child speaks. Jeremy for some time endured these irrelevant caresses with that unruffled patience he always displayed in life, but finally interrupted her.

'But, Mother,' he repeated, 'why does it?'

That evening Mr and Mrs Sybba discussed Jeremy and his future as they sat in rocking-chairs on the porch.

'And why in the name of mercy,' said Mrs Sybba, at the end

of a long monologue, 'the child couldn't speak out sooner and save me all the days and nights of worry, and the neighbours all talking about it, and the disgrace to the family having a child that wasn't perfect in all its faculties, though as I said to Mrs Glawney this evening, the Pratts and the Sybbas for generations have always done things in their own way and always will, I can't think.'

'Well,' remarked Mr Sybba, whose slow country New England drawl contrasted with the Boston volubility of his wife, 'I guess there's no further occasion for worry now.'

'Indeed, John Sybba, but there is!' she exclaimed, rocking more rapidly. 'I knew all along that Jeremy was no ordinary child, with a family like his you have every right to expect a child to be bright, with two of his ancestors State Governors and one of his uncles a College Professor, and his own mother a Daughter of the Revolution, and even his Paw the best thought-of attorney in the County, and his coming out with the words so pat and clear, and his dear little face that serious, there's plenty to worry about, and if we fail in our duty and don't give him the education he has a right to expect for the great career he's going to have ...'

'There's time enough for that,' interrupted Mr Sybba practically.

'Indeed, there is *not*, John Sybba, and well you know it, many a time I have heard my dear father say that the Reverence Scharnhorst, he was a Unitarian, and I've often heard him say that the family were Counts before they came to America, and he was a most intimate friend of Mr Russell Lowell the famous poet and ambassador, told him that Mr Emerson often said to Mr Lowell that you couldn't begin a child's education too early, and from what Jeremy said this afternoon it's a shame and a disgrace if he doesn't get every opportunity and not be held back from taking the place that one of his family's entitled to take ...'

'Well, well,' said Mr Sybba, yawning, 'we'll see, we'll see.'

But though this conversation, prolonged as it was for some hours, seemed to break down on male apathy and selfishness, Mrs Sybba was not to be put off. And it is a fact that from the very beginning she insisted on having and did obtain the best education for her son, thus well and truly laying the foundations of that extraordinary career.

As with other saintly men, Jeremy Sybba's youth was not remarkable for religious fervour. But, one feels, an element of dramatic intensity would otherwise be lacking in his conversion. Not that Jeremy ever failed to receive religious instruction in the home or that any sort of looseness can at any time be imputed to him, as to St Francis of Assisi and other even less reputable saints. There was a 'consistency', as he would have called it, throughout Cibber's life, which preeminently befits the first American Bienheureux. Cibber was always remarkable for prudence and decency. Everything he said and did bore the mark of careful premeditation. He left nothing to chance, never abandoned himself to any of those spontaneous impulses which, once yielded to, leave a lifetime of regret. Nobody could claim ever to have found Cibber off his guard; and his emotional life, like his charity and his writings, showed all the sober parsimony of a refined classicism.

His mind was never polluted by attendance at the Public Schools of America, which in England would be called the Free or National Schools. As his mother never wearied of pointing out, through the Sybbas Jeremy was related to Sybba, the Saxon King of Kent (Eng.), who is buried in Westminster Abbey; while the Pratts were descended directly from Emperor Pertinax of Rome (Europe), whose name had become corrupted, in accordance with Grimm's law, during the confusion of the Dark Ages, first to Pratinax, then to Prantx, and finally to Pratt. 'Never forget, Jeremy,' she would say to him, 'never forget you are a Pratt.' And he never did forget.

He was sent to a 'pay school', or Select Academy for Young Gentlemen, established at Colonsville by a learned Episcopalian clergyman. Can we trace to this preceptor the seeds of Cibber's subsequent piety? Apparently not. Enquiries have proved that he was not a man of high moral character and, indeed, that he had left Philadelphia some ten years earlier in circumstances which can only be described as regrettable. He was seen by one of his parishioners dining at a restaurant with a woman who smoked a cigarette. He hid his disgrace in Colonsville. But, weak as he was morally, his attainments as a scholar were considerable, and he gave lavishly and of his best to the young aristocrats committed to his charge. It would be an exaggeration to say that Jeremy was his favourite. Indeed an old fellow-pupil informs us that the schoolmaster more than once referred to Jeremy as an 'oily little pup' and a 'crawling microcosm of Chadband.' This sort of thing Jeremy quietly ignored, as was always his wont, especially with men of low moral stamina; and the only revenge he took was the highly creditable one of winning the prize for good conduct and attendance. As he grew older, his surprising intellectual capacities asserted themselves. He took prize after prize, diploma after diploma (all framed and exhibited in the parlour), until the Academy for Young Gentlemen admitted that it could teach Jeremy no more, and requested his 'removal to higher educational spheres'.

At this crisis in his life, young Sybba owed much to the indomitable determination of his excellent mother, and still more to chance. Indeed it is not remarkable that his more pious hagiographers (for such we must now call them) have seen the Guiding Hand of Divine Providence in this chain of circumstances. Who could then have foreseen that this bright-eyed American lad would play so conspicuous a part in the intellectual and moral life of Europe and, indeed, of the world?

In the comfortably overheated parlour Mr and Mrs Sybba discussed their son's future, while he sat still, an observant but almost silent witness. Mr Sybba was reading the Colonsville *Sentinel*, Mrs Sybba was crocheting a black silk cravat, and Jeremy was perusing a volume of *Great American Thoughts*, when she abruptly broke out:

'Now, what's Jeremy going to do, for he can't go back to the Academy after they've as good as admitted they can't teach him anything else, and I never really liked the man, although he's well-connected and a gentleman, but there was something queer about leaving Philadelphia like that, and a boy like Jeremy ought to be given every opportunity for culture and progress?'

Mr Sybba and Jeremy both looked up, and Mr Sybba laid the *Sentinel* slowly on his knees with an inaudible sigh.

'Well,' said Mr Sybba in his slow, pleasant voice, 'I guess it wouldn't hurt him to come into his Dad's office. I started life at fourteen without a cent and no prospects, and I picked up my education as I went ...'

'Pshaw, John Sybba!' his wife interrupted vivaciously. 'I'm ashamed of you bringing all that up before your son, it isn't his fault if you didn't have the advantages of a gentleman's education, though I'm sure you've done better than many a man who has, but you ought to be glad that we can give him what most members of his family have always had, and send him to College.'

'College?' Mr Sybba pondered a little. 'The most advanced and successful men in this community never saw the inside of a College, but I don't see why the boy shouldn't have a year at the State Institution. I've done business for one or two of the College Profs., and I'll ...'

'A year at the State College,' cried Mrs Sybba vivaciously.

'Why, John Sybba, what are you thinking about? Jeremy must take the full course at one of the best *Eastern* Universities, have you forgotten that one of his uncles was at Cornell, Ithaca, and I always remember him telling me that the new State Colleges were vastly inferior, that's what he said, vastly inferior, to the older establishments in the East?'

'And who's going to pay for it?'

'Now, John dear, you know you can afford it. A man who makes his five or six thousand dollars a year can give his son the best, that's decided, and Jeremy can take his examination at once, but what worries me is that I've found out that although he's above their standard he's nearly a year too young and I've been thinking how he can put in that time most profitably, and not lose touch with the finer things.'

Mr Sybba reverted to his former notion:

'He can spend the time in the office with me, and then he'll know something about the work he'll have to do when he leaves College. He'll inherit a dandy business.'

'Nonsense!' exclaimed Mrs Sybba, 'working in an office isn't culture, and I'm quite determined that Jeremy shall have culture, there isn't enough regard paid to culture in the Western States, and I made up my mind yesterday when I was reading *Sesame and Lilies* while I was peeling the potatoes that Jeremy and I will go to Europe ...'

'Gee!' exclaimed the startled gentleman, 'what in hell ...!'

'Now, John, I've asked you a hundred times not to swear in front of me or the boy, I won't have these coarse manners in my home.'

'But who's going to pay for that sort of monkeying around? I'm darned sure I'm not!'

And Mr Sybba thumped his fist on the table with all the emphatic authority of an American husband and father. Mrs Sybba tightened her lips, and rocked a trifle more rapidly. There was an electric silence. Mr Sybba felt the foolishness of a man who lets slip an advantage by unnecessary violence; Mrs Sybba was busily nailing her star-spangled banner to the mast; and Jeremy looked on mutely but anxiously at this battle whose stake was his destiny.

'Besides,' Mr Sybba went on, trying to cover his error of tactics, 'how do you know he wants to go?'

'Would you like to spend a year in Europe with your Mother, Jeremy?' asked Mrs Sybba, not looking at him.

'It'd be bully!' said Jeremy, who had not then acquired the chastity of diction for which he was afterwards famous. 'But if Dad can't afford ...'

'Never mind that,' she interrupted, 'if the money question is settled, would you like to go see all the picture galleries and quaint old places and customs and meet some of the cultured Europeans?'

'Yes,' said Jeremy, with a gleam in his intellectual eyes, 'I've wanted to go ever since ...'

'What have you to say now?' Mrs Sybba asked her husband triumphantly.

'Only that I can't and won't pay for such goddam fool notions, especially if he's going to laze around three or four years at some highbrow College out East ...'

'You won't be asked to pay a cent,' remarked Mrs Sybba, with her lips yet more tightly closed.

'And where'll you get the dollars?' roared her husband irritatedly.

'That's where I come in,' she retorted. 'I won't have my child grow up like a hobo, I owe it to the family ...'

'Um,' grunted Mr Sybba, 'if you get a nickel out of your family you'll be pretty darned lucky, I'm telling you. But I won't interfere with your fool notions. You can go, if you can get the money – *if,* I say.'

'Yesterday,' said Mrs Sybba sweetly and placidly, 'I went and saw the real estate agent, and my plot of land at the corner

of Maple and Twenty-Second has gone way up in price, because I heard from Mrs Shepherd that her husband has bought
the other half of the block because he knows they're going to
build a big department store there, and the real estate man
offered me five thousand dollars for it, but I wouldn't sell out,
and he's going to raise me two thousand five hundred dollars
on mortgage, and I've seven hundred and fifty dollars in my
bank pay account, and I guess Jeremy and I can mosey around
Europe on *that*.'

Mr Sybba shifted his quid to the other cheek, and spat
thoughtfully into the stove, but made no remark. Jeremy
went across the room, and silently kissed his mother's
brow.

Thus, about thirty years ago, Jeremy Cibber for the first
time stood on the soil of that Europe which he was destined
to illuminate by his intellect and to purify with his morals.
The America he had left was very different from the America
of to-day – an America of free immigration and violent
saloons, where sky-scrapers were still only a few hundred
feet high and automobiles a novelty. And so too was the
England where he landed – a purse-proud, confident ant-hill
of imperialists who believed that for ever the waves and
world markets would remain like dead Lacedaemonians,
obedient to their commands. It was the calm, effortless
superiority of the Victorian sunset which most impressed
the young American's keen mind. At a glance he saw that a
cool, even modest certainty of supremacy was far more effective than a striving and uneasy self-assertiveness. And Jeremy
knew that he had found his spiritual home. Here, in the ancient
matrix of his race, he felt that the genius within him would
be recognised, would be effective in a way impossible in a
cruder and more turbulent land; and here the rewards offered
to a noble life were worth winning.

It would be tedious to describe at any lengths the phases of this Wanderjahr, which undoubtedly inspired young Cibber with the ideals and ambitions which he pursued with calm consistency throughout his life. Yet at least one incident must be mentioned, for Cibber himself has told us what a profound impression it made on his mind, erroneous though his vision of it was. After lunch on their first day in the beautiful and famous university town of Oxbridge, Jeremy went out alone while his mother rested. He wandered through the medieval streets, looking up at the restored Gothic or crumbling classical facades of the Colleges, venturing timidly into quadrangles, until at length he was collared by a servant and forcibly shown the hall and every one of the forty-two portraits which hung so crustily on the panelled walls. There was a faint odour of stew and mustard, and the men's beer tankards had just been collected on a table for washing. With reverence Jeremy ascended the dais and beheld the oak chairs of the dons, thinking in his complex way of the austere peace of Learning and whether the officious guide would take sixpence or insist on a shilling.

As he came out of this College, with a mind occupied by lofty thoughts, there approached him two Proctors in their robes preceded by a beadle carrying a small silver mace. Jeremy paused to look at them, so awed by this display of academic splendour that he hardly noticed the undergraduates scooting off along side streets or one exceptionally vulgar youth making a long nose at their impressive rears from a safe distance. Cibber's mind, like that of the historian of the Roman Empire, was little susceptible of enthusiasm; but on this occasion he was moved. Remember, he was still only a precociously intelligent boy, ignorant even of the university life of his own country, and greatly impressed by the stately pageantry of English public life. As he stood in the cool grey shadow of the old wall, conscious that he was that most abject of Oxbridge's temporary population, an American tourist, fevered with all the splendid antiquity of this great seat of Learning, and a little flustered in the matter of the tip, he gazed at the two elderly and somewhat infirm gentlemen with their silver-bearing herald, and saw them as gods walking upon earth. One of the hasty hypotheses of youth formed in his mind. He concluded that this must be the University ceremonial laid down for the progress of the Poet Laureate and the Historiographer Royal from luncheon in Hall to their several apartments. Ludicrous as this must seem, it was nevertheless a noble error. And noble too was the ambition which instaneously formed itself in Jeremy's mind – he determined to give his life to humanity by becoming either Historiographer or Laureate.

Jeremy kept this incident and his determination to himself, with a reticence exceptional in a boy – but if he had not been exceptional we should not now be his humble admirers. Reticence was in a sense forced upon him during this tour, and came to be an essential part of his character. Mrs Sybba was so much stimulated by the aristocratic culture of Europe and by meeting several lovely Americans of high standing in the East, that her already remarkable eloquence was stimulated to the majesty of Niagara. She talked so continuously that Jeremy, in the vulgar phrase, couldn't get a word in edgewise, and found himself limited to monosyllables of assent or polite evasion. Almost a year of this regime rendered him exceptionally silent, a habit which merely reinforced the native caution of his soul. In later life those who met him casually were often disconcerted by this monosyllabic reserve, and often had not the patience to wait for the lapidary phrase which crushed an opponent or illuminated a world.

Mrs Sybba approved of this silence. Not only was it convenient to herself, who disliked both interruption and contradiction, but she felt that only in silence could Jeremy drink in all the culture that she was giving him. 'Drink in' was the phrase she always used. In cathedrals, in galleries, in cloisters, at Chamonix and Fiesole, on Salisbury Plain, and at Carcassonne, she would invariably say: 'Now, Jeremy, sit still and drink it *all* in.' And then she would talk herself. It is easy to exaggerate early influences, even when maternal, yet any observer of Cibber's life must be struck by his obedience to this command. To sit still and drink was more than a discipline with him, if was second nature. Is it too far-fetched to see in this maternal influence the origin of the now famous motto he chose for himself in later life? When, as every one knows, Cibber was recognised as the greatest historian of his age, he allowed the College of Heralds to blazon his coat-of-arms, but insisted that the motto must be: *Qualis Tacitus Sedeo* – which happily alludes to his imperial ancestry, his historical eminence, and the stillness wherein he sat.

It is always pleasant to linger over these early stages of a great man's life. We see him looking forward to life with the appetite of genius and of youth, which is itself another kind of genius. He is not yet on an eminence, not yet cut off from us of the commoner sort by his lofty if dread distinction. He is conscious of powers, but anxious for the future, for how can he tell if the fickle race of men will acknowledge the god within him? In retrospect we watch him, borne down by no such fears, for in Cibber's case at least we know that he is to win two glorious crowns – of intellectual superiority and of conscious holiness.

Ambition and ideals Jeremy brought back with him from Europe, yet as he stood on the deck of the ship as it steamed heavily into the busy harbour of New York he felt anxiety too. New York Harbour was not then what it is now, but it was even then a terrible and impressive spectacle of material energy. Young Cibber felt it hostile to him. What had he in common with these restless builders and un-builders of new Babylons? How could he hope that such men and women would even listen to the message he left within him? His mother stood beside him, pointing out all the most conspicuous and famous buildings by the wrong names, happily excited to be home once more. For a moment Jeremy was tempted to confide in his mother, but prudence and self-restraint warned him to be silent. *Qualis Tacitus Sedeo*. How proud a ring of self-discipline sounds through those appropriate syllables! In silence young Cibber vowed to himself that he would return to Europe, and return this time not merely to admire but to conquer.

Little need be said of Jeremy's career at the great nation-famous university of Kail, since other and more learned biographers have dwelt with peculiar relish and insight upon the progress of his studies there. It is enough to say that he won high academic distinctions, and, though he was oddly unpopular with the men, was the pride and pet of the whole faculty with the exception of the Dean, who once remarked privately to a colleague that 'sucking Jesuits revolt all my Americanism'. Cibber was peculiarly fortunate in winning the judicious affection of the celebrated Tibbitts, at that time the foremost historian of the United States. Tibbitts had known Fustel de Coulanges and Acton, and had been the first to introduce to America the improved historical methods of the Ecole des Chartes. Most of his knowledge he kept sedulously to himself, conceiving that it was no part of a professor's business to reveal valuable secrets of scholarship to young men who were destined for the pursuits of commerce. But in Jeremy's case he made an exception. The lad's eager face, with its faintly Emersonian nose and tight lips, immediately caught his attention; and he was not long in guessing the high intellectual ambition which it masked. He laboured to develop young Cibber's intellect with almost fatherly assiduity. He spent at least two evenings a week in conversation with his pupil, urged him to attempt brief papers on minute but disputed points of history, and corrected them with the closest attention to exactness of thought and precision of statement. Some of these early papers have been preserved, and are exhibited to the public in the Library of Kail. Arranged in chronological order, they are of the utmost importance to students, for they show the cautious but regular waxing of Cibber's powers; the more so, since they constitute the bulk of his writing.

These happy years of intense study were only once interrupted. During Jeremy's third year his beloved mother suddenly passed over, leaving him a few thousand dollars, a small but refined library, a pre-Civil-War silver tea-set, and the family tree handsomely inscribed upon an immense roll of parchment. It would be unjust to say this sad if inevitable event had no effect on Jeremy. Like so many great men, he owed much to his mother, and was conscious of it. She had first discerned the stirrings of genius within him, and had done her best to foster them. But true to his nature and self-discipline, he allowed no trace of emotion to appear, though he was supposed to suffer all the more behind his appearance of self-possession. This, as we now know from Cibber and his followers, is the mark of true greatness – to restrain not only the outward expression of emotion but emotion itself, until nothing remains but the pure intellect and the pure spirit of contemplation.

On the night before his return to Kail, when all the pious ceremonies of final valediction had been discharged, Jeremy sat with his father in the parlour. John Elias, never a talkative man, sat silent, apparently deep in reflection. Jeremy was only too glad to be relieved of the necessity for making conversation — always so painful an exertion to him. While he felt all dutiful respect for his father, he never allowed their relationship to degenerate into sentimentality. So he too sat in his wonted stillness, meditating a destructive essay on the alleged incorruptibility of Robespierre. This, in fact, was the famous 'oblique' method which Cibber made so formidable, i.e. always to create by destruction, to seek truth for oneself by exposing the errors of others.

Some twenty minutes of mental polishing had almost brought a sentence to the peak of efficiency, when Jeremy found his labour wasted through an irrelevant remark from his father.

'I'm sorry she's gone,' said Mr Sybba, breaking out of his reverie and dabbing his eyes with a large white handkerchief. 'When I come to figure it out, she was a good wife and a good mother. I'm a sight sorrier than I ever figured I should be. Death's a fearful thing, Jeremy.'

'Yes?' remarked Jeremy, very non-committal.

'It's like — it's like an earthquake, which tears away the side of a man's house and leaves him naked to the world.'

'Indeed?' asked Jeremy, with a faint trace of satire in his voice — such displays of vulgar feeling being always distasteful to him.

'She was a wonderful woman,' continued Mr Sybba, who was too coarse-grained to notice these finer shades in his son, 'yes, sir, a wonderful woman. I don't know that I ever tasted pumpkin pie as good as hers, and her hot crullers died with her — she never would give any one the receipe. If I'd had that woman's personality and culture and natural eloquence, believe me I'd be United States ambassador to England by now or even State Attorney.'

'Yes?' said Jeremy.

'But there,' said Mr Sybba, blowing his nose loudly as

if summoning a garrison, 'as Bryant says in *Thanatopsis* "Death sets his icy hand on kings." '

'Shirley, Father,' Jeremy corrected him.

'She was wonderfully fond of you,' Mr Sybba proceeded, ignoring the interruption. 'I drew her will up for her myself as clear and comprehensive a document as ever left a lawyer's office. She's left everything she had to you, and ... '

'Need we discuss that now?' asked Jeremy, whose taste was offended by this sudden introduction of a will and testament into Mr Sybba's funeral oration.

'Not if you don't want to,' said Mr Sybba, pained and surprised by his son's attitude. 'I'll see all the formalities through for you. But don't you want to know what she's left?'

'Later on,' said Jeremy, 'perhaps you'll be kind enough to write me about it.'

'Oh, if you want it all in black and white ... ' said the old gentleman, rather deeply offended.

'No, no,' exclaimed Jeremy in distress, 'you mistake my precise meaning ... '

'Well, it don't matter. But there's something else I want to ask you, since you're going back to College to-morrow.'

'Yes?'

'It concerns me as well as you, so I'd like an answer, though I don't want to hurry you. You're of age, but you're only just of age, and what you've seen of the world don't amount to five cents. I guess it's up to me to give you a guiding hand. But when she was dying, I gave her my solemn promise I'd leave you free to choose your own way in life and not force you into the business against your will. Now, listen here, Jeremy ... '

And Mr Sybba, in his pleasant even voice, rambled off on a long monologue, to which Jeremy hardly listened – that subtle mind of his, which always found decision so difficult, needed silence and reflection. At last, when his father paused, he said gently but with his crisp exactness of diction:

'I have already given this matter much anxious thought ... '

'Quite right,' said Mr Sybba approvingly.

' ... And I wish to avoid making a hasty decision ... '

'Good lad.'

' ... And so, with your permission, I shall think it over during the remainder of the session, and write you at length about it.'

Jeremy stood up to say good-night.

'Well,' said Mr Sybba in some perplexity, 'we don't seem to have gotten any place, do we? But you know the position. Here's a prosperous business if you want it, bringing in ... '

'Yes, yes, I appreciate that, and I'm deeply grateful for your consideration and kindness, deeply grateful, but ... Well, good-night, Father, *good*-night.'

Old Sybba, a man of affairs accustomed to make quick decisions on the material plane, could not be expected to understand the more delicate and idealistic texture of his son's mind or the resultant hesitations. He was much perplexed some six or eight weeks later when he received the following letter from his son:

MY DEAR FATHER, – The final examinations for my degree have prevented my answering your letters and queries as promptly as I wished. Moreover, I was anxious not to be too precipitate in committing myself to a course of action.

I have to thank you for your two letters, informing me of the disposal of my inheritance and of your generous offer to continue to me an allowance of twelve hundred dollars. This I accept, temporarily, with considerable respect and gratitude.

My perplexities in the choice of a career have increased rather than diminished, and they have been the more painful since you say that your own decision to retain or sell your practice as an attorney rests upon my decision. I need scarcely say that I am deeply conscious of the affection implied by this, which only adds, if possible, to my gratitude and perplexity.

My studies here have been chiefly historical, and I am encouraged by Professor Tibbitts to push them further. I have no positive distaste for the Law, but I find that my interest is drawn rather to the contemplation of legal theory than to practice in the Courts. Business, in the usual sense of the word, is not attractive to me, though I am fully conscious of the importance of practical affairs. And indeed I feel that some training in them would be of great value to me.

Professor Tibbitts and the President of this University have jointly undertaken to arrange for me to take a post-graduate course at the Sorbonne in Paris, with the possibility of proceeding afterwards to a German or English University. But to what does this lead? History, though a discipline of paramount importance, leads only to an academic career, and I am not certain that I am fitted for the responsibilities of a Chair, even if I could obtain one. Europe beckons me, but America holds me; History allures, but the Law and a solid position in honourable society oppose it. If I go to Europe I venture upon the unknown, and, which would be extremely painful to me, separate myself from my only near relative. Yet if I return to the office, I must waste all the results of three years' sedulous labour, with the painful uncertainty of not knowing if I am qualified to sustain a legal career.

In these circumstances, I feel it would be a grave mistake for you to abandon or to sell your office and business, since, even if I proceed to Europe, as I may, there is every possibility that at the end of a year I might (though I might not) desire to return to America and a practical career as a lawyer. – I am, your affectionate son,

(Signed) JEREMY SYBBA

Mr Sybba slapped the letter down on the table, and spoke aloud:

'Well, darn it all, what in hell does he want?'

Here, in the current phrase, we are 'up against' one of the most puzzling aspects of Father Cibber's character. On the one hand, everything forces us to see in him a man with a fixed ideal and ambition, one who foresaw and predetermined every step of his way; and, on the other hand, irrefutable evidence proves that throughout his life he had a profound dislike for committing himself, seemed to enjoy perplexing

himself and his followers with protracted hesitations. 'Irresolution', 'paradox', say the constipationists; 'mystery', 'divine
waiting upon the Divine Will', cry the hagiographers. But
for us, every character, however subtle, is capable of a
rational explanation. In Cibber's case there is no need to
plunge into cynical materialism or irrational mysticism.
Jeremy Cibber was a man conscious that he was called to
high destiny, and almost from boyhood aware of the form his
life ought to take. But a man so unworldly was inevitably
uncertain of the means – the practical means – to the desired
end. We may liken him to a great general, who is certain of
his strategy, but sadly perplexed as to his tactics. And something must be allowed to the modesty of great minds. We,
who look back upon Cibber in his triumph, can scarcely
understand the doubts which must have thronged his mind –
at the instigation of the Evil One, say the hagiographers –
when he contemplated the possibilities of a young Middle
Westerner conquering the intellectual dictatorship of the
Anglo-Saxon world. The chances of success must have
seemed remote indeed, and we cannot rationally be surprised
that here, as always, he displayed a caution which amounts
almost to timidity and irresolution.

The alternatives before him were clear but by no means
simple. If he entered his father's profession, he was almost
certain of a decent competence and an honourable status,
while in his leisure he could pursue the historical criticism so
dear to his heart. But the isolation from centres of learning,
the contamination from brutal and vulgar minds, the haunt-
ing doubt that he might fall down in important deals – all
these gave him pause. The other course of pure learning had
its dangers too, for while seeking the intellectual kingdom of
heaven he might suddenly find himself very much on the
rocks. He solved the problem with characteristic subtlety.
On a Wednesday he cabled his father: 'Returning to-morrow

explain all later Jeremy'; and on Thursday took the boat to Cherbourg.

II

Legend has very freely distorted the history of Cibber's early years in Europe, and this is the less surprising since we know so little of that period. One important fact is established beyond doubt. He definitively changed his name from Sybba to Cibber, probably because his intellectual ambitions suggested to him that even this slight link with a defunct English literary man would be of assistance to him. In this he was right, since in England – his ultimate goal – it is socially far better to be the grand-daughter of a poet than to be a poet. Some have even gone so far as to doubt that he was ever named Sybba at all, but this is disproved by the passport which is now one of the treasures of the Library of Congress, and by the numerous hotel registers purchased by public subscription and presented to the Vatican. In all these official documents the name is invariably spelled 'Sybba'. Why he did not legalise the change of name when he became a naturalised British subject, we shall never know; probably he lost sight of this smaller matter owing to the immense difficulty of deciding upon the step of naturalisation. And it might have been well for the world's peace of mind if Cibber had continued to hesitate. Many of us are still in a state of palpitation over the threatened war between the United States and the British Empire, which arose entirely out of the dispute as to whether the Bienheureux should be described as 'American' or 'British'. The peace of the Nordic world was only saved by the tact of the American Ambassador who found a formula acceptable to both Powers by describing Cibber as 'Nordic Christian Nationalist'.

If only John Sybba had preserved his son's monthly

letters, we should be fully informed about this interesting period; but unfortunately he always destroyed Jeremy's letters as soon as he had answered them, and thus much must be left to conjecture. The legend that he made a pilgrimage barefoot to the shrine of Our Lady of Lourdes may be dismissed as a pious distortion of a trip to Biarritz with an English Countess, whose name has hitherto baffled the efforts of the acutest scholarship to discover. Equally fantastic is the assertion that he filched by bribery the tibia of St. Thomas Aquinas from a Church in Naples. This, of course, is another low constipationist calumny. Cibber was never in Naples until long after his conversion; and if further refutation is necessary, the simple fact is that the diminutive tibia in question (no larger than a turkey's drum-stick) is still in the shrine with the Papal certificate of authenticity.

What is self-evident is that Jeremy Cibber must have read with incredible pertinacity and speed in Paris. How otherwise can we account for the universal and awe-inspiring erudition which subsequently he rather kept in reserve than displayed? Almost every other period of his life was either tempestuous, privately infelicitous or absorbed in outward activity. His more pious followers believed and still believe that he was supernaturally inspired with the knowledge of tongues and the arcana of science and history. But it is plain that they overlook the advantages of the 'oblique' method. Cibber's positive contributions are little short of meagre. Where he excelled was in pointing out the errors of others. Thus, while a man may spend eight or ten years in the composition of a book, Cibber could pick out all its faults in as many days, while the writing of one of his brilliant 'exposure' essays would not occupy him more than six months. Thus, he acquired the reputation of always knowing more than the most learned, of possessing more abilities than the most talented. He was, so to speak, the Guardian of the Guards

– the critic of the critics, whom there was none hardy enough to criticise.

This absorption in study left little time for outward incident. Jeremy soon found out that Professor Tibbitts cut very little academic ice at the Sorbonne, but was too cautious to betray his surprise. Instead, he set himself patiently to work to discover the defects in the methods of the Ecole des Chartes; and his unpublished (and regrettably lost) paper on this topic won him a great reputation among the students of his class. 'Ce Sibbère,' they said to each other, 'est très fort. Il sait préciser admirablement les défectuosités de la méthode. C'est fantastique, c'est formidable!' To their urgent entreaties that he would publish something, Jeremy opposed a smile and shrug of modest deprecation. *Qualis Tacitus Sedeo.*

Yes, intense and arduous as his studies were, he found time to become an enthusiastic and ardent follower of Monsieur Charles Maurras, defender of Nationalism, Monarchy and Catholic Discipline. Since Cibber was not French he could not be regularly enrolled among the Camelots du Roi, but his touching personal devotion to the great doctrinaire earned for him the nickname of 'the Master's Orderly Man'. There was no service from which he shrank, and he was equally proud to buy the Master his packet of Caporal cigarettes and to assist him in denouncing the errors and crimes of the Third Republic. Moreover, a curious document seems to prove that at times he made one of the bodyguard of loyal Camelots who watch over the Master's personal safety. There is in existence a photograph of the guard-room of the Action Française, taken a year or so before the War. Three Camelots are lying down wrapped in blankets, but fully dressed; at a table sits Jeremy Cibber on guard between a copy of the newspaper and a half-empty bottle of gin. *Qualis Tacitus Sedeo.*

In this manner eighteen months passed rapidly, and the lean melancholy figure of the young American became familiar to all the more serious student gatherings of the time. Cibber made few intimate friends and spoke very rarely, but listened carefully. Yet already he was able to make his influence felt, and time and again would ruin an argument or wreck an enthusiasm by a well-placed criticism. His thoughts, however, turned more and more towards Oxbridge and London; and he was almost eager to take his place among the new school of historians who were rapidly revolutionising methods in England. Between 1909 and 1912, there had suddenly arisen such eminent exponents of the new method as Tregson, Hough, Skeffington, Grynt, and Lucas Cholmp; while, as frequently happens, the older school was stimulated to a last flicker of vitality by opposition and produced the popular figures of Hubbley, Frammel, and Clabber.

By instinct and training all Cibber's sympathies went to the older school. He had a profound admiration for the incisive coldness of Clabber, who at twenty-five had received a Chair in a provincial university. But Chance – or shall we say, Providence – directed him to the newer school where his remarkable gifts more easily made themselves felt. His letters to Clabber remained unanswered, for this petted scion of Oxbridge could scarcely be expected to take the slightest interest in the opinions or existence of an unknown American student at the Sorbonne. Lucas Cholmp, on the other hand, was an American who had won much praise in England by his vigorous exposures of Washington and John Paul Jones. Yet he felt keenly his position of comparative isolation among his European colleagues, and was – and indeed still is – planning ardently to found a Cholmp school of historical writers to act as a counterpoise to Tregson and Hough and their satellites.

Cholmp replied to Cibber's first letter by return of post

and a very brisk correspondence began between them, laying the foundations of a friendship which endured for some time after Cibber had wrecked the hopes of the Cholmps by out-manoeuvring them. From the first, Cholmp was urgent that Cibber should come to England, and, though this was Cibber's dearest wish and purpose, he delayed so successfully, discovered so many motives for hesitation, that the unlucky and impatient Cholmp became half-frantic and committed himself to all kinds of pledges to assist Cibber's career in England. Even then, Cibber acted without precipitation. During his correspondence with Cholmp, he was receiving more and more and more urgent letters from John Elias, demanding to know what course Jeremy intended to take in life, announcing the imminent sale of his practice, and the reduction of the allowance, unless Jeremy returned to Colonsville immediately.

In this crisis, Cibber acted with remarkable prudence and decorum. He telegraphed to Cholmp: 'Detained continent urgent affairs coming England immediately,' and sent a deferred cable to John Elias: 'Starting as soon as possible do nothing drastic'; and took the train to Geneva to think out the situation.

The malignancy of faction and envy has been fully exerted in an effort to depress Cibber's reputation in the matter of what is sometimes called 'the disaster of Geneva'. The hagiographers are discreetly silent; the constipationists exultantly vocal; the world perplexed. The holders of the True Faith are naturally struck by the fact that temptation came to him in *Geneva* – the citadel of heresy. One ardent spirit, since gently censured, presumed to draw a parallel between Cibber's six weeks in Geneva and the forty days in the wilderness. In any case, the fact cannot be blinked that at this period Cibber was at his farthest from holiness.

It was at any rate a period of intense intellectual activity, for in that short time Cibber wrote the first page and a half of his (unfinished) essay, 'A Plea for Royalism in Western Europe', an exceedingly able paraphrase of Maurras. Considering the storm and stress of his mind, this is little short of miraculous. On the one hand, he had financial worries, the growing hostility of his father and agonising doubts about his vocation in scholarship; on the other hand, he had the acute personal problem of Miss Adèle Paleologue.

Through a friend in Paris, Cibber had been introduced to the Heely Brewsters, a wealthy and prolific American family, summering in a large villa near the lake. With open-hearted American hospitality, Mr Brewster cordially welcomed his young and worried compatriot, and made him free of the house. This large and somewhat tumultuous family included two grown-up daughters by a former marriage, and two children, whose governess was Miss Adèle Paleologue. Several young men, more or less earnest suitors of the girls, were undergoing their preliminary trials under the discreet but shrewd surveillance of Mrs Brewster. Needless to say, Cibber was never for a moment seriously considered – all his matchless if hidden gifts could not atone for his penury and lack of prospects. Indeed, to be just, he never thought of either of the two Brewster girls. As he put it, they were 'not serious'. But from the first he was attracted by Adèle's exquisite melancholy. In order to escape the drudgery of her position Adèle was thinking of marrying an American footballer of the most repulsive mediocrity who had an income of about sixty thousand dollars. Almost from the first Cibber felt that this would be wrong.

While the other young people stood about the piano singing the popular songs of the day or played tennis, Cibber often sat with Adèle and talked to her in that soft winning voice he unconsciously adopted when he wanted something.

He was delighted with her intelligence; and his sense of historical romance was stirred by the discovery that she was an authentic descendant of the last Emperor of Constantinople reduced to servitude by her father's unlucky speculations in Rumanian oil.

'My life,' said Adèle one day, with that exquisite foreign accent she cultivated rather than concealed, 'has always been an exile's. My family has so many different nationalities in it that my blood must be a kind of rainbow.'

And she laughed in a self-depreciatory way.

'It has a very noble origin,' said Cibber gravely.

Adèle looked at him with the deep grey eyes which were so effective under her neat black hair, and made a little gesture of half-comic pleading.

'Oh, don't let the others know that I told you that! They'd think I was fibbing or trying to impress them. You know what Americans are – or perhaps you don't, you're so *different*. But *please* don't speak of it.'

'It would be quite useless to tell them – they would not appreciate it. The American always depreciates every aristocracy but his own.'

'How true that is!' exclaimed Adèle. 'But tell me, is it really, really true that you are an American? I can scarcely believe it. You're not a bit like the others.'

'I was born in a crudely commercial part of the United States,' Cibber admitted, 'but my mother at least was connected with a distinguished European family. We travelled together in Europe – and then my interests have always been intellectual. Besides, it is very unfair to judge America by the worst type of newly-enriched tourist. Suppose we judged Europe – as indeed some of us do – by the immigrants you send us?'

'How well you put it! I had never thought of it in that

way before. Of course, it is provincial of *us* to pass judgment so recklessly. America must really be a *wonderful* country.'

'Ye-es,' said Cibber thoughtfully, 'ye-es, but it has many defects. It is essentially a country with too many moralities and too few manners. It can only be rescued by a disciplined aristocracy and a dogmatic Church.'

He was about to continue, a little didactically, but checked himself and took delicately in his fingers a piece of needle-work which lay on her lap. Their fingers slightly touched.

'What is this lovely piece of embroidery?' he asked.

'You like it?' she asked vivaciously. 'It's copied from an old Byzantine design – one of the few poor relics I have left. As I work at it, I think of those distant ancestors of mine ... '

'La Princesse lointaine!'

'How understanding you are, how kind!'

She squeezed his fingers softly, and then dabbed her eyes with a very small white handkerchief which had worked in the corner an 'A' and a tiny imperial crown. Cibber was inspired to considerable respect by this restrained and aristocratic grief.

'Do forgive me!' Adèle brightened through departing tears. 'So foolish of me! But, as I said, I'm an exile and my life's a lonely one. It means so much to me to be spoken to as a human being. Yet I ought really to make you go after the others, instead of sitting here wasting your time with a mere – nursery governess!'

Again she turned on him the emotional spotlights of her large eyes, which Cibber in his excitement felt might be those of the mosaic Madonna in Sant' Apollinare. He was possessed by an insensate wish to embrace her and to beg the privilege of devoting his life to her welfare. But even in this crisis, when most men make double-dyed fools of themselves, Cibber retained his composure and gift of ambiguity. Far from clasping her to him or uttering wild words, he said with grave courtesy:

'Education, even of the very young, is a responsible and serious task.'

Adèle, whose tempered experience had expected something very different, looked at him with as much surprise as if he had handed her a frog instead of a cup of tea. She had never given the footballer half as much encouragement. Not being able to think of any suitable reply, she picked up her needle-work and began stitching. Cibber contemplated her, and the *asinus* of St. Francis and Uncle Toby was powerful within him. Yet he was so far from plotting any dishonourable action that his mind was chiefly engaged in figuring whether he could possibly afford to marry on no income and uncertain prospects. He leaned towards her, and spoke in low but precise tones:

'There are many things I should like to discuss with you, in private if possible. Here we are liable to interruption. It is important to us both. Could you meet me after dinner this evening?'

Adèle glanced at him sharply – really a very odd young man. She said:

'Yes. I can say I want to go to the new Kineema. I shall have to be back at ten.'

'Where shall I find you?'

'Be outside the upper entrance at half-past eight.'

Just before dinner that night a letter marked 'urgent' was brought to Adèle's room by one of the servants. She opened it, and read:

MY DEAR MISS PALEOLOGUE, – If I were not afraid that you would consider it a presumption, I should be tempted to say 'My dear Adele' – I write in considerable haste and confusion, not to say deep distress. On my way back this afternoon I called at the American Express, and found mail of the utmost importance awaiting me. I have no right to expect that you should take that interest in me which I have sometimes hoped you might feel, and therefore I shall not try to explain the very complicated and painful situation in which I am suddenly placed.

If it were not that I must leave Geneva at once, I should have been delighted to meet you this evening, as you so graciously permitted, and should have endeavoured to explain my perplexity. All I can say here is that a letter from my father gravely embarrasses me and will probably make it impossible for me to return to my studies in Paris. On the other hand, my friend Cholmp sends me an urgent communication which seems to promise a way out from my difficulties.

If I were not urgently pressed for time – my train leaves in an hour – I should endeavour to see you, or at least attempt to give you some idea by writing of the deep impression you have made on me. But either is impossible, so I shall not make the attempt. Yet I would ask you not to forget me, and even to hope, as I do, that we may soon meet again in circumstances more favourable to conversation and intimacy.

With every expression of regard and esteem,
Faithfully yours,
(Signed)   JEREMY P. CIBBER

Adèle snapped the letter into her handbag, and after dinner was very gay and cordial with the footballer, who had begun to get a little sulky from jealousy. This pleased him so much that he consumed several whisky highballs, and worked himself into a state of almost baresark eroticism. So much so that Adèle had first to fly from his faun-like pursuit along the garden paths, and later to use every device of cajolement and threatening to prevent his breaking into her bedroom during the night. So different are men's temperaments, and so wide the gulf between virtue and its opposite!

There, so far as Cibber is concerned, the matter might have ended – but for the whim of Hazard or the Hand of Providence.

Although Cibber's letter to Adèle did not contain the whole truth, those thousands personally acquainted with his character will know that it was true as far as it went. He had called at the American Express, and had found letters from his father and Cholmp; but it may be seriously doubted whether the news they contained made any real difference to his situation. John Elias a little more explosively and impatiently demanded to be told whatinhell Jeremy intended to do; Cholmp a little more urgently (if possible) besought him to come to England, where, he asserted, a man of Cibber's intellectual eminence 'would be received with open arms'. And that was all. Except that the situation was six weeks older, it was very much what it had been. Obviously, the new element of action was supplied by Adèle. Just as Cibber had been compelled nearly two years earlier to go to Paris to think out his relation to his father, and then to go from Paris to Geneva to think out his relation to his father and Cholmp, so he now took the express to London to ponder what, if anything, he should do in the matter of Adèle.

Lucas Cholmp and Hough met Cibber at Victoria in response to the agitated telegram he sent from Paris. They had some difficulty in picking him out from the crowd, despite the fact that he wore in his buttonhole a red rose and a white one. They were a little surprised to find that he was wearing a new and ceremonial bowler (bought in Paris for the occasion) and a short but goat-like beard, which he had suffered in Geneva. Mr Hough belonged to the clumsy-silent breed of intellectual, the kind of man who wins an immense reputation by smoking a pipe without speaking in company, and then destroys it by knocking down the fire-irons or upsetting his tea when spoken to. Lucas Cholmp, on the other hand, was a neurasthenic American with a perpetual dry cough and an affectation of epigrammatic and allusive speech which was at once irritating and obscure. Finally identifying Cibber by his Tudor buttonhole, they greeted him with affable condescension, to which he replied with an exaggerated Continental politeness which rather baffled them. So if they secretly felt that Cibber was probably as much of a freak as he looked, he had no doubt whatever that they were pretentious bores.

Nevertheless Cholmp was very glad to have caught at last what he thought was a pupil. In fact, so obtuse is vanity, he never could be made to see that Cibber was by far the greater man, and persisted to the last in thinking as well as asserting that Cibber was a horse foaled in his stable. And there can be no doubt that Cholmp did work very hard to establish his protégé in England, by finding him a small, dark, tank-like flat near the Euston Road, by trying to find him jobs and by introducing him to the New School of historians. In this way, Cibber was early made acquainted with important pioneer work which at that time was unknown to the public and not much regarded even in the learned world where all the men of established reputation did their utmost to discourage and suppress the innovators. Here again he was served by his gift of sitting still. While not so portentously dumb as Hough, he was generally a silent witness of their ardent debates on the papers they read to each other, while he, with characteristic modesty, contributed nothing. Sick of the eternal cold shoulder of the academic world and confident that their methods were the right ones, these young men were arranging for the publication of a joint work, to which each would contribute some characteristic specimen of historical analysis or interpretation. Cibber did not join the enterprise, pleading that he had nothing good enough to add to their collection – an excuse which seemed more than reasonable. In private, however, he made a number of notes in which the faults of each of his new friends were brought out with masterly incisiveness.

He was still uncertain of his career. Oxbridge seemed more remote from London than from Paris or Colonsville. At that time it quite frankly would have nothing to do with him. John Elias, weary of tergiversation, had sold his business, and reduced the allowance to a mere five hundred dollars. This Jeremy supplemented by giving lessons in English to South American students. Though he thus preserved a measure of independence and leisure, he was characteristically unhappy. Here the constipationists conspicuously come into their own again. Naturally, no clue must be neglected in an attempt to elucidate Cibber's life, but is it not absurd to explain away every action, every mood, every aspect of a great Leader by a single fact, a proceeding as childishly primitive in psychology as the old ruling passion idea? There are a dozen possible explanations of the slow, silent misery which seemed to soak into Cibber until he reached saturation point, when he slowly exuded it. Was not the innate consciousness that he was picked out as a Man of Destiny sufficient to fill him with melancholy forebodings? And his pessimism was never of the exuberant, fruity kind which calls upon Heaven and Hell in fury; with him it was restrained, almost morose, tart and acid like very green apples.

Probably it was the pessimistic feeling that the action would be useless which prevented his writing to Adèle.

It was towards the end of September, 1914, that Hazard or Providence interfered with Cibber's life. He was walking to the British Museum when he most unexpectedly met Mr Brewster, who shook him cordially by the hand, and almost in the same breath enquired after Cibber's health and expressed his own deep satisfaction that the British were being well whipped in France. On grounds of prudence in an alien country, Cibber demurred, but Mr Brewster swept all that away with heartiness:

'What are you doing here, eh? On your way Home, eh?'

'Well,' said Cibber, 'not precisely.'

'Quite right, sooner the better. We *did* have a time getting here from Switzerland. Those darn Frogs are suspicious as hell. But come along, come along! Gee, the family'll be pleased to see you.'

And in spite of Cibber's demurs, Mr Brewster swept him into a taxi, hustled him into the lift at the Savoy Hotel, and hurled him into the family suite.

There is no need to enquire into the motives which caused Mr Brewster – in spite of Mrs Brewster's opposition – to offer Miss Paleologue a refuge in the United States during the few months for which, as was then generally believed, the military troubles of Europe would last. The gallant footballer had rushed into the French Foreign Legion; and Switzerland, like a prim Brunhilde, was surrounded by the balefires of War. So what else was there for Adèle to do? Adèle herself developed strange atavistic fears; nightly she dreamed of the horrors of the sack of Byzantium, and her fear of fire-arms was such that the slamming of a door made her bolt like a rabbit. She wanted to get as far away as possible from the scenes of violence in which Europe was idiotically destroying itself. Adèle, in fact, was a model to us all – if everybody had felt as she did, the War would not have lasted ten minutes.

After the ghastly feeling of the Continent, London seemed in another hemisphere, so unconcerned was it then, so disposed to consider the War as a crusade for others and a bit of fun for yourself. Even so, Adèle felt she was not far enough away. Great then must have been Cibber's power of seduction, since he persuaded her to forget his affront to her in Geneva and to endure all the possible horrors of War on the London front for his sake. Nevertheless, this marriage is one of the major mysteries of Cibber's life. On Adèle's side we may perhaps explain it by pointing out that for most women any sort of man and a shack are better than being a nursery governess. But how about Cibber? How explain this infatuation in so cool a fish? All men and large numbers of women are human, but when we consider the profundity of Cibber's studies, the growing New England austerity of his appearance and morals, the almost arid bleakness of his life and the imposing nihilism of his philosophy at that time, this marriage can only be explained as a savage freak of Hazard or as the Hand of Providence using strange means to bring a Great Soul to God.

At any rate, they were married.

III

The Abbé Sieyès, asked what he did during the Reign of Terror, replied with admirable simplicity: 'I kept alive.' So might Cibber have answered, if he had had children, and if they had asked the question: 'What did you do in the Great War, Daddy?'

Continuance of hostilities between the Powers regrettably interrupted the scholarly proceedings of the New School. Hough disappeared early, and was never heard of again; whence it was concluded that he had discovered one of the numerous heroes' graves at that time so lavishly provided by Government. And one by one the others fell away, until only Cholmp and Cibber remained to carry on the Tradition. During the War years they did not carry it very far. There was a discouraging lack of response to their efforts. A small instance will give some idea of their difficulties. At Cholmp's suggestion, Cibber offered to lecture (gratis) on the Influence of Sidonius Apollinaris on Gallo-Roman Culture in the Last Quarter of the Fifth Century before the Canterbury Literary Society – and the offer was unanimously refused! The paper appears among Cibber's 'Remains' in its amended form as Christian Evidence in Heathen Gaul, and received the posthumous award of a gold medal from the Historical Society of Keppwee, Illinois. Which only goes to show that even genius must await its hour.

Moreover, even Cibber's lofty courage was oppressed by public calamity and domestic distress. London was raided by Zeppelins and Fokkers, and Cibber could not soothe his nerves by evoking any historical parallel, except the doubtful one of Carthaginian elephants; and even then the ingenious study remains unfinished. What is significant is that here for the first time he shows a serious interest in theology and hints that the sufferings of London might possibly be attributed to the scourge of God. Some writers dismiss this as no more than a glancing blow at the ex-Kaiser as another Attila, but others incline to think it shows which way the cat was jumping. Moreover, the responsibilities of matrimony weighed heavily upon him. John Elias did not increase his allowance, and prices were rising, rising; historical genius had no commercial value; a household had to be supported somehow. With superb energy, Cibber made a decision and – what a mad world it was! – accepted work as the guiding spirit of a haberdashery department, where his courteous manners and distinguished appearance found full scope. Yet even this noble sacrifice obtained no earthly reward. The truth, for truth must out, is that Jeremy and Adèle did not hit it off so happily as might have been hoped.

Like the wives of many great men, Adèle has been severely blamed. The topic has even been vulgarly debated in one of the cheaper newspapers under the heading: 'Should Our Saints Marry?' Enthusiastic admirers naturally enough feel that intimate companionship with one of the Immortals should be gratefully repaid in every manner possible, and that the tenderness of a spouse should be doubled with the respect of a disciple. They forget that in these days the hero's inevitable valet is nearly always his wife. And they forget that Adèle was one of the earliest to proclaim Cibber's peculiar genius and to push him on in the world. Is she really to be blamed because she, an ordinary woman, could not dwell happily on the austere mountain heights of spiritual elevation? Could she help it if his presence – owing to the will of God, no doubt – drove her into wild neurasthenia? After all, it must be rather a shock to think you are marrying a nice young American and then to discover that you have bedded with an angel unawares.

Cholmp, who had been rather in favour of the marriage as a means of linking Cibber with Europe, watched their dissensions with growing dismay. In the evenings, after the haberdashery was disposed of, he and Cibber took long walks in the darkened London streets, dashing down into Underground stations when the maroons went off.

'You ought to do something about it,' Cholmp urged. 'What I mean is, haven't either of you got any sense?'

'A situation so complicated ...' Cibber murmured.

'But you can't go on like this. You're driving each other crazy.'

'Ye-es,' said Cibber.

'Well, can't you do *something*?'

'What is there to be said, what is there to be done?' Cibber retorted languidly.

'Well, you can't go on like this, can you?'

'No-o, no-o, probably not.'

'Then you'll have to do something.'

'Ye-es, ye-es, no doubt.'

'Well, what are you going to do?'

Cibber raised his arms slightly, and let them fall limp against his sides with the mute eloquence of despair. Cholmp restrained his impatience.

'Look here, what I mean is, why don't you send her to the country for a month?'

'What! In cold weather like this?'

'Why not?'

'She wouldn't like it.'

'Well, she'll have to lump it.'

'But she wouldn't go.'

'Damn it!' exclaimed the irascible Cholmp, 'make her go.'

'But I don't know anywhere to send her.'

'Hell! You've got the whole miserable little island!'

'Ye-es, ye-es.'

'She could go to Swanage.'

'Yes?'

'Is that decided?'

'So complicated a situation ...' Cibber muttered again, 'and this Registration of Aliens is distracting. Isn't Swanage a Prohibited Area?'

'Well, get naturalised and try Cheltenham.'

'Yes,' Cibber agreed, 'one might do worse than Cheltenham.'

'Well, there you are,' said Cholmp triumphantly. 'All you've got to do is take a ticket, and pack her off for a few weeks.'

'Ye-es,' said Cibber dubiously, 'ye-es?'

Debates of this sort occurred almost weekly, invariably with the same result. Cibber would agree that something ought to be done and would assent faintly to whatever Cholmp proposed. But somehow nothing ever was done, and unfortunately the pair, though wedded in the sight of God and man, grew more hysterical daily simply through having to inhabit the same tank-like flat. Cholmp was so much annoyed that only his sense of duty prevented his joining the Army.

The Armistice, when it came, was a distinct relief all round.

From this time onward the private life of Cibber is more and more rapidly lost sight of in the golden halo of his career as a public figure; and it would be impertinent and tedious to trace with the same minuteness events which are still so fresh in the public memory. Yet the *miracle moderne* (so named by an eminent historian in allusion to the *miracle grec*) remains, and we have to explain why a man who was totally unknown when the Armies limped home is now revered throughout the civilised world. Something, perhaps, may be conceded to the dearth of Great Men during the sinister and futile decade of the twenties; something may be allotted to the spiritual disarray of those times; but more, much more, must be attributed to the grandeur of Cibber's personality.

For all her neurasthenia, Adèle had not been idle. In spite of the haberdashery, which he clung to with rare self-maceration, Cibber ranked as an intellectual on the strength of his Plea for Royalism and other unpublished works. Moreover, Adèle's position as an exiled Princess naturally gave her prestige in a country which specialises in such matters, though the prestige was severely weakened owing to the fact that she had no money and no aptitude for sport. Nevertheless, she made her way into one or two of the Best Houses and was almost on terms of intimacy with a number of Really Good People. Her greatest attainment was the Duchess of Camperdown, an extremely amiable hag with many vague good intentions. Only her blameless life and immense wealth enabled the Duchess to maintain her social position, which was seriously menaced by her unfortunate weakness for intellectual society. She was greatly attracted by Cibber's good manners – 'so different from all these brutal and boisterous young men coming back from the wars, my dear' – and was ever faithful to him, an ardent worker in his cause, and one of the first of his Distinguished Converts.

Scarcely less important, though in a very different way, was the exquisite Catholic poetess, Cecilia Myrrhwell, the daughter of a Don, the wife of a Don, and the mother of sons who were born to be Dons – and indeed those who survived the War became Cibber's staunchest supporters at Oxbridge. Although Mrs Myrrhwell died an octogenarian in the odour of sanctity, she did not live to witness Cibber's final apotheosis. This was indeed bad luck, since it was she who first detected Cibber's vocation, and who never ceased to urge him along those ways of righteousness which are also paths of peace. Through her influence, Cibber captured the Universities, just as he captured the high world through the Duchess of Camperdown. And as for the mere mangy world of unattached intellectuals, there was Cholmp, ever ready in those days to preach the doctrine of Cibber and almost ruining himself by standing lunches to editors of periodicals who influenced what they wistfully but hopefully described as The Thinking Public.

With these valued allies, Cibber exactly at the right moment produced his epoch-making Notes on the Provincial Itinerary of the Emperor Antoninus. At first sight it seems impossible that so abstruse a work should have epoch-making consequences; but then, as we all know, it is the method and not the substance of a work which makes its value. And Cibber had method. The Itinerary itself was relegated to footnotes, while the notes, cast in the form of a commentary, became the text. In the opening pages Cibber politely but decisively annihilated every living historian of eminence except Cholmp. Then, in passages of unparalleled eloquence, now known to every schoolboy outside the great Public Schools, he lamented the decay and disappearance of so many once great and prosperous cities. In prose which moved with the stately tread of conscious superiority, he lamented the degradation of Kingship and the fetid growth of democracy, and pointed out that the ruinous European War had been the combined work of the Socialist Free-thinkers and the Jews. But the War, he insisted, was but a trifle, a mere symptom. Without the authority of an Aristocracy, welded to a King by ties of enthusiastic interest, England and the Continental states would collapse in a welter of blood and crime. Then deepening his organ-notes in a diapason of despair, he almost groaned that it was Too Late, that all Authority was doomed, and that nothing was left for the Noble Spirit but contemplation of the grave and the scurry of rats over the withered hopes of Mankind.

This work had the sort of bad press which is very good for a reputation. The cheaper papers ignored it; the old hack reviewers who were not in the know scoffed at it; two of Cholmp's stand-bys praised it extravagantly. But behind this was a *susurrus* of comment which started from the merest whisper and in time became a positive gale. The Camperdown set talked about it at dinners; the Myrrhwell set at Oxbridge lifted their eyebrows at those who did not admire Cibber; Cholmp gave the tip that Cibber was *the* coming man. In a short time five thousand people were talking Cibber, and nearly five hundred copies of this book had been sold. People greeted each other: 'What do you think of Cibber?' and the correct answer was: 'Oh, my dear, a marvellous man, so original and *depressing*.' Anybody who was silly enough to ask: 'Who's Cibber?' lost caste in a frightening way.

Within a fortnight Mr Ashleigh Hill-Peck, the Guardsman poet-raconteur, had fourteen absolutely *priceless* stories about Cibber.

Wherever you went in evening dress you were bound to hear people discussing Cibber.

In the House a highbrow Labour back-bencher described him as a menace to working-class mothers.

Yet with all this fame he refused to leave the haberdashery, while Adèle's humours wore him to the bone. Was this inability to make up that mighty mind, or was it a supreme touch of chic? In either case it turned mere publicity into fame.

A great genius in a haberdashery department! How too remarkable! What a disgrace! Why doesn't somebody do something? People became most agitated:

'Do you know Cibber's *still* in the haberdashery?'

'*No!* You *don't* mean it?'

'My *dear*, I thought he was *scraping* it in by thousands!'

'Oh, it's that awful wife of his.'

'How I loathe that woman!'

And so on.

Almost every amateur job in England (except those of Speaker and door-keeper to the Ritz) was offered to Cibber – and refused.

Qualis Tacitus Sedeo.

The Duchess was almost frantic. She almost besought Adèle:

'My dear, you must *make* him leave. Believe me, I know these men of genius. The sheath wears out the sword, the sheath wears out the sword, you mark my words.'

But she didn't guarantee an income.

At length the desirable happened. A deputation from Oxbridge waited upon Cibber, and offered him a Supernumerary Chair of Religious History at £1,000 a year for three years or the duration of the Peace, whichever proved the longer period.

It was accepted.

Normally, one would expect the gale of whisperings to lapse into complete silence as soon as Cibber had done violence to his nature and made a decision. But this was far from being the case, for a number of reasons. True, some of the younger and more frivolous elements of the ruling classes tried to start an anti-Cibber Five Minutes Silence at all parties, but this was promptly squelched by the still younger and serious group. Otherwise Fame continued her triumphant course.

Some of our elder critics, nettled at being left out of the plot, would have loved to wipe up the literary arena with Cibber's body. But they were afraid to oppose the powerful interests supporting Cibber, and added their praise (which was the more fulsome in that it was insincere) to the raucous voices of Cholmp's literary leaders of The Thinking Public. Thus Cibberism spread to the suburbs and provinces, without losing any of its aristocratic prestige. The Duchess and Mrs Myrrhwell were staunch as great black oxen, and ruthlessly trod down opposition. Oxbridge itself, amazed at having been intrigued into doing something unprecedented, felt bound to back Cibber, in spite of the aggrieved snorts and characteristic *bons mots* of several ferocious old Dons.

And, it must be admitted, Cibber rose splendidly to the situation. He was fully aware of the difficulties of his position as a sort of alien amateur in an old and haughty Seat of Learning, proud in peers. He therefore combined extreme caution and superiority with *un extérieur très pimpant* and perfectly lovely manners – such a change from the usual eccentricity and boorishness of the greatest living experts in everything. Oxbridge held the world's record for the lifted eyebrow, but Cibber raised his at least a semi-tone higher. His cool American wit, polished among the Camelots du Roi, enabled him to score off even his most hirsute and erudite opponents, and soon made him a dreaded power. People grew very cautious about starting little mots against Cibber, when they found that they were invariably the victims of more formidable sarcasms from him. Truly, in those days he fought the good fight, and the hosts of holy angels were with him.

Within a year Cibber was the acknowledged if unofficial Social-intellectual Dictator of England. Matters the most remote from historical scholarship were submitted to his judgment, and invariably treated with distinguished caution. His opinions were expressed in pithy epigrams, of Delphic subtlety and profundity. Very wisely, he backed all the influential scientists; and they, delighted to be mentioned outside laboratories and abstruse periodicals, began to talk of him as the Great Moral Leader who would bring England out of the post-war desert into a promised land of pure morals, booming trade and welfare work. At this period Cibber had not yet found God, although as always he went in for a high moral tone, on the ground that it was bracing to the intellect.

Foreign countries heard rumours and became curious. Anxious cablegrams were wafted across the Atlantic, offering ten thousand, twenty thousand, thirty thousand dollars for a series of Cibber Lectures. They were not even answered. The Germans, with characteristic interest in science, sent over a small committee of psychologists to enquire into this new manifestation of English Volksgeistdummheit. In France, Monsieur Julien Benda said in a manifesto that Cibberism was one more example of the regrettable influence of Monsieur Bergson; and Monsieur Bergson said in an interview that Cibber ought to read a little philosophy – an ambiguous remark which was interpreted in England in a complimentary sense. During a visit to Italy, Cibber was received by the Head of the Government (who gave him a signed photograph) and by His Holiness, who bestowed his Blessing. The former King of Spain wrote to ask Cibber's advice on how to deal with the University of Salamanca.

Cibber engaged two faithful secretaries, and became the-most-difficult-man-to-meet-in-England, which was a tremendous triumph for the Duchess and Mrs Myrrhwell, who were flattered and fêted everywhere in the hope of an introduction to the great man.

Yet it would be false to say that amid all this glory Cibber either was or seemed happy. Much of his time he appeared to be plunged in thoughtful gloom, probably of a religious nature, from which he only emerged to slaughter a reputation with an epigram. Some writers say that it was because he deserted gin for port. Now, it is true that gin is diuretic, silvery and pungent, whereas port is a bowel-wearying liquid. But the explanation is altogether too simple and unreflecting. Cibber would have been Cibber on lion's milk and moonshine. To find the better clue we must rise from the liver to the heart. When Cibber looked into that alleged mirror of the emotions, he found, so to speak, a vacuum. In spite of his intellectual and social triumphs, life for him was almost equally compounded of dust and broken bottles. Broken bottles and dust he gave his followers, and that apparently was what they wanted and could enjoy, so long as they were presented with polished indifference.

Adèle became more and more unhappy. It is always *rather* unpleasant to live with a genius, but quite awful when he is a Cibber. Few persons now take the view that marriage is or should be a merry bacchanal, accompanied by flutes and the capering of panisks to the tune of 'Hymen Hymenæe!' But Cibber considered it as an inviolable legal contract, implying none but social obligations. So long as Mrs Cibber had the honour to be inscribed in the correct register, got her oats and fig-leaves, and received social consideration by reflection, what the devil else could she want? So, many a time poor Adèle gazed into the mirror, clutching her hair distractedly, and whispering: 'I'm going mad, I'm going mad, I'm going mad.' Cibber invariably stood up when she came into the room, and their quarrels were conducted on coldly intellectual lines.

Cibber's hierarchal passion led him to identify his despair with God, in whom he did not believe. For him God was not a passion, but a theorem; and he could never quite prove the theorem. Nevertheless, his house became rapidly crowded with the instruments of the cult. Cibber disliked the Madonna, but his walls were hung with crucifixes, arrow-smitten St Sebastians, martyrdoms of this, that, and t'other, and bleeding, emaciated Christs of the school of Cranach. Even the hat-rack looked rather like a wooden crucifix, placed in readiness for everybody's calvary. Cibber's own room, got up like an over-furnished monastic cell, was a capharnaum of ascetic objects – a *prie-dieu* with little sharp points to make the knees holy, several 'disciplines', a chasuble, an incense-burner, a reliquary containing the forceps of St Fallopius, and works on such agreeable and saintly persons as St Elizabeth of Hungary who liked to embrace lepers and ulcerated patients, and St Lydwine of Schiedam whose gangrened flesh grew into her rough wooden bed. On the mantelpiece were a skull and a stuffed rat – emblems of Life and Death. The house itself was fre-quented by unwashable Franciscans, learned Benedictines and smart little Jesuits dressed as parsons of the Church of England.

Cibber's lectures became sermons of gloomy piquancy and epigrammatic misery.

Once more the thoughts of intellectual England were feverishly concentrated upon Cibber. Was he going to declare himself? Would he abjure the errors of the world and be 'received' or wouldn't he? Was he really going to lead England to Rome? Oddly enough, he appeared unable to make up his mind. Even the Jesuits got fearfully agitated and impatient, and sent long cipher reports daily to the Superior by devious ways – when the penny post would have been cheaper, quicker and rather safer. On Monday Cibber had been observed to scratch himself so often that he was ob-viously wearing a hair-shirt, and had taken communion in the highest obtainable church of England. But on Tuesday he came out in a silk shirt and spats, said that St Francis of Assisi was a sentimentalist, and got drunk on port with the Greatest

Living Expert on rusts and mildews. On Wednesday morning, the swish of a lead-laden discipline and horrid groans were heard through his bedroom keyhole by the Jesuit-butler. On Thursday he went to a Thé Dansant, but on Friday he abstained from all nourishment except the Sacrament and a bottle of port. On Saturday he complained that the Pope was uneducated, but on Sunday edified the company at a cold supper by his exegesis of certain knotty points in the works of St Thomas Aquinas.

Nobody concerned quite knew where they were or what to do. The priests were frantic. Nearly fifteen thousand conversions of important and frequently wealthy people were being indefinitely held up by Cibber's procrastination. 'If he goes on delaying,' they said to each other, 'our labours will be wasted, and these thousands of precious and thirsting souls will lose the waters of Eternal Life'. They blamed the Jesuits, who in turn blamed the precipitation and rude zeal of those who tried to shove Cibber into a formal declaration. Mrs Myrrhwell, who saw him every day, found difficulty in concealing her impatience; while the Duchess, who had planned a select and enormous party of new converts to celebrate her own conversion, was quite furious at the delay. But nothing definite could be obtained from Cibber. *Qualis Tacitus Sedeo.* The turmoil and public uncertainty were almost inconceivable, and Trade suffered as badly as from a General Election when the Socialists seem likely to get in.

This tragic situation of almost national suspense was solved unexpectedly by the one person almost everybody had forgotten, viz. La Princesse Adèle. She ran away with a young man, and plunged into a life of hectic dissipation in Berlin. As the sole reward for years of misery she begged Cibber to divorce her.

It almost looks as if Cibber had been waiting for an event

of this kind to make his decision, though here again it is always possible that the real difficulty was to resolve into harmony the innumerable subtleties of that great and wonderful mind. At any rate, a fortnight after Adèle's desertion, Cibber was 'received' – thereby making the divorce impossible.

The ceremony was deeply impressive when Cibber, having confessed and received absolution, first received the sacrament in accordance with the rules laid down by Peter and thereafter never altered in the minutest detail. All those present – and Westminster Cathedral was packed – felt that they were witnessing a solemn and dramatically decisive moment in the history of England.

Following Cibber's lead, the fifteen thousand notables plunged into the purifying waters of the church like one penguin. Renewed prayers for the complete conversion of England were ordered all over the world, and enthusiastic relays of religious kept the prayer fires burning by many a holy shrine.

Among the converted was that enlightened Prince, the Duke of Pulpory, who controlled the three large syndicates which controlled every periodical in the United Kingdom. Splendid and impressive descriptions of Cibber were written up by the yellowest journalists obtainable for money, and all the details of his private life (excluding Adèle) were exhibited to the Thinking Public, with photographs. A vast new religious campaign was started with two slogans: Turn To God And Save Your Investments, for the better-class papers; and The Catholic God Will Raise Your Screw, for the journals of the lower orders.

England was swept by enormous and palpitating waves of religious emotion, which recalled the finest days of Smithfield. Millions were converted in sobbing masses, while the whole Catholic clergy was exhausted by its duties, and phalanxes of recruits were rushed from every part of the Christian world. Obstinate nonconformists, who refused to abjure, were forced to bolt like rabbits in all directions; and the Red Peril was finally averted by lynching every one who refused to kiss the sacred objects which were continually being carried in procession by enthusiastic mobs of converts.

His Holiness (by birth a Prince of Massa-Carrara) was forced to issue a message to his dearly beloved English lambs, ordering them to abandon unauthorised processions, and to return to their work on wages reduced by twenty per cent.

British Government Stock went to a premium, and a new Peter's Pence 8% Loan, recommended by Cibber himself, was twenty times over-subscribed.

The sublime height was reached when His Holiness visited England, and Cibber, converted Englishman and naturalised Catholic, knelt before him on the platform of Victoria Station between the Cardinal Prime Minister and the King to receive a Benediction which had been specially reserved for the occasion.

By special request of the Pope and Cibber, England declared war on France, the last stronghold of intellectual paganism in Europe. America, thrilled to the marrow at learning that all this had been accomplished by one of her ex-sons, joined in; and an immense crusade for the forcible conversion of the world was started. The Russians proved to be the toughest nuts but even they were cracked eventually.

After these tremendous scenes which have shaken the world and made it the pious place we now live in, all else must come as an anticlimax. Cibber, at his own request, retired to a Roman monastery where, as we are told, Divine Visions were frequently vouchsafed to him. On his deathbed he received Full Absolution and the Apostolic Benediction from the Pope, and at his own request was buried in the little cemetery of the monks. But the gratitude and piety of the world could not be satisfied with such lame honours. Public subscriptions were started and large sums were raised for the purpose of getting Cibber made a Saint. The aristocratic education of His Holiness forbade his making a full Saint of an American, but the sums of money raised were so enormous and the long-desired conversion of England so great a miracle that he graciously yielded to the prayers of the faithful and the recommendation of the Curia, and pronounced the Beatification of Jeremy Cibber.

Beate Cibber! Ora pro nobis.

SALAR THE SALMON
Henry Williamson
712

In this engrossing chronicle Henry Williamson takes us once more into that world of river life which he has so intimately studied and which he first revealed to us in *Tarka The Otter* (now available as a Puffin Story Book and specially illustrated by C. F. Tunnicliffe). With a literary method which is the equivalent of a slow-motion film, Mr Williamson describes the typical battle for survival of Salar and his kind. And *The Beautiful Years* (Penguin edition in print) is perhaps the most perceptive book on childhood and country living ever written.

*

THURSDAY AFTERNOONS
Monica Dickens
714

The personal and professional life of a successful consulting physician, written with all Monica Dickens' flair for characterisation and vivid story telling.

*

THE PURSUIT OF LOVE
Nancy Mitford
711

By the author of the best seller *Love in a Cold Climate,* this is a sophisticated novel of our times, distinguished by candour, vivacity and a notable insight into the feminine temperament.

WITHOUT MY CLOAK
Kate O'Brien
716

This distinguished novel (awarded the Hawthornden Prize in 1932) is a spacious history of an Irish family which will remind many readers of *The Forsyte Saga*. It is a work as absorbing in its detail as in the broad sweep of its narrative, and confirms the tribute paid to Miss O'Brien by J. B. Priestley who wrote: 'She seems to have been designed by nature to be a really good novelist. She writes well; she can create a character; she has an eye for a scene and a period.'

*

THE HORIZONTAL MAN
Helen Eustis
718

This unusual story of a murder, which takes place in an American women's college, has been hailed in America as the most promising first novel of its sort in recent years.

*

DON'T, MR DISRAELI
Caryl Brahms and S. J. Simon
715

Those who enjoyed the same authors' skit on the Elizabethans – *No Bed for Bacon* – will relish this spiritual pantomime of Victorian England. When it first appeared The Evening Standard said '*Don't, Mr Disraeli* is a masterpiece of wit. This is a book for the connoisseurs of wit'.

AUGUST FOLLY

Angela Thirkell

732

This is a tale of the brighter side of life, carefree and vivacious yet told with the author's usual accomplished style and uncommonly good sense of character. Admirers of Angela Thirkell will suspect that lighthearted romance is the keynote of this engaging chronicle of rural and social life in the village of Worsted.

*

STRAWBERRY ROAN

A. G. Street

731

The scene, as in 'Farmer's Glory', is the Wiltshire countryside which A. G. Street knows so intimately. This time the main link between the events he chronicles is Strawberry Roan, a calf which, in the course of agricultural routine, passes from farm to farm until its animal destiny is fulfilled. By this method the author depicts for us the problems and the preoccupations of an English farming community and brings us into vivid contact with the men and women who labour on the land.

*

VERDICT OF TWELVE

R. W. Postgate

730

'It seems more than likely that *Verdict of Twelve*, by Raymond Postgate, will be judged the best mystery of this year and many years to come ... It is a superb piece of writing and makes other horror stories seem flat and undiscerning. – The New Yorker.

ILLYRIAN SPRING

Ann Bridge

713

'Women in the early forties who have been wives and mothers for over twenty years are liable to suffer from a slight sense of guilt whenever they embark on any purely self-regarding activity; but Lady Kilmichael had better reasons than this for her desire to avoid the eyes of acquaintances on her journey. She was leaving her home, her husband, and her family – possibly for good.' With the opening words the problem and indeed the plot of this book is set forth, and the difficulty of so many women in middle life who try to reconcile the past with the changing present is reflected in a most charmingly civilized novel.

*

ROYAL FLUSH

Margaret Irwin

733

One reviewer wrote of the book that 'it took me quite five dazed minutes after I had read the last sentence to realise that I was not really in seventeenth-century France.' Minette was the nickname Charles II of England gave to his sister Henrietta, the youngest child of Charles I and his French wife Henrietta Maria, and *Royal Flush* is the story of Minette's short but historically important life.

'It is a magnificent theme and Miss Irwin has dealt with it magnificently. Only a high and subtle imagination joined to a feeling for strict historical truth could have produced this result.' – Francis Iles in Time and Tide.

A WRITER'S NOTES ON HIS TRADE

C. E. Montague

A 219

By long meditation, as well as by long practice, the author explored the values and techniques which produce good writing. His purpose was not to compile a mere manual of Do's and Don'ts, but to examine the complex discipline which a writer must learn and accept if he is to use the English language with power and precision and also to guide readers as well as writers about such matters as narrative, over-statement, realisms, lucidity and slang. His analysis will sharpen our critical observation of whatever we read.

*

OF MICE AND MEN and CANNERY ROW

John Steinbeck

717

Of Mice and Men is a story of the strong and the weak, and their dependence upon each other. It revolves round the characters of Lennie and George. Lennie is a man with the strength of two, but with the mind of a child, whose whole world centres round George who tries to protect him and steer him away from trouble caused by his superhuman strength and simplicity. Of *Cannery Row* John Steinbeck said he just 'opened the pages and let the stories crawl in by themselves'. Cannery Row is a street bordered by houses, shacks, and boiler pipes, in which live all kinds of people who have one thing at least in common – their poverty. It is written with all John Steinbeck's deep understanding of vivid and curious personalities.

THE MEANING OF ART

Herbert Read

A 213

When this book first appeared it was described by the *Star* as 'the best pocket introduction to the understanding of art that has ever been published.' A compact survey of the world's art, from primitive cave-drawings to Salvador Dali, an exposition designed to show the persistence of certain principles and aspirations throughout the history of art, and to summarise the essence of such movements as Gothic, Baroque, Impressionism, Surrealism ... Readers who follow this progressive and concise analysis, with its 64 pages of pictures, will find it a valuable and stimulating guide to the visual arts.

FROM 'THE MEANING OF ART'